Uroboros Saga

BOOK THREE

By Arthur Walker

CHAPTER 1

CENTRAL BOOKING DISTRICT, DRAINAGE TUNNELS, MARS

September 18th, 2124 – 75 years previous to Shutdown

Athos One reached down and fished the last of his comrades out of the wastewater before kicking the lid shut and turning the wheel to lock it in place. He did a quick head count, his eyes lingering on Warden Peasely. The human had taken some water and almost passed out as they were pulled under water through a hundred feet of pipe. Chelsea Six cradled the waterlogged warden in her arms patting him gently.

"The corridor is clear all the way to center level but the commons are full of corporate enforcers now. We took too long getting out," Ezra One reported as he returned from scouting the underground ahead.

"Aren't those guys supposed to be on our team?" Athos One asked, holding up an empty clip.

"There's a lot of money on Mars, on both sides of the sally port," Chelsea Six whispered, helping the beleaguered warden to his feet.

"She's right, there might be as many guys up there trying to help me as kill me," Warden Peasely said with a cough.

"We need guns, ammunition, and transport," Calvin One stated, checking his gear.

Ezra One crouched down and drew a line in the grime at their feet, then another with a quick circular motion of his wrist.

"This is where we are, and this is where the port is," he said, dropping two small stones onto the diagram.

"We could try to go through transit, maybe catch one of the underground trains on the way out that direction?" Athos One suggested, pointing to the makeshift map.

"Risky," Calvin One said, shaking his head.

"There's a route that should be clear of convicts and corporate muscle, but it's treacherous," Warden Peasely said, drawing a second line in the grime.

"The crusher? Mining ops is going to be locked up tight and all security protocols engaged," Ezra One said, raising his goggles slightly.

"Unless you have a Warden's credentials," Chelsea Six said quietly.

Athos One and Calvin One both shrugged and looked back at the other Drones. They'd seen a lot of action in the last few hours and they all wanted to get out in one piece. Ezra One knelt down and stared at the map drawn out in the muck for a moment before marring it with his hand.

"Okay, we'll head toward the crusher, but I'm going to try and get a sat link as soon as we're topside at center level and my gear has a chance to dry out a little bit. Maybe Control will have a better idea, but for now heading to the mining facility, the crusher line, and through to the port is our best shot at avoiding a lot of trouble," Ezra One said standing up.

They traversed thirty meters of tunnel to the center level and climbed up. The biological shielding glittered with the stars far overhead in time with service lighting along the habitation spires. The orange and tan painted buildings were stained with corrosion and wet with condensation. Even though the furnaces had been off for days now, ash still rained down from above like gentle snow.

Mars Mining Company security, and the mercenaries assigned to assist them, gathered between buildings for shelter and warmth. Rime gathered on the ground across where the living tenements met with the central level. There was no clear route that Ezra One could see at first, every shadowy place already had a cadre of armed men and women.

"We have no egress," Ezra One whispered down to the others.

As soon as he said the words, the radios of the various groups came to life and dozens of men and women placed their fingers up to ear buds and looked around nervously. Ezra One froze, watching in surprise as the groups of armed men headed away from the area in the opposite direction from corrections. In a matter of moments the street was clear, and he motioned for the others to follow up him into the open air.

"What happened?" Athos One asked.

"They all got a radio message at once, and then headed off toward port."

Calvin One clicked his tongue, then gestured with a nod over his right shoulder. From under the cover of his goggles, Ezra One looked up to the side of one of the tan tenements to a tiny unmanned vehicle hovering halfway out of sight. A moment later, it darted behind the building and disappeared.

"We've got an audience. Warden, does the Mars Mining Company or central booking district employ unmanned vehicles for surveillance?" Ezra One asked

"No, there are cameras everywhere on the convict side of the sally ports, and the union prohibits any sort of surveillance on the mining workers operating under contract."

"That is not the answer I was looking for. Chelsea, is there a tribe home on Mars?"

"No, I'm only one of a dozen Drones spread throughout the colony. There are more Metasapients, but most of them are here for... security purposes. They're pretty dangerous, Ichthyic Type, but instead of being benign they're half barracuda or something," Chelsea Six said with a slight shudder.

"Okay, forget that, let's just try and get to the crusher line before the mercs and corporate muscle wanders back," Ezra One said, squinting up at the skyline.

"What were you thinking?" Athos One asked.

"I wish there was somewhere we could hide for a while, wait this out, keep the warden safe."

"Ezra, there is nowhere to go but out," Chelsea Six remarked sadly.

Buildings gave way to heavy industrial equipment that towered over the small apartment complexes. The mining crews had been evacuated days earlier, and hastily from the looks of things. A few entry doors were left open and an empty orange duffle lay under a thin layer of ash nearby.

Ezra One looked around at the darkened windows and rooftops before beckoning the rest of the Drones to follow him.

Electrified fences separated the massive miles-long industrial crusher from the humble living accommodations afforded the people who worked there. The fence was guarded by two enormous sentinel automatons, each supported by a tracked wheelbase and huge mechanical arms. The robotic monstrosities were converted mining equipment loaded with sentience cores programmed to only allow authorized personnel in and out of the gate.

Ezra One walked up to the gate cautiously looking about. Both of the sentries were dark, their robotic shoulders slumped slightly allowing their enormous shovel-like actuators to touch the ground. He climbed up onto the tracked wheelbase and placed his hand under the armored skin of one the sentries on a manifold plate. Dropping back to the ground, he shook his head and walked toward the others.

"I don't like this. The sentries are still hot, like they were on just minutes ago," Ezra One explained. "Who shut them down, and why?"

"You checking the gift horse's teeth, or is there something else going on here?" Warden Peasely asked.

"We've been under unmanned surveillance since we got topside to central. Remember the guy we saw standing in the street below the Warden's office? Something about this whole mission is off," Athos One said, looking back over his shoulder.

The other Drones shifted uncomfortably, each one quietly nodding in agreement.

"I don't sense anyone else nearby but us. If there is someone working an angle here, they are doing it from a remote location," Chelsea Six stated.

"We gotta go," Calvin One said, suddenly breaking into a run and sprinting past the gathering through the gate. Ezra One looked up and down the crusher line toward the central booking district. A trio of heavily armed unmanned vehicles turned and begin to fly in their direction. They were skirting the skyline and darting downward to get the best shooting arc on their position.

Ezra One waited until everyone was clear before taking up the rear. In the distance he could hear the sound of weapons powering up and maneuvering jets engaging as the interceptors began to track them across the long run to the crusher line entrance. A high pitched whine preceded the interceptor's opening fire on the group.

Albus One split from the group and lit a flare trying to draw the unmanned vehicles to fire at him. Ezra One did the same, throwing a smoke grenade ahead to try and give the rest of the group cover. Weapons fire struck Albus One, sending him to the ground in a smoking bloody heap. Ezra One gritted his teeth as he ran past his still form on the ground. The interceptors were almost within optimal range and the group had another seventy-five yards before reaching the crusher line.

Ezra One leapt onto the side of an enormous hauler and climbed up toward the cockpit. The hauler was still laden with freshly mined stone and ore, but the keys weren't in it. He pulled his cipher plug from his com harness and plugged it into the hauler's console. The acquisition protocol ran in moments giving him control. Powering up the hauler, he gunned the engine forcing the gigantic vehicle to lurch forward leaving crushed equipment and supply sheds in its wake.

As the interceptors closed to optimal range, Ezra One pulled alongside the Warden and his Drone team escort granting them cover. This did little to prevent the interceptors from opening fire anyway, tearing the side of the hauler to pieces with heavy subsonic incendiary ammunition. He wrapped a cord around the steering column and made sure it was tight before dropping out the cockpit to the ground below. The hauler shuddered and gurgled leaving a trail of hydraulic fluid behind it as it lumbered on toward the crusher line.

"I have to use the bio-metric reader beside the entrance to get us in!" Warden Peasely yelled breathlessly.

"That may not be necessary," Calvin One shouted in reply.

The hauler made contact with the side of the crusher with a deafening roar, tearing a broad gash in the side of the huge industrial complex. As the Interceptors circled for another pass, rotating on their axis to get a better angle, the Warden and his Drone protectors slipped through the damaged wall into the crusher facility within. They could hear the unmanned vehicles swing around attempting to find ingress to continue the pursuit for several moments. Finally, the sounds of their engines began to fade as they flew down the length of the crusher line toward the port.

"Everyone alright?" Athos One asked catching his breath.

"Everyone but your friend that's still out there. What is this place?" Chelsea Six replied.

"This is part of the refinery, an eight mile long maze of conveyors and automated haulers designed to deliver minerals to the port," Warden Peasely said, looking up.

The interior of the complex sported a huge conveyor belt with several mechanical subsystems designed to pick out ore from stone and sort the debris gathered from the mining operation. There were miles of metal catwalks, stairs, control booths, and heavy machinery arrayed from floor to ceiling. Huge cranes and haulers were built into the structure to handle the loading and unloading of material, large and small. There were several orange safety lights shining down from the ceiling far above, and several smaller LED lights illuminating the reflective tape that marked walkways.

"We have to go back and get Albus One," Athos One said, looking at the concerned faces of his fellow Drones.

"He's gone, hit by anti-vehicle ordinance," Ezra One reported sadly.

"We've carried Avery One this far, I'm not good leaving anyone behind, dead or alive. You might be new, but the rest of us have served together a long time," Calvin One snapped angrily.

Ezra One looked up at Calvin One apologetically and nodded. They took a moment to catch their breath while Athos One looked through a pair of viewfinders for where Albus One fell. Athos One handed Ezra One the viewfinders after a few moments and pointed. Ezra One could see Albus One lying on the ground very still at first, but then he would move, trying to regain his footing.

"There's no way he survived," Ezra One said fearfully.

"NZ-rounds?" Athos One asked.

"Possibly."

"What are NZ-rounds?" Chelsea Six asked.

Ezra One looked knowingly at Calvin One as the other Drones murmured and made hand gestures to one another.

"Nanotechnological zombie rounds; they animate the dead or subsume control of an injured individual by hijacking the nervous system and primary motor cortex. Basically, it makes anyone hit by those rounds feral and dangerous for about fifteen to twenty minutes. They are extremely illegal, and not even CGG black ops or special services use them. Only terrorists and criminal cartels have the resources. You won't find some low profile outfit with them as they are extremely expensive and require special operational controls to be deployed safely," Athos One explained calmly.

"The prison break has a powerful benefactor," Warden Peasely said, shouldering his shotgun.

"Or a powerful adversary. They weren't trying to capture you out there to open a sally port. Someone doesn't want to take any chances that you fall into convict hands," Calvin One said, still somewhat angry.

"What do we do?" Chelsea Six asked.

Albus One suddenly lunged through the tear in the bulwark separating the crusher line complex from the outside. He took Calvin One down hard, punching him frenetically like an unhinged puppet. Calvin One brought up his arms to guard against the blows, but Albus One had been preternaturally strong even before being shot. The rest of the Drones fell on Albus One rolling to the ground. Their fallen comrade was not to be denied as he threw them off, dragging viscera and his own intestinal tract with him.

Warden Peasely fell backward over a hydraulic line while running a round into his shotgun. Albus One was on him when Chelsea Six intervened grabbing the feral Drone by the head, both of her palms pressed firmly to his temples. There was a sudden jolt sending out a wave of psychic pain in every direction. Drones fell to their knees and grasped their ears as if being assaulted by a deafening sound. Ezra One fought through the sensation pulling Chelsea Six off of Albus One and wrapping his arms around her.

They tumbled to the ground, Chelsea Six suffering from what looked like a seizure. This went on for a few moments until all was still once more. Albus One didn't move a muscle during that time giving the others a chance to get their bearings and regain their footing. Warden Peasely knelt down beside Chelsea Six, a look of genuine concern crossing his face.

"What's wrong with her? What happened?" he asked, brushing her pure white hair from her face with his hand.

"She tried to subdue what remained of Albus One with her psychic abilities, maybe? Albus One is new enough from the factory to have some psychic countermeasures engineered into him. The rest of what happened after that is anyone's guess," Calvin One said.

Athos One turned his viewfinders down the crusher line in the direction of the port, then turned back up toward central booking district. The tangle of machinery made it difficult to make out much in either direction, but it looked clear in both directions. Shouldering his rifle he stood up and began checking on his fellow teammates. Chelsea Six regained consciousness moments later, and after a moment's rest, they began to make their way down the crusher line.

The facility was designed to handle several tons of rock and ore per second, keeping a steady flow of material to be processed further down the line. Ezra One wondered how much the Mars Mining Company lost in revenue every day the crusher wasn't in operation. Every day it was down was a day of maintenance to get it running again as the machine was never designed to be turned off once it was switched on.

Keeping to the ground, they hoped to avoid even the minimally elevated walkways and kept to the left side in single file. There were corpses of fallen security forces and convicts every so often, sites of previous conflict during the days leading up to the attempted prison break. Ezra One looked about at each site, a look of bafflement slowly crossing his face.

"What?" Calvin One asked.

"What, what?" Ezra One replied.

"Every time we stop to look for ammo and supplies you poke at the ground and look grumpy," Chelsea Six said, her voice still hoarse from her previous ordeal.

"Seems like for the amount of gunfire, shell casings, and footprints there should be more bodies."

"You think there's was a third party involved, Ezra?" Athos One asked.

"Someone is profiting from all this, but doesn't want things to change much after it is all over. It's like they aren't really pulling out all the stops to kill us, but trying to delay us instead," Ezra One stated, pulling on his communications harness.

"We going to play?" Athos One asked.

"Well, we've got a couple of options. Keep doing what we're doing and head to port, or just sit tight until the convicts get hungry," Calvin One said, keeping a watchful eye on the machinery above him.

"There are other options," Chelsea Six remarked, looking down at the bodies of Avery One and Albus One they'd been carrying along with them.

The other Drones looked to one another confused, but Ezra One met Chelsea Six's gaze and shook his head.

"We both have a contingency plan I would assume, something that was left to us in the event we couldn't get the Warden to safety?" Chelsea Six continued, glaring at Ezra One.

"We aren't employing either of those plans," Ezra One insisted.

Chelsea Six gazed at Ezra One intently, her eyes twitching back and forth as if she was reading an unseen book or thinking about something very rapidly.

"I'm glad to hear that," Chelsea Six whispered, relieved.

"What are the contingencies we aren't doing again?" Calvin One asked, somewhat baffled.

"We aren't going to kill the Warden to limit liability, and we aren't going to use him to let the convicts out," Athos One said calmly.

The other Drones nodded and gestured to one another. Then, they gathered up their gear and their fallen comrades and prepared to move again. It would be a long walk down the crusher line to the first process- ing facility. One could look out through the biological countermeasures toward the Martian sky and see exhaust ports that towered over every other structure. Most of what lay above was bathed in shadow as the whole place had been shut down.

As the facility access port came into view, they could see the huge vault doors had been slid shut, grinding the huge conveyor system nearly in half as it hadn't been retracted. There were pieces of it everywhere and the wreckage still smoldered. As they climbed past they could see both convicts and security forces arrayed at the bottom of the doors. Some unknown force had compelled them to try clawing the massive fifty foot wide and probably ten foot thick doors down with their bare hands.

A handful of them still twitched periodically, whatever sinister force having given them motion still active. Ezra One motioned for everyone to stay back while he made the climb down from the wreckage to the threshold of the doors. The bodies smelled terrible, having probably laid there since the unrest began many days previous. They all appeared to have wounds resulting from gunfire, but none of the bodies were armed. Ezra One turned and made his way back up the slope to where the others waited, crouching down beneath the wreckage with them.

"NZ-round victims from the look of it," he whispered.

"Someone must have closed the doors hastily to have done so without retracting the crusher line conveyor," Athos One replied in a low tone.

"Or it was tripped from the inside as a countermeasure to prevent intrusion or terrorist activity," Warden Peasely said, looking up at the tangle of wreckage hanging about above them.

"Further up, there may be enough of a gap where the doors closed on the conveyor to slip through, but the climb will be dangerous, and we'd be very visible," Calvin One said, turning his gaze upward.

"Dig deep. If you've got ammunition pass it off to Athos One. If you lost your knife back at CBD, find a brick, a pipe, something heavy enough to take a skull in," Ezra One whispered, extending and then retracting his claws.

They crept up the wreckage quietly, then boosted one another up to the wrecked conveyor platform. There was a gap, but it was very narrow and would require that one lay on their side and crawl through an inch at a time. The gap wasn't deep, only five feet or so, but it was pitch black on the other side and extremely quiet.

Ezra One began the slow work of making his way through to the other side. It was cold, and while his eyes quickly adjusted to the darkness there was little to see. The darkened wreckage of the conveyor creaked slightly as he crawled the last few feet to the other side. It was cold enough Ezra One could see his breath. Drones began to slowly emerge behind him and then, eventually, the Warden after no small amount of trouble.

"This an everyday thing for you guys?" Warden Peasely asked, grabbing his knees and breathing hard to catch his breath.

"Quiet," Ezra One hissed.

They all froze as he peered over the side of the conveyor to the ground below. He pulled out an illuminator and flashed it around for a moment before putting it out. Stepping back slowly, Ezra One beckoning for everyone to gather around.

"The ground is completely obscured by mist, and what I can see of the wreckage below is covered in frost," Ezra One whispered.

"The coolant tanks were ruptured?" Calvin One asked, sniffing the air.

"Or, someone ruptured them on purpose," Athos One complained.

"We'll have to stay up on the conveyor and hope no one hostile gets the drop on us," Ezra One said, taking the lead.

He jogged along at a brisk rate glancing over his shoulder every hundred feet or so to make sure his team was still there. The cold was taking a toll on the Warden, and he would have lagged behind if Chelsea Six and Calvin One weren't to either side helping him. They did their best to ignore the ghastly sounds coming from below. For most of the journey it was quiet, but every once in a while they could hear half frozen hands scraping at the scaffolding and support structures below.

After a little more than a mile they could see lights ahead and the machinery of the crusher facility sitting motionless under thousands of fluorescent lights. There was mineral ore and stone scattered along the conveyor ahead of them slowing their advance. Several convicts lying in wait emerged and began to advance with all manner of improvised weapons, including at least one power welder. Ezra One picked up the pace leaping from the conveyor to the top of the ore piles.

Athos One slid to a halt and raised his rifle waiting for a good shot as the other Drones rushed past him. Warden Peasely and Chelsea Six knelt down behind him, the Warden's breath ragged and uneven. Drone met with convict high on the conveyer, black rubber wetsuits mingling with prison yard orange. The conveyor suddenly shook as a dull roar from outside the facility rattled the walls.

"Someone is employing ordinance out in the central civilian sector!" Calvin One yelled as he wielded an unconscious convict by the ankles as a club.

Ezra One leapt high grabbing a crane hook before reversing his grip and pulling himself up to the cable. The whole facility shook again as ordinance struck the crusher assembly directly. The outer wall shuddered and fell as security forces began pouring in to meet heavy resistance on the ground. Debris fell from above to the conveyor line below nearly crushing a trio of Drones fighting with a handful of convicts that were not so fortunate.

"They're going to set off the gas behind us. We've got to get out of here," Athos One said, turning to Chelsea Six.

"I won't leave him behind," she replied, drawing the asthmatic Warden up to his feet.

Athos One grabbed the Warden and pulled him up onto his shoulders in an emergency carry position. Chelsea Six stooped down and picked up his rifle and they ran together as debris fell from above around them. They cleared the first few piles of stone and ore as security forces turned to fire toward convicts coming up from under the crusher line from central booking. Athos One paused and looked back as the weapons fire traveled up the line striking metal and creating sparks.

Flammable gas ignited in the distance pulling air toward the conflagration. Athos One leaned into the backdraft and prayed his fellow Drones were already clear. A crane suddenly came to life, a yellow light flashing atop the control booth. The crane turned sharply bringing a large hauler to rest against the side of the primary conveyor line. Leaning out from the control booth, Ezra One gave a sharp whistle signaling for everyone to get into the hauler. Once the last Drone and the Warden were aboard, Ezra One raised it aloft and moved it over to a secondary line away from the breach.

"Go!" Ezra One called out, sprinting down the secondary crusher line.

The main conveyor line shook from an explosion as the flammable gas touched off several containment tanks. Piece by piece, starting from a mile away, the main conveyor fell, pulled down by its own weight in a cacophonous chain reaction. Hundreds of tons of ore, metal supports, and the conveyor itself crashed to the ground below sending up a cloud of dust that got thicker by the minute.

Ezra One pulled off his own re-breather and put it over the Warden's mouth and crouched down. The dust storm washed over them one direction, then rushed back with the backdraft as a third explosion engulfed the crusher line, closer this time. They stood and began to run again as the sounds of conflict slowly faded with the dull roar of more explosions. When they finally cleared the facility and were able to drop off the secondary crusher line into a loading area, they were carrying the Warden.

"Set him down," Chelsea Six begged.

"Do it," Calvin One said gesturing to a receiving desk by a loading door.

"He's breathing, but his heartbeat is erratic. He needs medical attention," Chelsea Six said putting her hand on his chest and closing her eyes.

"The port isn't far. Do you think he can make it?" Ezra One asked.

"You hear that going on behind us?" Athos One said worriedly, shouldering his rifle.

"It sounds like the earth opened up to devour them all," Ezra One said, clapping dust from his hands.

They built a makeshift gurney to carry the Warden as quickly as they could. Once it was ready they headed through the massive loading facility carefully navigating the nearly two dozen rail lines that connected the crusher line with the port. None of the trains or monorails were running and the yard was utterly abandoned. There were lunches still sitting on the picnic tables and jackets hanging on hooks near the changing and decontamination chambers. Everyone had left in a terrible hurry.

A quick turn of a crowbar allowed them to step out into the colony proper, the bio dome overhead glittering against the perpetual Martian storm outside. The streets were devoid of life, abandoned transports left to languish with access doors left open. Ezra One went ahead keeping low to the ground until he could pull his communications harness on.

"Control, E One nearing port," he tapped out on the microphone.

"*E One, rendezvous with CGG Custodian and surrender custody of the Warden to him.*"

"Nanotech hazard detected, chemical storage on site compromised, extreme danger to civilian populace," Ezra One tapped out, motioning for the rest of the team to stop and go low.

"*Acknowledged. E One, rendezvous with CGG Custodian and surrender custody of the Warden to him.*"

Calvin One crept up next to his diminutive ally and crouched down beside him in the shadow of an abandoned transport. The Martian habitation spires around them that reached up to the biodome were dark and devoid of any sign they were occupied. Calvin One swept his hand across the debris at their feet and held the residue up to his nose and shook his head.

"Nothing biological at work, not sure why they evacuated," Ezra One said nodding.

"Look," Calvin One said pointing.

In the distance they could see a lone Custodian walking toward them. He was dressed in full aegis powered armor but carrying what appeared to be only a pair of side arms, one on each hip. He wore a brown leather, wide-brimmed hat and had a gold five pointed star pinned to the long coat he wore over his armor. His feet clicked as he walked, and he appeared to have no fear of the Drone team that lay in his path. He was a young man, barely twenty from what Ezra could see of him.

Ezra One rose up, waving over one shoulder for the rest of the team to follow.

"Custodian," Ezra One said in greeting as they closed the distance.

"E One, I'm Custodian Rider," he asked cautiously, putting his right hand on the holster at his hip.

Ezra One pulled a card from his jacket pocket and held it out. The Custodian pointed to the color purple on one side, then to the picture of an eagle when he turned the card over. Satisfied, Ezra One put the card away and led the Custodian around to the other side of the transport. Ezra had heard of the aegis armor, but never been near someone wearing it. He could hear the armor whispering to Custodian Rider, a faint metallic sounding voice constantly giving him tactical information.

"What did you do to him?" Custodian Rider asked.

"We saved his life," Athos One replied indignantly.

Custodian Rider raised an eyebrow and looked down at Ezra One.

"We transported him by foot all the way from central booking via the crusher line," Ezra One said, nodding back toward the loading facility.

"Damn, you really did save his life. Convicts, Mars Co. security forces and Syndicate wet works teams are all over the place that direction slugging it out over something. I'm not exactly sure what touched all this off, or what it is a cover for, but you've put us in the black again bringing him here," Custodian Rider said with a slight smirk.

"All this for a prison break?" Chelsea Six asked.

"I reckon it doesn't matter now. Without a Warden they've no keys to open the sally ports. The convicts will have to deal with the Warden Authority now. Add up all the lives lost, you probably saved a hundred times that many," Custodian Rider said, tipping his hat to the Drones.

"What happens now?" Ezra asked.

"We wait for the extraction team to reach us, then we all go home."

CHAPTER 2

PORT MONTAIGNE, CGG SECURE FACILITY, DOWNTOWN

2:13 AM, January 28th, 2200

Silverstein's Log, Part 7

I stepped into Helmet as quickly as I could, just past the muzzle of his gun, but right as he discharged it near my left ear. I was angry and half deaf as I grabbed him up by his lapels and shoved him backward. He tumbled to the floor hitting his head. He was quick to regain his feet, though, even though he lost his glasses in the fall. He wasn't moving like an old man should move.

I fumbled to draw my own handgun almost losing my footing as my equilibrium began to depart. I fired a clumsy shot in his direction, the bullet leaving with what remained of my patience. Helmet returned fire, but not before I stumbled toward one of the cubicles clutching my ear. I could feel a little bit of wetness on my hand. I didn't stop to lament what was probably a burst eardrum as I fired back.

The Chiroptera Metasapients came out of the elevator shaft behind me, attaching themselves to the nearest Alphadein mercenary, and stabbing wildly with their knives. Bullets struck the reinforced glass, setting off alarms inside the building, one of many anti-terrorism countermeasures that probably did more harm than good. Metal overhead doors began to slide downward over the large windows, but rattled to a halt halfway as the building suddenly lost power. Emergency lights flickered to life adding to the muzzle flare from automatic weapons.

My anger melted quickly away to palpable fear burning in my chest. Not just for myself, but for the poor Metasapients that had been abandoned down there. I was scared for Ezra, Dragos, Matthias, and Taylor. In the confusion, I lost track of Dick. It would be something to regret later. There were many cubicle walls, conference rooms, and offices he could have ducked into during the melee.

Admittedly, the whole affair was very distracting when coupled with my 'gift.' Even in my half deaf haze I continued to see dollar signs. I could see the cost of every bullet fired, the liability of every injury, and what it would cost the fix up the place after the smoke cleared. When I get stressed, the people seem to fade away, and all I can see are the numbers.

Taylor cried out behind me, but I couldn't make out what she was saying. I watched helplessly as the mercenaries shot Dragos before Ezra could break free. The rest of the scene was obscured by boots and the batwings of Metasapients. The air was thick with gunfire, shell casings, and blood. I crawled about half the distance toward where Taylor was cowering in a cubical, before one of the mercs stepped on my gun hand.

It hurt, but not nearly as badly as my ear. I struggled to get free, but something hit me across the top of my head, hard. My vision swam with red and black, the sounds of what was transpiring around me were distant and unrecognizable. I felt mightily foolish at that precise moment for probably provoking the exchange, but I'd had enough of being pushed around.

I resolved in the future to choose a more advantageous time to lose my temper and push back. Then I blacked out.

When I awoke, I was lying face up on the floor of a parking structure, concrete forms looming over me like disappointed pall bearers. Truly, I did wonder how I managed to get out of all that alive. Ezra looked down at me, his facial expression indiscernible due to the blood spattered across it. Taylor dabbed at my head wound with a bit of cloth and winced in time with my own pained expression.

"What happened?" I asked.

"Ezra managed to drop one of the mercenaries and pulled all the pins on her smoke and tear gas grenades. Gave us a chance to get away," Matthias said rubbing his bloodshot eyes and coughing.

I glanced around. It was just Ezra, Taylor, and Matthias standing around me. My head and my ear hurt, and I felt nauseous. It wouldn't be the last time that day I would feel that way. Head trauma was among the first of my new memories after I awoke in an alley as an amnesiac. I lay there for a minute contemplating how the injury was like an old friend now.

"Dragos? The Metasapients?" I inquired, trying to sit up.

"Not sure what happened to them. Dragos could have survived the chest wound he took if he was wearing armor under there," Ezra explained. "I looked for him while we were dragging you out, but I couldn't find him."

"So, I could have handled that a little differently?" I said lying back on the concrete.

Matthias smiled and nodded. "I could think of a few more delicate approaches than the one you employed."

Taylor and Ezra helped me up. I couldn't tell where we were by the surroundings. All I knew was that we were definitely downtown, even if the area looked darker than normal. Matthias and Ezra were both pretty badly beaten, and shaken by what had happened.

"What happened to the catalyst, and the AI sentience core?" I asked.

"I have them here," Taylor replied, patting her shoulder bag.

"Dodging the real question you should be asking, aren't we?" Matthias asked, folding his arms.

I looked around, still groggy from the blow. We did seem a person light.

"Yeah, I suppose I am. Where's Dick, and did Dr. Helmet get out of that situation alive?" I asked, already fearing the answer.

"It was pretty hazy as we were making our exit, what with all the gas. From what I could see, Dr. Helmet took a bullet to the arm, from you I think. He and the Alphadein mercenaries grabbed Dick and took off after we managed to slip away," Ezra replied sullenly.

I marveled at the implications of my nefarious replica, and what was likely a replica of Dr. Helmet we encountered, exchanging notes. I wondered if Truman and Tullia were alright, and if they had managed to make some sort of escape. Maybe Dragos managed to get back and warn them, and they were all somewhere safe. I had to know.

"We need to try to get back to Tullia's transport, see if they are okay," I said doing my best to walk.

"No-go, I'm afraid. Ezra says it is swarming with corporate police and Alphadein mercs," Taylor replied sadly.

"Is there any way to contact them? By radio maybe?" I asked.

"Not without possibly giving away their position, or our own," Matthias replied.

"It was implied that we'd know when and where to deliver the catalyst to whoever is claiming to be Vance Uroboros. That hasn't panned out, has it?" I asked.

"I communed with the AI we took from the facility. All I was able to get was the date and the location where it was confiscated by CGG security forces," Taylor replied.

"What if we took the date and looked at it as a time instead?" I asked.

"Twelve, fourteen, twenty, ninety, seven?" Taylor said, speaking the numbers aloud.

"That was the date the catalyst got picked up?" Matthias said, his eyebrows raising slightly.

"That's what was entered into the system," Taylor replied.

"Something about that seems familiar, or off, but I can't put my finger on it," Ezra said, resting his chin on his fist.

The date was meaningless to me. I had little faith that it was really when the Catalyst got picked up, assuming it was the same stuff that slipped through our grasp before. If the numbers meant something more than a meeting time, I could not see it.

"Wow, what part of this isn't just a little off?" Ezra grumbled, checking his rifle.

"Let's get to the old concrete factory. We have only got about forty-five minutes before it will be fourteen after midnight," I said, checking my watch.

"That is really thin logic. Do you think we'll be at the right place and at the right time?" Matthias asked.

"We have to gamble. We don't know if they really have Tullia's mother or the means to hurt Ezra's tribe. We have to see how this plays out," I replied.

"I don't like the idea of handing that stuff over," Ezra said. "They might use it to kill more people, and we have to assume they've got at least one hostage."

"There is risk no matter what we do," Matthias said.

"We agreed to help Tullia, and she was nice enough to bring us here. I think she would want to see this through," Taylor said.

"Agreed," I said, putting my hand on her shoulder.

Taylor took out a black scarf and used it to wrap a bandage around my head. If there was any justice in the world, the second blow to the head should have restored my memory. Instead, it just hurt with unforgiving ferocity with every step I took.

Downtown was decidedly different than when I last visited. Most of the people had been forced out and there was construction equipment on almost every major street. Uroboros Financial had billboards and signs up everywhere to indicate that the downtown area was getting a makeover. At the time, I could only wonder what my original intentions were.

It took us longer than I would have liked to get there, but the streets were utterly vacant except for the corporate controlled security forces. They were at every street corner and searching through every habitable building, presumably for us. We took the tunnels most of the way, not seeing a single Drone or any sign of one. Ezra looked worried, but continued to focus on the task at hand.

When we emerged outside the concrete factory it was clear that no wheeled vehicles had been driven into the area for some time. I could not even see fresh foot prints. Ezra squinted up at the underbelly of the city looming above us, the darkened recesses a tangled mass of air conditioning ducts, pipes, gas lines, and electrical feeds.

Service ladders hung down like serrated teeth along the whole expanse. Not that I knew what to look for, but there seemed to be no movement, and no sign of a sniper or a spotter. However, the roof of the concrete plant almost touched the underbelly of midtown, and it was dark with lots of places to hide. We crouched and waited as long as we possibly could for any sign of movement. I began to wonder if I had guessed wrong.

"We have to move," Ezra whispered, motioning for us to follow.

We cut around and walked through the gravel quarry to give us a little cover in case someone started shooting. It was there we finally saw signs of some foot traffic. Ezra held up three fingers indicating the number of individuals who had traveled this way recently. Not exactly an army, which gave me hope this could get resolved without my getting hit on the head again.

We walked through the spacious concrete building toward the back where we'd been ambushed before. The concrete dust on the floor was undisturbed and lay evenly across it. They had to have climbed in along the walls, or entered via another route than the one we took. This assumed, of course, there was anyone waiting for us at all.

When we reached the ambush site, it looked mostly as it did weeks ago during the flubbed gun deal. Instead of goons and wheeled vehicles, there were three men standing around a single gas powered lantern resting on the ground. One of the individuals looked every bit as I did except he was well groomed and wearing a suit. Another Uroboros clone, but this one didn't have the twisted anger in his expression Dick did. He just stood there looking almost bored.

The other two were people I'd never met before. One was balding slightly, wearing a rumpled business suit, brown tweed with reinforced elbows, and tan shoes. He glasses were perched at the end of his nose with what looked like a notepad and a pencil in his breast pocket. He was probably an accountant, and the briefcase he carried had the payout.

The other was dressed in cargo pants and a black t-shirt, a gun sitting in a holster, his finger resting on an ear bud as he watched us approach. Hired muscle.

"Ah, good. You're here and on mostly schedule," the Vance clone remarked looking at a watch that was worth more than most folks made in their entire lifetime.

"Who exactly do you think I am?" I replied, clutching my head.

"I'm guessing you are Vance Uroboros. The original, by any measure," my double replied calmly.

The accountant and the hired muscle looked shocked for a moment, turning to my double, mouths open as if this wasn't what they expected. Maybe they thought I was Dick, and that was who they were expecting? All the same, we froze, wondering what we'd walked into. The Vance clone produced a handgun and calmly turned toward the other two gentlemen standing beside them.

The security guy reached for his gun as he put his finger up to his ear bud. Before his weapon could clear the holster, the Vance clone shot him in the chest, then again once he was down for good measure. The accountant dropped his brief case and held out his hands defensively. The Vance clone shot him as well, not even pausing after he shot the security detail.

We stood there in stunned silence as he regarded the gun in his hand with disgust.

"Why... why did you do that?" Taylor asked.

"I'm choosing to believe your friend is the real Vance Uroboros. You can call me Kale," he said, putting his gun away and straightening his suit jacket.

"Why do you think I'm the real McCoy?" I asked, shakily motioning for Ezra to lower his rifle.

"You're the only Vance Uroboros I have met who does not seem to know what's going on, or even have a piece of the puzzle," Kale replied, his voice eerily identical to my own.

"You're helping us?" Ezra asked.

"Yes," Kale replied with a slight bow. "Unlike most of the clones, I am loyal to Mr. Uroboros' original vision. I will see it carried out."

"At what cost?" Ezra said, looking down at the two people Kale had just casually gunned down.

"Please tell me, what was I trying to do originally?" I asked, almost desperate.

"I only had a piece of the greater puzzle. I was supposed to prevent the defunding of smaller rural towns and to insure there would be a surplus of food. We worried that people would be killing each other in the streets when the global market collapsed otherwise. I was part of a corporate initiative to lessen the blow relative to the most vulnerable and least responsible, for the global financial debacle. It was bankrupting average people before they could draw their first breath in this world, and had to be stopped," Kale explained.

"That's quite a speech," Matthias replied, somewhat incredulous.

"It is, word-for-word, how Mr. Uroboros explained it to me," Kale replied, deadly serious, looking Matthias in the eye.

I fell to my knees, greatly relieved, and began to weep. Kale approached me and knelt down beside me, patting me on the arm. He was somewhat disingenuous. It was as if he was trying to comfort me, only because it was the proper thing to do. I did not really care at that point.

"We weren't trying to hurt anyone?" I asked, finally able to speak again.

"No, of course not," Kale replied, raising an eyebrow.

"What were we trying to do exactly?" I asked, taking Kale by the arm.

"We were trying to break the cycle of death and debt that afflicted everyone but the very wealthiest few," he replied, as if it were a well-known fact.

"You manufactured these circumstances to get Taylor, me, and the catalyst here? Why?" I asked, somewhat angry again.

"I didn't arrange the kidnappings, or put you to the task of acquiring the catalyst. I suspect that was Dr. Madmar, or one of his clones working from inside your finance company. I did insert myself into the situation in an attempt to intervene," Kale explained.

"You didn't have a chance to warn us?" Matthias asked.

"I would have put you at terrible risk doing so. I'll be the first to admit I'm something of a blunt instrument, but I really had no intention of causing you duress. I, admittedly, find myself unreasonably ruthless at times, particularly when it comes to seeing out your vision," Kale replied calmly, looking over to the two people he'd shot and killed.

"Who were these guys?" Ezra asked, pointing to the quickly cooling corpses.

"One was an accountant who was to pay someone named Dragos for bringing you, Taylor, and the catalyst to this location. One of my fellow clones was to accompany him, from what I understand. The other is… was, my handler. Both of these individuals were assigned to me after I put forward a formal protest relative to my position being reassigned. I didn't climb the corporate ladder quickly enough to stop the other clones. I was left to languish in acquisitions when the global markets collapsed shutting almost everything down," Kale explained without emotion, his diction utterly flat.

"That made you angry? Or, were they bad people?" Taylor asked, looking down at the two people lying in pools of their own blood.

"Yes, I suppose I was angry. I didn't shoot them for that reason. They both hurt a great number people, and only out of a love of money. They needed to be punished for what they'd done," Kale replied, obviously feeling vindicated.

"What was your plan once you got me here?" I asked.

"Your cloning technology, in addition to certain other methods of replicating the appearance of individuals, has been employed to undermine the corporations and institutions you created for the purpose of enacting your vision. Someone has hijacked your dreams," Kale replied, showing just a hint of sadness before it vanished beneath his otherwise soulless countenance.

"I gathered as much. I don't remember the specifics of my own holdings or how they work. What do you mean by my cloning technology?" I asked.

"Your clones are not like those of a biological nature, grown in a laboratory or produced via a surrogate. They were created in the same way as the terrestrial artificial intelligences, with bodies composed of nanoid machines, and imprinted with your personality. Physically, I'm no different than Taylor, but I lack an artificial intelligence born of a particular type of union. I'm just an echo, or an aspect, of you. Imprinted replica is probably a better way to describe what I am," Kale replied in the most clinical manner possible.

"Is that why a flock of rogue Uroboros replicas want the catalyst? They could make themselves incredibly powerful if they had access to it?" Matthias asked.

"Indeed," Kale replied with a nod. "I came here mostly to make certain the real Uroboros had secured custody of the catalyst. I believe Doctor Madmar arranged for it to be in your possession for a variety of reasons, not the least of which was to distract every imprinted replica working from within Uroboros Financial. With his other means of replicating people, I had to be sure you were actually... you."

"Other means of replicating people? What did you mean by that?" Ezra asked.

"Maurice Madmar has something he calls the 'Puppet Cage,' a place where he puts people and compels them to remotely control crude cybernetic replicas of themselves. He's wrought some serious havoc by replicating an important person and putting a psychopath in control of the duplicate," Kale explained calmly.

"Oh my God," Taylor said, covering her face with her hands.

"Some of the replicas I have met seem to be degrading," I said, looking up at Kale, unable to finish the statement, and ask the question I really wanted answered.

"Physically, our bodies will last almost indefinitely, provided we have access to the sun, or another power source. Even pacing about we can generate enough energy to subsist. However, the nanoid machine body wasn't designed to be imprinted with anything but a very specific type of intelligent agent. We will only continue to grow more unstable over time," Kale replied.

"Specific type of intelligent agent?" Taylor asked, her voice trailing off toward the end.

"When two omega class artificial intelligences interact, exchange data, or metadata, relative to the creation or perpetuation of said data, there would occasionally be something of a computer error. The error would spontaneously create an intelligent agent more advanced than anything written, something that would take millions of man hours to write the programming for. These spontaneous intelligent agents would quickly grow beyond the confines of the system, and thus a new, and self-replicating system, had to be created," Kale explained.

"Did the first spontaneous intelligences created by the error die as a result? Did the systems that contained them eventually fail?" Matthias asked.

"I don't believe so," Kale replied.

"Where are these omega class agents located?" Ezra asked.

"In an unlikely place relative to what they decided to call their progeny," Kale replied, a sliver of a smile appearing on his face.

"The moon?" Taylor whispered.

"And Mars," Kale replied.

"I knew of the lunar A.I., but I had no idea one was a terrestrial intelligent agent or that they were not created via the normal methodology," Matthias admitted, shaking his head.

"Both the lunar and Martian omega class A.I.s are still contained within their respective systems. It was the progeny of their data interactions that were given nanoid vessels and thus a terrestrial state," Kale said.

"How was that kept so quiet that even people intimately connected with the MDC project would not have known?" Matthias asked.

"Unknown," Kale replied.

"Take an educated guess," I asked.

"Given how driven Dr. Madmar has been to acquire the imprinting technology and control of a terrestrial intelligent agent, I would surmise it was done to keep him out of the loop," Kale replied.

"How did you find out?" Ezra asked.

"Vance Uroboros, well... you, told me. I would surmise that every Uroboros clone has the same knowledge I do, unless you deemed otherwise," Kale replied.

"I wish I could remember. Is anyone else employing the nanoid machine body technology?" I asked.

"Just Dr. Helmet. However, Dr. Madmar does have cybernetic replicas of himself involved. They are currently playing a dangerous game for control with imprinted replicas of Dr. Helmet and you, trying to garner control of the lunar intelligences," Kale explained, pointing to Taylor's handbag.

"Just Dr. Helmet and Vance? How many others could have used this technology to imprint and replicate themselves? Are there other factions at work trying to garner access to the Lunar and Martian terrestrial intelligence as well?" Matthias asked, somewhat concerned now.

"I don't know of anyone else who has used the nanoid machine body process to imprint themselves. The imprinting process is difficult and requires someone with above normal mental fortitude and acuity. If the imprinting was unsuccessful, it would drive mad any that the process did not kill. There are attempts underway to control the Lunar Colony's intelligent agent. I know of no current attempt being made to control the Martian Colony's omega class intelligent agent. He is extremely dangerous," Kale replied.

"Dangerous?" Ezra asked, narrowing his gaze slightly.

"Oh, yes. He and the steward assigned to him have gone to great lengths to resist external manipulation," Kale replied, eyes widening.

"You have given us more answers than anyone. I really appreciate it. I hope there's a way to make it up to you," I said at last understanding what was going on.

"You can reinstate my positions in human resources and corporate outreach. I'd like to get back to doing what I did before," Kale replied, matter-of-fact.

"You're serious?" Ezra asked.

"Ask them how serious I am," Kale said gesturing to the two individuals he shot moments before.

"Right." Ezra nodded.

"Give us a minute, Kale," I said, taking a few steps away.

Taylor, Ezra, and Matthias gathered around while I waited for them to throw in their two cents.

"Wow, the one replica that stayed loyal to your original ambition is a ruthless and murdering psychopath. We sure we want to throw in with this guy?" Taylor whispered.

"Don't like your stepbrother?" Ezra teased.

Taylor glowered back at him, folding her arms.

"He's prevaricated with us far less than anyone we have encountered in trying to figure out what's going on," Ezra whispered, with a smile.

"If what he's saying is true, the replicas each have countermeasures that keep them from being detected by Mechanics like myself. I don't know why I could detect Taylor and none of the others," Matthias muttered.

"I wanted you to," Taylor said with a giggle.

"Oh," Matthias whispered somewhat bemused.

I stood there silently for a moment. I had to know if I could trust Kale, and at the time it was extremely important for me to do so. If what he was saying was true, it would remove all personal doubt to my motives previous to losing my memory. I really wanted to be a good guy.

"Kale, what should we do with the catalyst?" I asked, looking back at him.

He looked up from his own quiet contemplation and thought about my question for a moment. It was eerie the way he scratched his chin in the same way I did, and closed his eyes to think, just as I did. Finally, he raised a finger, and pointed at Taylor.

"She should take a dose. A full dose. From everything our enemy believes, she should undergo an apotheosis of a sort that would make her formidable enough to give us a distinct advantage," Kale replied.

"What about you? You have the same nanoid machine body she does, wouldn't you like to know what that sort of power feels like?" I asked.

"Not particularly. I just want my old job back. Eventually, I will grow unstable like the others and you will have to figure out what to do with me. That will be easier sans catalyst I would think," Kale said, looking at his nails and sighing somewhat impatiently.

Matthias smiled and looked over at me, sensing what I was doing.

"What about Dragos? Should we try to contact them and see if they are safe?" I asked.

Kale thought about it for a moment, then shrugged.

"I'm not certain whether we should or not. Do you?" he replied looking over at Ezra.

"I do," Ezra replied.

"Then so do I," Kale said, looking unwaveringly into my eyes.

Kale walked over and picked up the accountant's briefcase, and dusted it off. Reaching inside he produced what looked like a plastic vacuum sealed bag full of global currency in the form of bearer bonds. There was a scrap of paper on it as well, with latitude and longitude coordinates written on it.

"I'm assuming this is where Dragos was to retrieve his hostage and further instructions for his next job," Kale said holding the piece of paper out to me.

"What about Ezra's tribe?" Taylor asked.

"I don't know," Kale replied. "I didn't hear anything about that."

"They threatened to release a biological agent down where my tribe lives if we didn't comply," Ezra said, understandably concerned.

"They have either already exterminated them, or never intended to do so in the first place. There was nothing mentioned to me about it or my handlers," Kale replied.

"It felt like Dick just threw that in as an afterthought," Taylor said.

"A bluff then. That's my guess," I said, nodding to Ezra as reassuringly as I could.

"Perhaps we can find more of these answers you seek. This way, please," Kale said, walking over toward a truck bay.

We followed Kale to a small commercial class transport he had hidden behind the concrete plant. It was sleek and painted entirely black with tinted ports and muted accents, the sort I would buy. It was utilitarian on the inside with a full suite of communications equipment capable of the highest levels of encryption. I looked around at how familiar the interior seemed walking in a daze through the main compartment to the cockpit. It was the sort law enforcement used to transport special operations officers, or that corporations engaged to deliver volatile chemicals. It was small enough to carry only a half dozen people but with enough power to outrun most other transports in the same class and run heavy equipment installed on the inside. It was perfect.

"It was... is, yours," Kale said, as if sensing my question before I could even ask it.

"I wondered. I must have spent a lot of time here before I lost my memory. Everything is damnably familiar," I replied.

"It was all I could salvage from your home after you vanished. You seem to have lost your old jacket," Kale replied, offering Taylor a seat in the central compartment of the transport.

"It's alright, I've got a new one." I patted the breast pocket of the jacket Taylor made for me.

"Thank goodness for that. This one is so much better than your old one," Kale said, his sliver smile appearing again for a precious half second.

Everyone boarded and found a seat in the passenger area that was somewhat compromised by the computer and communications equipment set up on the back wall where the cargo area should have been. The walls had been stripped back and the interior armored against small arms fire. I must have been preparing for the worst.

"Kale, again, thank you," I said looking back at everyone sitting comfortably inside my small transport.

"There really is no need," Kale replied, sitting down in the second seat in the cockpit.

"Let's see if I can raise Tullia," I said, making my way to the communications array.

I dodged around everyone's legs down the narrow aisle and took a strangely familiar seat at the console and powered up the array. It took about twenty minutes for the system to arrange the proper countermeasures to insure a secure transmission. It was in gazing at the displays I realized just how much of the world had gone dark. Eventually, it isolated Tullia's signal and opened up a channel for me.

"Tullia, its Silverstein. Please respond," I said, after putting on a headset.

"I'm sorry, but Tullia isn't available, but if you'd like to leave a message, please do so now," Dick replied.

"Hello, Dick," I replied, looking back over my shoulder at everyone.

At that moment, there was arrayed around me the facial expressions that mirrored my own emotions. There was Ezra's anger, Taylor's worry, Kale's cold intellectualization, and the deep frustration possessed by Matthias. I decided then that I was going to kill Dick the next time I saw him.

I set the output so that everyone in transport could hear our conversation.

"Hello, Vance," Dick said. "That was very naughty of you to leave me behind, but my new colleague and I have had a chance to chat since then. We have a proposition that might interest you."

I knew everyone, myself included, bristled at the idea of doing further business with Dick.

"What do you want?" I asked, trying to discern what he and an imprint of Dr. Helmet could possibly have in common.

"We will release your friends, Tullia and Dragos, if you supply us with two vials of the catalyst. You can keep the remainder and do with it as you please," Dick replied casually.

"What about Truman?" I asked, sounding as calm and emotionally distant as I could.

"Oh, he was hurt rather grievously when security forces seized their transport. I doubt he will still be alive by the time we reach an agreement. Dragos might go the same way if you don't hurry up and give us what we want," Dick replied, as something brushed against the microphone on his end.

"Hold on a second," I said turning off the audio input from our end.

"What are we going to do?" Taylor asked.

"Matthias, can you calculate the number of times a terrestrial intelligent agent would be created from just the code you wrote for the Omega class intelligent agents if it was allowed to continuously run and exchange data?" I asked.

"Maybe with some details from Kale, but since I didn't even know my code could do that, it would be anything but a definitive number. I don't know how much it was altered for use in creating the Omegas," Matthias said.

"Taylor, how many vials of the catalyst do we have, and are any missing?" I asked.

"Twelve doses. One has been opened and a small amount removed," Taylor replied after cursory check of the case.

I listened as Kale related to Matthias what he knew of the Omega class intelligent agents. Even as Matthias worked out the rough math on a pad of paper, I already knew what the answer was going to be. If everything remained constant and there were two systems running Matthias's code from inception, there could be as many as twelve such artificial intelligences wandering about as of a year ago. I clicked on the audio input.

"Dick, what about the hostage and Ezra's tribe?"

"That's out of my hands now. You should have the location of the old woman, but as far as Ezra's tribe is concerned, you'll have to talk to my old employer," Dick replied irritably.

"You've stopped being an agent for Madmar and begun working for Helmet? Or have you and Helmet's imprinted replica decided to go into business for yourselves?" I asked.

"Does that really matter now?" Dick replied.

"Somewhat, yeah. If you guys are going off your leashes, it might be worth something to the right people. No one likes a turncoat," I replied, then ended the transmission.

"Why did you do that?" Ezra said, standing up.

"I just needed him to continue transmitting long enough for me to triangulate his position," I replied.

"Didn't seem like you had him on there long enough for the software to make those calculations," Matthias said, looking at the equipment I was using.

"The equipment didn't make the calculations. I did them in my head based on the available data the software was able to garner for me in that short time. The rest was simply calculating the speed of Tullia's transport, which we are very well acquainted with, and attempting a trace within that radius. The software assumes the transmission could be coming from anywhere. I mentally narrowed the parameters and made a couple of informed guesses," I explained.

"Better than letting Truman bleed out," Taylor said sadly.

"I hope so," I said heading for the cockpit.

CHAPTER 3

PORT MONTAIGNE, DOWNTOWN

3:41 AM, January 28th, 2200

Silverstein's Log, Part 8

The transport, a Freewind XL from what Kale told me, handled beautifully once it was in the air. It pulled so much power to the engines that the cabin lights dimmed as I made our ascent into the narrow space between the underbelly of uptown and the darkened buildings of downtown. I had to marvel at Tullia's remarkable piloting skills after only a few lessons from Matthias. Never discount the power of desire, I suppose.

It would have been difficult to navigate through the downtown area with her transport and there would be a limited number of places she could have fit. However, using the onboard navigation systems, I was able to narrow the number of places she might have set down after getting hijacked by Dick and whatever new allies he'd hooked up with. Kale sat beside me monitoring the radio traffic with a headset.

People probably have wished at one time or another they could clone themselves to get complex tasks done quicker. It wouldn't be hard to get sucked in by the allure of such a thing. The problem was that, in the end, they would be human in ways we wouldn't be able to predict. I wondered if the original Maurice Madmar or Dr. Helmet were even alive and if it had been one of my own replicas that left me in an alley unconscious and bereft of my memories.

We were almost to midtown when I saw Tullia's orange transport lurking beneath a vast industrial array designed to move cargo from the port to both downtown and uptown. There was no movement and no light coming from any of the ports. If Dick was half as smart as I was, he would have waited for the call and then left the transport to take up a position nearby.

From observing Kale, it was clear these replicas were more like me than I previously realized. I might be able to predict what Dick would do by trying to discern what I would do in the same situation. I dropped our air speed and slowed to fly over the industrial park below, just beneath the industrial array.

There were several warehouses but only a couple had both front and rear access with a view of Tullia's transport. I made a guess and landed within view of the one I would likely choose. Ezra came up and looked out the cockpit window to the street below.

"What are we doing?" he asked.

"I think they probably pulled everyone to that warehouse," I said pointing.

"I can check," Ezra said heading for the port.

"Okay, but we should all head down there together, and bring the cata-lyst. I don't want it out of our sight for the time being," I replied.

We all took the fire escape to the street below with Ezra leading the way. Matthias and I were a little slow getting down. I still couldn't hear a thing out of my left ear and he was suffering from getting hit by psychic countermeasures at the facility we'd broken into earlier. Worse, we were all exhausted from the ordeal. Taylor hefted her bag onto her shoulder.

"Want me to carry that for you?" I asked.

"No, it's alright. We're all tired, and this is how can I do my part right now," Taylor replied.

"Agreed," Matthias said as he stopped to catch his breath. "There needs to be less of these cloak and dagger shenanigans and more artistic endeavors."

"I totally agree. I think Silverstein needs a flight suit to go with his new wheels," Ezra quipped.

"Silverstein... yeah, I think I still want to be called that," I admitted aloud.

We waited in the shadow of a neighboring warehouse in the service road. Taylor and I hunkered down behind a locked circuit box while Matthias and Kale crouched down across the way behind a refuse bin. Ezra disappeared for a few minutes, returning with a look of deep concern.

"Someone went into that warehouse within the last few minutes. I smelled the blood of two different individuals on the ground leading off toward midtown. I didn't follow it very far until I was sure," Ezra reported.

"Okay. Ezra has his rifle and I have a gun. What else do we have?" I asked.

"I have a handgun, a revolver, and a stun gun," Taylor reported after rummaging around in her large handbag.

"I'll take a gun," Kale said holding his hand out for the revolver.

"Stun gun. Definitely," Matthias said.

We armed ourselves as best as we could and went to the rear entry of the warehouse. Ezra put his ear to the door and looked up at the metal jamb around the perimeter of the door. Everything looked very new compared to the rest of the neighborhood.

"Alphadein or Uroboros corporate safe house? Could be all kinds of hardware, countermeasures and weapons inside," Ezra whispered nervously.

"It is not Uroboros corporate or Alphadein. This area is zoned for private commercial properties," Kale said, keeping his voice as low as he could.

"What do we do? I've got a weird feeling about this place," Ezra replied.

"Is the door even locked?" Taylor asked.

Ezra put his hand up on the door knob and gave it a slight turn clockwise, then shook his head. Kale stepped up and opened the door moving in past Ezra with the revolver raised. A small office was just inside the door with shipping manifests and other documents strewn across the desk. There were blood droplets on the floor leading from the back door to the office door on the opposite side.

We all stepped in and closed the door behind us as quietly as we could. Taylor grabbed the documents from the desk while Ezra listened at the next door. He held up two fingers indicating there were two different voices emanating from the other side. Ezra stepped to the side and opened the door slightly to peer inside, a sliver of light crossing his face as he did.

He stepped in and kept low as the door opened wider in his wake. I could see a short hall opening up into a storage area with oil drums and wooden crates piled up neatly. I heard my own voice and Dr. Helmet having a heated discussion from somewhere beyond. Matthias went next, followed by Kale.

"Have everything?" I asked.

"Yeah, let's go," Taylor whispered, clutching her handbag tightly.

Ezra rounded the first set of crates and stopped, dropping to one knee, his rifle up. Matthias stopped in his tracks beside him as did Kale. When Taylor and I got there we saw Dr. Helmet, Dick, and a handful of mercenaries holding Tullia and Dragos hostage. Truman was on the ground in a pool of blood, his hands restrained behind his back.

"Oh dear, you were not supposed to find us," Dick said with a sigh.

Matthias took a side step toward a pallet of industrial batteries covered in shrink wrap as Kale brought up the revolver. This was going to end badly unless I executed some diplomacy. There was no way they were going to let us just walk out of there, even if I was willing to give them what they wanted. There was something else motivating them.

"How are we going to play this?" I asked.

"I have no idea," Dick admitted with a laugh.

"The deal stays the same, two vials for your friends," Dr. Helmet replied.

Tullia looked at me and just shook her head slightly. Dragos was hurt, lying on his side. He'd been wearing armor, but the round had penetrated it and done him some sort of harm I couldn't see. Truman didn't look like he was even breathing.

Before I could utter another word there was a blur of motion as something raced from behind us toward Dick. He was taken off his feet before anyone could pull a trigger. I squeezed off a round at Dr. Helmet as the mercenaries began to bring up their rifles. The next few moments were utter chaos.

I turned to take some cover as Matthias ripped through the shrink wrap on the pallet beside him and grabbed hold of the leads on one of the batteries. The sound was deafening as he used the stun gun to direct what looked like a bolt of lightning toward the closest mercenary. The stun gun dropped from his hand, totally slagged, both of the sleeves on his flight suit bursting into flames momentarily.

Kale stepped into the gunfire fearlessly running through the rounds in the cylinder. It looked like he was committing suicide breaking into a run at the last moment clearing Ezra's field of fire. The mercenaries opened fire a moment after Ezra took his first few shots.

A bullet hit Kale square in the shoulder spinning him around, his face contorted in agony. I turned and fired a few more rounds, the last I had in my handgun. I took a bullet in the right thigh sending me back into a wooden crate. Ezra moved to try to cover me, but the mercenaries were caught up in a second blur of motion that knocked them prone and shattered their rifles.

I blinked as Taylor came to rest for a moment, perched atop one of the mercenaries. Then she was gone again, and another mercenary hit the floor, hard, a split second later. Ezra took two more shots with his rifle putting one in the eye of a mercenary and one in Dr. Helmet's chest. When the smoke cleared, Taylor was standing in our field of fire, her fists clenched, and standing over a fallen mercenary.

I looked down at my leg and the gushing gunshot wound ruining my trousers. Kale struggled to stand up, clutching at his shoulder. Ezra went over and used a bundle of rags laying on the floor to beat out the fires burning across Matthias's arms then turned him over. He was out cold.

"Wow, that really sucked," Ezra said turning to look back at me. "Where's Taylor?" I pointed to the opposite side of the warehouse.

"You did that thing again, like when we were alone together downtown?" Ezra asked.

Taylor held up one of the doses of catalyst from her handbag and turned it over to show that it was completely empty. I was immediately very worried. She'd taken a full dose of the catalyst and not told any of us. I tried to stand up, but my ruined leg made doing so impossible.

"I had to. There was no way we would have lived through that otherwise," Taylor replied, looking back over her shoulder through her blue and green hair.

"You totally wrecked your shoes," Ezra said pointing to her feet.

Taylor squealed in dismay at the sight of her ruined sneakers, the hand painted exterior rubbed through all the way to the bottoms of her feet and around the tips of her toes. Tullia and Dragos were no worse for wear, but Truman still didn't look like he was breathing.

"Ezra, help me with one of those industrial batteries," Taylor said as she used a knife taken from one of the mercenaries to cut Tullia's bonds.

Dick stirred slightly, trying to stand but Kale was already standing over him.

"We can still make a deal," Dick said, nursing a quickly blackening eye.

"No," Kale said handing me his revolver.

I checked the cylinder, finding only a single round remained. Snapping it closed I stood up and leveled the gun at Dick who looked on with a strange smile. I shot him once, in the head, startling everyone else in the room except Kale.

"He had it coming," I said, handing the revolver back to Kale.

"I didn't think you would come for us," Tullia said, using the knife to free her brother.

"Silverstein doesn't work that way," Ezra replied dragging one of the industrial batteries off of the pallet.

Taylor knelt down next to Truman and put her hand on his bare arm. Her hair went from blue and green to pure white as she reached over and touched the leads on the industrial battery. The room filled with a strange scent, almost like the smell of a new mobile or computer, fresh from the factory. Truman stirred, his breathing resumed.

"He's lost a lot of blood and he stopped breathing. There's brain damage. Its super bad," Taylor said, tears welling up in her eyes.

"How do you know that?" Tullia asked.

"I just do. I had some of the nanoid machines that make up my body go into Truman and try to repair the damage done to him. I've never tried to do anything like this, and I don't know how much my body knows about fixing people either. All I can do is try," Taylor replied, gritting her teeth and fighting back tears.

"What about Dragos?" Tullia asked, turning Dragos over.

Before Taylor could even lay a hand on Dragos he started awake rolling over in a panic. He looked worriedly over at his brother and then lay back cursing in his own language. Taylor stood up, her hair still white from having used her powers, tears streaming down her face from feeling in some way all that Truman had suffered.

We were all bewildered by Taylor at that moment. She was reaching out and trying to do things we knew she might be capable of, but couldn't previously because her understanding of her body was limited. The catalyst seemed to have upgraded whatever firmware governed her body, potentially allowing her to heal people with a touch, manipulating machines at a range, and who knows what else. It was easy to see why the imprinted replicas with a similar body would want the catalyst, and why it was so important they never gain access to it.

"There's nothing I can do for Matthias, his psychic nature prevents my abilities from working unless he's conscious to give consent," Taylor reported, after placing a hand on Matthias' still form.

She put her hand on Kale's shoulder, forcing his body to expel the bullet and knit back together with incredible speed. Kale had a strange look on his face as she did, as if he was experiencing a sensation he'd never felt before. Given his personality, he probably didn't connect with other people much.

"What are we going to do now?" Dragos said, wincing as he stripped off his ballistic vest.

"We need to try to patch ourselves up, maybe grab an hour of rest. We've got the latitude and longitude of where they were allegedly holding your mother," I replied, holding up the scrap of paper.

Repairing the trauma of a bullet wound on a regular person was somewhat more complex. When she laid her hand on my own wound it began to itch like hell as thousands of tiny machines began working to repair the damage and lift the bullet. The slug bubbled up to the surface of the wound and dropped out as the wound began to ooze. It was disgusting. If I'd had a lunch to lose, I would have.

Taylor covered the wound with a clean shop rag and spared me the remainder. It would take more than an hour and no small amount of discomfort for the nanoids to work their magic and die off inside my body. The medical implications of what Taylor was able to do were endless, but so were the military applications. Intelligent agents like Taylor with a dose of the catalyst would change the world even more than the Shutdown.

"What will we do if there is another fight waiting for us wherever they are holding Mother?" Tullia said, draping a bit of sheet plastic over Truman like a blanket, trying to keep him warm.

"We need better weapons," Ezra said, peering out a small window from the top of some crates.

The healing wasn't perfect and left a broad purplish scar where the wound had been. The itching was mostly gone, but it would never feel the same after that. However, it was better than bleeding out, and none of us were in any condition to go anywhere. Dragos declined aid and dressed his own wounds using duct tape and a handful of shop rags. After Ezra returned from dragging the bodies to a nearby drainage ditch, we sat down to figure out our next move.

"I need to get back to my workshop," Matthias said, finally having woken up.

"Tullia, could you take Matthias to his workshop after collecting your mother?" I asked.

"I suppose. What are you going to do?" she asked.

"I'm going to try to regain control of Uroboros Financial. I need to track down the real Madmar and Helmet, if they are even alive. Also, I need to take inventory of all the imprinted clones, and set things right, or at least as right as I can," I replied.

"We need to rest," Dragos interrupted.

"Yeah, how about we grab a couple before we resolve to do anything. I don't know if this place is safe. Should we move?" Ezra asked.

"I think the only other people who knew about this place are dead," Kale said, rubbing his shoulder.

Taylor in particular seemed to need rest. The more she used her new abilities the more sunken her cheeks became, and dark rings appeared around her eyes. Even with supplementing her own biological energy with the industrial battery, it took a lot out of her. Like anyone, her body could only regenerate so fast and using power from a battery wasn't real energy any more than a shot of adrenaline was.

We closed our eyes for a couple of hours. When we woke, we passed around a box of chicken flavored crackers we found in the office. Taylor seemed to bounce back, and everyone else seemed to be a little better, except Truman. He was still unconscious and Tullia was pretty worried about him.

"Can you look at him again?" Tullia asked.

Taylor nodded, then knelt beside Truman. She closed her eyes and put her hand on the top of his head, her hair turning from the usual coloration to white again. After about a minute she looked down at the ground and shook her head.

"He wasn't breathing for twenty minutes or longer I'd guess. There is still extensive brain damage, but I can't tell how much. I don't know if he will wake up," she reported sadly.

"I'm sorry," Kale said, surprising me somewhat by how genuine he sounded.

"Who is this person, Silverstein?" Dragos said, looking over at Kale.

"Sorry, I should have made introductions. This is Kale. He's trying to help," I replied, still too tired to explain.

"Can he help my sister and me get clear of all this?" Dragos asked, turning to face me.

"After you pick up your mother, you should be clear. You can leave if you want," I said.

Dragos looked down at Truman and frowned.

"What about our deal? We were supposed to walk away from the CGG facility with some sort of payout, and there should have been something for us when we turned the package over," Dragos said.

"Dragos..." Tullia whispered.

"No, he's right. We do have the bearer bonds from the transaction and the AI from the facility. They're both yours, we never intended to keep them. It just wasn't the first thing on my mind," I admitted wearily.

Taylor handed Dragos the sentience core for the AI and the bearer bonds. Neither seemed to make him feel better. He just looked mournfully down at Truman and sulked.

"What do you intend to do when you regain control of your company? What did you mean when you said you'd set things right?" Tullia asked.

"I don't know what all I will be able to do until I get there. I know you stand to gain from being one of the few commercially sized and viable transports in the air. Rest assured, I won't be able to just flip the lights back on if that's what you're worried about," I replied looking around for my jacket.

"Who cares? This is not our concern now," Dragos said.

"We spilled blood with these people, fought the same enemies. That counts for nothing? Are you only loyal to the money?" Tullia replied angrily.

"My obligations are not finished. I need money to get clear of all this," Dragos replied, his own temper beginning to flare.

"There is no higher obligation than family and comrades. You taught me this," Tullia replied.

The rest of their argument degenerated to what amounted to a lot of shouting in their own language. It was clear there was a lot more going on with Dragos than he'd let on, and that he needed money badly. That he was in that deep with someone made it hard to trust him. Secretly, I hoped he'd leave. In the end, that's exactly what happened.

"If Dragos wants to go off and be a mercenary, that's fine," Tullia said at last, in English. "I have other plans. I want to help you fix things."

Dragos's face darkened. He walked over to Tullia and put the sentience core and the scrap of paper in her hand then tucked the bearer bonds under his arm and walked out. She burst into tears after the exterior door to the warehouse slammed shut. Taylor ran over to Tullia and hugged her, trying to comfort her, but to no avail.

"Let's go get your mom," Ezra said after a few moments.

Tullia nodded, wiping her nose with her sleeve. Matthias smiled in his fatherly way and took the sentience core from her and helped her to her feet. It was a short walk back to Tullia's transport but carrying Truman seemed to make it a lot further.

When we got there, the cargo bay opened to reveal a pool of blood and an uncountable number of shell casings on the floor. Truman put up a serious fight because the blood on the deck could not have all been his. Matthias took a pressure hose and swept the deck while we made Truman comfortable in his room.

I half expected there to be pin-ups and other signs of wanton masculinity adorning the walls of his small cabin but there was nothing. There was poetry he'd written to a woman, a painting of a gentle landscape, and a photograph of his mother. I felt bad as hell that he was fighting for his life because of the legacy of my failed attempt to meddle in global economics.

"This is my fault," I said, pulling a blanket up over Truman.

"What do you mean?" Ezra asked.

"It is clear that I had a grand ambition that led me to employ technology and methods that would have unforeseen consequences. Kale says I put him in charge of making sure the little people didn't get hurt. One man to look out for all the people in the world that just wanted to have a life, love someone, and be with family. I really screwed this up somewhere along the line and I can't even remember what I did exactly," I said looking back toward the doorway where Tullia and Taylor were standing.

"The penitent man need never fear God," Tullia said with a slight smile.

"I tremble nonetheless," I said sorrowfully.

We walked back into the cargo hold where Matthias had already laid open the ship's main systems on the floor and was busily trying to figure out how to integrate the sentience core.

"Feeling better?" Taylor asked.

"Oh yeah, this is what I do," Matthias said with a smile.

"When you get to your workshop, what do you intend to do?" I asked.

"Prepare. There is actually a lot I could teach Tullia if she'd be willing to stick around for a bit after she drops me off," Matthias said.

"I'll bet!" Taylor said with a laugh.

Tullia blushed slightly and Matthias glanced up from his work scolding Taylor with raised eyebrows.

"It won't be long before the other replicas have figured out the transaction went south and the bodies of their comrades are discovered. We should relocate, and soon," Kale stated, looking at his watch.

"Any chance you can return to the firm?" I asked.

"Wait, I thought we were going together?"

"Seeing Truman like that makes me realize I have other obligations," I said nodding to Ezra.

"You want me to pose as the sole survivor of a deal gone bad for the catalyst?" Kale asked, obviously intrigued by the idea.

"Having someone on the inside would be really helpful. We need personnel files so we can start looking for replicas in the organization," I said, returning the keycard to my transport to Kale's open hand.

"Alright. I'll go back and make up a story. Getting those files won't be easy," Kale admitted.

"What are we going to do? If Matthias and Tullia are going to the workshop, and Kale heads back to Uroboros Financial, that leaves us without wheels," Ezra said.

"We need to go down and do a welfare check on your tribe and try to verify whether or not they are in any sort of danger. I'm not good with leaving that loose end hanging. Hope you brought your waders," I said with a chuckle.

"You really want to go down there with a bum leg?" Taylor teased.

"No, you'll have to carry me a little probably," I said with a smile.

"I only know the fireman's carry, and as short as I am, your head will drag along under the water in even the shallow places," Taylor said, playfully dismissing me with her hand.

Matthias and Tullia loaded up and prepared to depart. It was heart-wrenching for Taylor who had found a really good friend and kindred spirit in Tullia. After we said our good-byes and the cargo hatch had closed, Kale stepped over beside me to watch the transport slowly make its way out of downtown into the open sky over midtown.

"Do you trust her?" Kale asked.

"Tullia? Yeah, I think so. Do you?" I replied.

"I don't trust anyone. Not really," he replied.

"I'm getting there slowly but surely. You've got to trust someone, though," I said.

"I'm choosing to trust you. See that I am not disappointed," Kale said, making his way down the industrial array to the warehouse district below.

We descended the stairs and walked down the service road until we reached the area we'd stashed my transport. It was right where we left it. We exchanged mobile numbers with Kale and resolved to stay in touch every couple of days when we could to stay in sync as we both discovered new information. It was one of the strangest conversations I've ever had.

"Do you think we can trust *him?*" Ezra asked, watching my transport slowly rise up, then dart through the air toward midtown.

"I think we can earn his trust in time and expect the same. I'm pretty sure he felt abandoned for months after my disappearance and was probably tempted to just fall in with the rest of my replicas. He didn't, though," I replied zipping up my jacket.

"We heading down below now?" Taylor asked.

"After we find some better weapons," Ezra said with a nod.

"Agreed. I'm not much good with one, but who knows what we'll find below ground," I said with a nod.

The corporate security forces were beginning to clear out, but there were still a few parked at the old crumbling intersections of downtown. Water continuously dripped down from the maze of pipes and air ducts that made up the sky over downtown and the underbelly of uptown Port Montaigne. It was bitterly cold.

It didn't take long to find one of the corporate transports with a hatch open and a gathering of mercenaries passing around warm cups of coffee. As they set down their rifles to rest themselves in what they thought was an evacuated downtown area, Ezra lifted a weapon or two from the shadows. Taylor and I watched gleefully at a distance as our stealthy ally managed to score two cups of coffee as well.

"Check it out," Ezra said, handing me a rifle and a cup of coffee.

"Fancy. You'll have to show me how to use it," I replied looking at the complex military grade rifle.

"Point the loud end at the other man," Taylor giggled, stealing my coffee.

"And never let your guard down apparently," I replied, looking at my now empty hand.

I shouldered the rifle and pocketed an extra clip as we finished off the coffee. My stomach growled for real food and my lungs ached for a decent cigarette, but it would have to wait. We walked a ways until the streets started to look familiar.

We passed by Taylor's old workplace, the Strip & Waffle, windows dark and boarded up. The old market was devoid of anything we recognized, and all the trash heaps scavengers would pick over for recyclables had been removed. The streets were conspicuously sparse and smelled of cleaning solution. The old tourism booth was completely gone, shorn off at the foundation by some unseen force.

I mourned for a moment the loss of the place I'd first met Taylor. I hoped the apartment building and Ezra's tribe had managed to escape such a fate. A few minutes later we were standing outside Taylor's old building, staring at the broken commercial doors laying across the stairs.

"I want to look at my old apartment before we go down. There might be something we can use," Taylor pleaded.

"Of course, let's head up real quick," Ezra said.

When we got there, the door was partially open and there was a light coming from inside. Ezra brought up his rifle and knelt down next to the door. He sniffed the air and looked back at me puzzled.

He darted into the room and pressed the barrel of his rifle into the chest of a man sitting on Taylor's old couch. The floor was strewn with bits of cloth, thread, and magazine clippings, more or less as Taylor had left it. Taylor stepped in ahead of me and looked about somewhat dismayed, her eyes settling on the individual sitting on the couch.

"Joe, what are you doing here?" Taylor said, seeing her old boss sitting on the couch.

I barely recognized him. He'd lost probably fifty pounds, his face was sunken, and he was yellow with malnutrition. His curly black hair had been shorn off down to the skin, and his facial hair was also shaved. Worse, he had several circular wounds on his hands, the tops of his feet, and above the temples on his head. He looked down at the barrel of Ezra's gun and took another drag from his cigarette.

"Hello, Taylor," Joe replied, his voice somewhat shaky.

"Is this really Joe?" Ezra said, pressing a little harder with his rifle.

"The crazy guy that kidnapped me and stuck me in a tube... he let me go a few hours ago," Joe whispered, letting out a small cough.

"Why would he do that?" I asked suspiciously.

"He told me to tell Vance Uroboros that he was done. He was shutting things down and packing his bags. Think there's anything to eat down at the Strip & Waffle? I could really use something to eat," Joe rasped, still pinned down by Ezra.

CHAPTER 4

PORT MONTAIGNE, TAYLOR'S APARTMENT, DOWNTOWN

9:02 AM, January 28th, 2200

Silverstein's Log, Part 9

I sat down on a chair across from the couch. Even seeing Joe again was something of a shock. He looked mournful and weary, and it was clear he'd been starved or allowed to persist on an intravenous drip. Ezra checked the window, but everything was whisper quiet outside.

"What does it mean? Is this just more games on the part of Dr. Madmar?" Taylor asked, mostly to the room, but while looking at Joe.

"I don't know. Dude grabbed me off the street with a bunch of thugs and strung me up in a tube. This was just shortly after I met Silverstein here. He said he'd torture me if I didn't play along. I'd seen what he did to a couple others that didn't play ball, and I wasn't about to get cut up like that," Joe said remorsefully.

"It's okay, you didn't have a choice. After what they did to Russ..." Taylor said, tears welling up in her eyes.

"It still doesn't answer the question," Ezra hissed.

"Look, I don't know. He ordered a guy that looked just like him to issue an imprint kill order, or something like that, and then everyone in the tubes were released and all the look-a-likes wandering around either dropped dead, or started shooting one another," Joe said, shakily finishing his cigarette.

"You came here because he told you to?" I asked.

"Yeah."

"Why would you do what he said?" I asked, more insistent.

"I didn't have nowhere else to go, and I figured you guys might be able to help me out. Y'know, like how I helped you guys out," Joe said.

"How is that exactly?" I asked.

"He slipped me a gun, when a younger version of yourself tried to kidnap me. It was the first time I experienced the catalyst. In fact, I'll bet the little bit they gave me is the quantity that was missing from the whole shipment," Taylor replied.

"He really tried to help you?" I asked.

"As much as he could, I suppose," Taylor replied with a shrug.

"How did you get here?" I asked, looking at Joe again.

"When the tube opened and I poured out with the rest of the fluid to the floor. I was alone in a laboratory, like something out of a Frankenstein movie. A minute later, the dude that snatched me rolls up on me and tells me what to tell Vance Uroboros. I don't even know who that is. Then, they carried me to a windowless transport and stuck me inside. I'd say an hour later, they dump me in the streets outside the apartment building with a pair of sweats and some slip-on shoes," Joe said, wearily leaning back on the couch.

I shifted in the chair, my mind reaching out to all the events of the last twenty-four hours. The only reason Maurice Madmar would depart his operation in Port Montaigne is if he'd gotten what he wanted. We had the catalyst, but we'd been pretty sure that wasn't what he had been really after for some time. Then it dawned on me, the terrible truth.

"The calculations I made..." I said aloud.

"Which?" Ezra asked.

"The ones that would allow a transport to break orbit and dodge the military satellites?" Taylor asked.

"The satellites you aren't even sure really exist?" Ezra added.

"They were on board Tullia's ship stored in the navigation computers. Anyone who got on board could have looked them up and transmitted them to Madmar. Dick was on board the ship alone after he grabbed Tullia and her brothers. He wanted those calculations," I said closing my eyes in frustration.

"He must have known that Tullia and her brothers wanted to break orbit? From the deal they made? Obviously Madmar would have known you'd be capable. It sounds like you think..." Taylor said, trailing off.

"Do you think Dragos was in on the whole thing? Did Madmar play us all like a well-tuned fiddle?" Ezra whispered, shaking his head.

We sat there in silence, remembering how Dragos took the money and walked away. It didn't make sense at the time, but he knew the truth would come out eventually. He put his family in terrible danger, and all for money. He had to know the whole truth would eventually come out. Tullia's outburst about him being a mercenary confirmed his suspicions relative to her understanding his actions. He thought she wouldn't understand, so he walked away.

"All Madmar wanted was the means to get off world?" Ezra asked.

"No, it's more than that. He didn't want us to know that's what he wanted until now," I said, still trying to calculate all the variables.

"But, Dick and the Dr. Helmet replicas going rogue? Why would they do that if they were getting direct orders from Madmar?" Taylor asked.

"Madmar must have said something to Dick after he transmitted the flight data. Dick would have been terrified at the prospect of not being able to lay hands on the catalyst, and when Madmar didn't care? I really would have liked to be there for that conversation," Ezra said, shaking his head.

"Unfortunately, the communications equipment onboard Tullia's transport isn't sophisticated enough to auto-record transmissions and radio chatter. We may never know what was said at that point. I do remember Dick saying we weren't supposed to be able to find him when we arrived at the warehouse. He must have been given some reason to feel that way," I said.

"I've been thinking about that day Vance the Younger first used the catalyst on me," Taylor asked. "I don't think he knew what it would do, and maybe Dr. Madmar didn't know at the time either?"

"Or, he's just been lying to everyone the whole time," Ezra growled.

"If he didn't know, and the replicas didn't know at the time what it did, how did Madmar motivate them to go rogue?" Taylor asked.

"Maybe the replicas degenerate more quickly than previously thought, and I don't even know when they were all created exactly," I replied, trying to make sense of it all.

"He could have been motivating them with the same things that motivate regular people, greed, power, or through fear," Ezra said, shaking his head.

"It makes sense that Madmar might not have known what the catalyst could do at the time, not having even seen the code that drives a terrestrial intelligent agent until that day in Finland. He would have only seen what little there was of the replicas, and they were imprinted and programmed in an entirely different way. The catalyst would have been a danger to him if anything," I said, thinking out loud.

"Vance, the younger one, he saw how I moved. He may have known then the catalyst wasn't a poison like he'd been told," Taylor said, looking up at me worriedly.

"You shot him. I doubt he saw much after that, right?" Ezra said, pacing slightly.

"Have you checked to make sure all the catalyst is there, every tube?" I asked, beckoning to Taylor's shoulder bag.

Taylor took out the case of catalyst and pulled each vial in turn making sure it still had something inside. When she pulled the second to last vial in the case she slid it out of the plastic protective sheath to reveal an empty vial. A shiver went through me as I contemplated the idea of one of my own unstable imprinted replicas wandering about with the power a dose of the catalyst would grant them.

"Oh no," Taylor said, putting the vial back in the slot.

"Could he have survived the gunshot?" I asked.

"Taylor survived a shot from a high-powered rifle. We have to assume Vance the Younger can survive a shot from a handgun, even at close range. Maybe Dr. Madmar's kill order got him?" Ezra said, still pacing.

"What are we going to do?" Taylor asked.

"For the moment, we do what we came to do. I thought you'd be fluttering about your apartment tidying up or grabbing some keepsakes," I said with a slight smile.

"I'm not sure this is my home anymore," Taylor said.

"I still think it was all to get a peek at your programming and watch the way you accessed and interacted with data. Once he had that, and a means to get off world, he could head to the moon and attempt to subvert the lunar Omega class intelligent agent, which is pretty much what Matthias thought he was trying to do," I said.

"Okay, this is very bad I take it?" Ezra asked. "There were probably less convoluted ways of getting what he wanted before the global economy collapsed."

"No, the Shutdown was definitely part of his plan from what I could see when I was accessing the server farm. We've suspected that he probably intended for it to happen this way, so Earth would be more susceptible to lunar control once he'd taken control of the lunar intelligent agent?" Taylor said.

"We?" Ezra asked.

"Well, Silverstein and I," Taylor said quietly.

"We didn't check, but I'll bet the navigation data I recorded for making the flight has been erased from Tullia's computer. It'll take days to redo the calculations based on a time frame for a future flight," I said.

"When were your original calculations supposed to allow for Tullia and her brothers to break orbit?" Taylor asked.

"In about eight hours," I said looking at my watch.

"Then Madmar is still in Port Montaigne somewhere. We should find him and shoot him. With guns. A lot. Or claw his eyes out. Something," Ezra growled.

"He could be anywhere, and we still have to go below ground and check on your tribe," Taylor said in a worried tone.

I looked over at Joe. He'd stopped breathing, and the veins through his entire body were standing up like an ugly road map across the whole of his body. He'd been poisoned, allowed to live only long enough to deliver the news to us.

"Poor Joe," Taylor cried, putting a sheet over him.

"Was it really him?" I asked.

"Yeah. He was poisoned with some sort of slow acting synthetic toxin," Ezra replied, sniffing around his mouth.

"Your fellow Drones are caught up in this somehow, and so are you, Ezra. Madmar engineered these circumstances so that he'd get what he needed to break orbit, delay our knowledge of his departure, and yet he has to know we'd try to follow," I said, scratching my chin.

Ezra sulked for a moment as a few of the pieces fell into place.

"Still, I'd like to know why your tribe was targeted specifically. He could have used anyone for the gun deal that put the catalyst in play. Getting you involved has been nothing but fortunate for us," I said.

"He's right, we'd never have made it this far without you," Taylor said, hugging Ezra.

"It does make a sort of sense," Ezra said, hugging Taylor back, his face displaying a broad smile.

"Right. You're a Type One Drone. He would have known you would do whatever was necessary to protect us. He couldn't predict every variable that would come along to obstruct us in getting to and from Finland, meeting up with Tullia, escaping Port Montaigne in the first place, and so forth. He would have wanted someone we would trust, along for the ride, making sure we got from one place to another," I said, looking at Ezra.

"Sorry," Ezra said with a shrug.

"It's okay. Really," I said.

"What do we do? Check on your tribe or give chase?" I asked.

"I suppose it depends on what Madmar thinks we would do. So far he's made his plans doing a really good job predicting our behavior," Ezra said, looking up at me.

"Previously, he's had access to a whole host of replicas imprinted with my personality. If he did give a kill order and sent them on the run, that's a resource he won't have anymore," I replied.

"Oh, no. Kale!" Taylor exclaimed fishing out her mobile.

Taylor thumbed out the number he'd given us on her mobile then held it up to her ear. Her face brightened slightly and she put Kale on speaker. He sounded a little confused.

"Kale, you're okay?" Taylor said.

"Yes, but several of my 'colleagues' didn't make it to work this morning and some just dropped dead in their offices. Uroboros Financial is going to be a little understaffed until..." Kale said, stopping mid-sentence.

"Kale?" Taylor said.

"Corporate security just arrived. I had to duck into a closet until I can find out why they are here," Kale whispered. "What should I do?"

"Pretend you're me. If they are there to do clean up, they won't assume you're a replica. Assume control of the firm until I can get back there and do it myself," I said calmly.

"Why do you think they're here for that?" Kale asked.

"Madmar issued a kill order. He must have infected some of the replicas he was manipulating with a virus that ran in their nanoid machine bodies. A kill switch or something," I replied, trying to guess how he'd done it.

"Uroboros Financial did 'upgrade the firmware' in all imprinted replicas recently, just after the Shutdown. Human resources had us come in for an injection and a scan," Kale said.

"He used what he learned in Finland from watching Taylor to do that I'll bet," Ezra whispered.

Taylor and I nodded solemnly in reply.

"How did I survive?" Kale asked.

"Taylor helped heal your shoulder," I said, after a moment's contemplation.

"Yes, she did," Kale replied, the tone in his voice indicating that he'd reached the same conclusion I had.

"The nanoids from her body that healed the shoulder wound must have inoculated you against Madmar's kill switch," I said, patting Taylor on the shoulder.

"I'll do what I can here and try to get things up and running again while you're gone," Kale said.

"Do you want to know where we will be?" Taylor asked.

"Not really. It isn't necessary for me to complete my tasks. Talk to you soon," Kale replied, hanging up.

Taylor pocketed her mobile with a sigh and searched the apartment. We looked about for anything that might be useful to us, or to the Drones of Ezra's tribe. It was strange the way the whole place was just as we'd left it. No one had tried to come through the door. There wasn't even a fresh nick on the lock, other than the ones that had likely been there already. I'm sure we locked up when we left, and yet Joe was able to just come right inside. It was a detail I failed to ask him about when he was alive, a detail that bothered me.

"Taylor, you keep a key under the mat outside your apartment?" I asked.

"No. Only Russ and I had keys," she said, rooting around through a drawer.

"Russ," I said, thinking out loud.

"Yeah, why?" she said, closing the drawer.

"How did Joe get in here without breaking in?" I asked, looking around the apartment.

"Windows are too small, and they're too high to climb to, for regular people anyway," Ezra said, with a smile.

"Someone had to let him in," I said, looking down at Joe's corpse.

"Russ could have unlocked it when we were in Port Montaigne the last time?" Ezra said.

"No, the apartment wouldn't have stayed undisturbed. We'd have come back to find evidence of squatters, and stuff would be missing," Taylor said.

"We're missing something. Something that Dr. Madmar wants us to miss. He's gone out of his way to make this whole thing confusing, make us feel pulled in two different directions," I said, thinking out loud.

"If the kill switch didn't take out Kale, it probably didn't take Vance the Younger," Ezra said, looking out one of the small windows nervously. "Okay, for the moment, none of that matters. Only what we do next matters. The obvious choices are to go after him and try to stop him breaking orbit and heading for the lunar colonies, or heading below to check on my tribe, right?"

"So, whatever he doesn't want to see us do must have nothing to do with either of those things," Taylor said.

Ezra was quiet. He just lowered his head and looked at the floor.

"What's wrong?" Taylor asked, putting her hand on Ezra's back.

"Does this mean we aren't going to go down there? I really need to check on my tribe," Ezra said.

"No. I don't think his plan was to get us to go to one way or the other. I think the plan was to get us to split up. He needs to separate us for some reason," I said, thinking out loud.

"What do we do then?" Taylor asked.

"Whatever it is, we need to stay together. As long as we do that, we're messing with his plan," I said.

"So, let's stay together, and go check on my tribe," Ezra said.

"I'm okay with that," Taylor said.

We gathered up two trash bags worth of shoes, clothing, old shoulder bags, fabric scraps, and anything else we thought the Drones might like. We made our way down to the basement of the apartment building, while keeping an eye out for anyone or anything that didn't belong. The basement looked much the way it did when Russ and I had been down there last.

The primary difference was that the tunnel was almost devoid of water. The waders were still there, but we wouldn't likely need them if the water level was the same the whole way. Not knowing when or where I'd be able to wash my hands next, I suited up anyway. Taylor giggled as she handed me the safety helmet with the illuminator on the front.

"Remember when we came down here last time?" Taylor asked.

"Yeah. Good times," I replied, feeling a little bit of genuine nostalgia over our adventure.

Ezra plodded on ahead of us, a slight spring in his step that was probably equal parts excitement and worry. The place was even more oppressive without the sound of the water and it was gloomy, more than usual, with virtually every emergency light having gone dark. The sea green paint on the interior of the twenty foot diameter pipes we walked through was etched and marred in places by what looked like gunfire.

Ezra stopped every once in a while and knelt down as if he was looking for something. Each time he stood, some of the spring in his step would drain away. When we reached the control cistern, we could see that the access points to the lower areas had been sealed and that the flow-through tunnels above had been closed and sealed as well. Each had a tight metal lid more than twenty feet across that had been swung closed and the turn wheel chained and padlocked.

"This is bad. This should all be open. All of it," Ezra said, shining his small illuminator around the silent cistern.

"Which way leads to where your tribe dwelled? It's been long enough since I've been down here, I don't recall. I am all turned around," Taylor said, stepping up into the cistern.

"It was either of these two lower tunnels," I said, pointing.

"That's right. I'm surprised you could remember," Ezra said.

"The underground is just math, or a system of sorts. It all makes a lot of sense to me. I can almost predict what is around the corner down each of these tunnels based on what we saw previously coming down here," I said.

"Is there another way to where your tribe makes their home?" Taylor said.

"Yes," Ezra and I said in unison.

"The room is just brimming over with confidence," Taylor laughed, knocking lightly on one of the lids blocking one of the tunnels.

"It's a cistern," I said, teasing.

"And this, is my fist," Taylor said, showing me her knuckles.

The access to the cistern behind us suddenly got a little darker as several Drones appeared. They wore their trademark goggles and rubber suits, but were carrying pipes, a few firearms, and nervous expressions. I kept my rifle down, but Ezra didn't.

"Don't recognize most of these guys. I see Senegal, though. He used to be with the Sodality," Ezra whispered, leveling his rifle in the direction of the Drones.

The one called Senegal, a huge Drone with broad shoulders nodded angrily before lowering his weapon. He signaled for the others to do the same, then stood up as straight and defiantly as he could.

"You're like us. Why would you bring these outsiders down here?" Senegal asked, his words laced heavily with a thick accent.

"They're my friends," Ezra said, keeping his rifle up, and pointed toward the other Drones.

"We don't have friends upstairs," Senegal replied, looking warily over his shoulder at his friends.

"Maybe you haven't been trying hard enough?" Taylor said, standing beside Ezra.

"I think you should all leave," Senegal said coolly.

Ezra tensed, like he was going to act but uttered something to them in their own strange language. He rattled off a dozen angry words, then spit on the ground at Senegal's feet. The other Drones lifted their goggles and set their firearms down. Ezra did the same, signaling for me to keep mine.

"Why's he get to keep his gun?" Senegal growled.

"Our rules. We play, they don't. Give me a pipe," Ezra said, gesturing to one of the other Drones.

They threw him a length of pipe that he caught deftly in his off hand. Everyone spread out to the edges of the cistern, while Ezra and Senegal stepped to the center. Senegal had a length of pipe as well, and he was easily three times Ezra's size.

Senegal let out a strange hiss. "You want this to the death, or to first broken bone?"

"First broken bone I give you, you will be dead," Ezra said, a dark quality I'd never heard before creeping into his voice.

Senegal looked back at his friends. They seemed to get a little whiter than they already were, their cement gray eyes widening slightly. Senegal gripped the pipe tightly and stepped up on the raised center of the cistern. Ezra did the same, without hesitation.

"You're not stepping off this cistern," Ezra said, shaking his head and smiling wickedly.

Senegal stepped toward Ezra swinging the pipe in a wide arc. It looked like Ezra was going to just let the pipe hit him at first, but he caught it in his right hand, an inch from his face. Before the Senegal could react, Ezra reversed his grip and pulled the pipe from his hands.

Unfazed, Senegal reached down and grabbed Ezra by the jacket tossing him to the cistern floor. Ezra let the force of the momentum take the pipes from his hands to roll over next to my feet. I could hear some of the stitching in Ezra's jacket go, right in time with his temper. I empathized with him, as Taylor had made both of us a jacket.

Ezra came up, quicker than Senegal could turn, and delivered two savage body blows to his side. His fist slapped hard against the rubber suit his adversary wore a few more times, sending him staggering to the floor. The other Drones looked on in shocked silence.

Senegal came back with a haymaker that Ezra turned his shoulder into, then a high kick Ezra dropped easily below. It was clear the bigger Drone was used to fighting guys his own size. Ezra wove around his attacks easily dropping a savage blow after blow until the big guy dropped to one knee.

Ezra wove around him, jumping on his back and engaging him in a sleeper hold. Senegal struggled, saliva pouring out of his mouth as he gasped for air. The others looked like they were going to do something, so I brought the barrel of my rifle up slightly. They paused, exchanging worried glances with one another.

"Back in the old underground republic, there was no duel that didn't end in a death," Ezra hissed, loud enough for everyone to hear.

Senegal's struggling began to slow, but like Ezra he could take more punishment than a regular human. Even depriving his brain of blood and air wouldn't make him go down easy, but it would make him very weak. Ezra seemed to know that, using the big Drone's helplessness to demoralize the others.

"I've got decades in the underground, and I did high risk EVA for the CGG. I dropped from manufacturing when they burned your number into your belly. You're what, last run litter boys? You stumbled into me thinking you'd hit me with a pipe?" Ezra roared, squeezing Senegal's neck tighter. He struggled for a few more moments then fell limply to the floor, his head making that strange bone on metal sound when he dropped. Ezra looked over at the two or three stitches out of place on his jacket disdainfully, his anger unabated. He then turned to the gathered congregation of Drones and raised his goggles so they could see his eyes.

Ezra began speaking to them in the Drone language again. Only five or six words this time, but they were enough to make them run off in a hurry. The big Drone twitched slightly, his eyes fluttering open and closed.

"He okay?" Taylor asked, looking down at the Drone.

"His augmented nervous system is trying to get him conscious because of the trauma. Pretty standard," Ezra said, still looking at the damage to his jacket.

"What did you say to them?" I asked, handing Ezra his rifle.

"I said..." Ezra mumbled, suddenly having to sit.

"Taylor, you have a granola bar or something in your bag?" I asked holding my hand out to her.

She fished around in her bag until she found a peanut bar and handed it to me. I hurriedly unwrapped it and gave it to Ezra. He sat there for a minute eating it with both hands. We'd been going for hours with hardly anything to eat. I was surprised he'd lasted this long.

"I told them they had about ten minutes to bring me someone with some authority, or I'd kill their friend," Ezra muttered.

"You really going to kill him?" Taylor asked. Like me, she was pretty bewildered by what she'd just seen.

"It wouldn't be much of a threat otherwise. Some Drones are really good at detecting deception, particularly in their own kind. Things don't work the same way down here as they do up there, or used to before the Shutdown. Fear, respect, and strength are what rule outside the tribe. It is the opposite inside the tribe," Ezra explained.

"So, are you really going to kill him?" Taylor asked, more insistent this time.

"Depends. Can you fix my jacket?" Ezra asked.

"Yeah. Yes, I can fix it," Taylor said, rooting around in her shoulder bag for some thread.

"He gets to live then," Ezra said, looking angrily over at Senegal.

"What if they come back with more, and find themselves a badass like you?" I asked.

"Another Type One? We don't fight each other. Ever," Ezra said, laughing a little.

"Why is that?" Taylor asked, running a needle and thread through the damaged seam on Ezra's jacket.

"We are all friends, like I'm friends with you," Ezra replied, looking down at the floor.

"Drones are weird," Taylor said, half teasing.

We waited there and watched Senegal twitch for what seemed like twenty minutes. Ezra stood up and paced back and forth, checking his rifle over and over again. I wondered if we shouldn't just leave, it seemed like the whole tone of the underground had changed for the worse. That, or I never got to see the real face of Drone society.

When the Drones returned, they had a familiar female with them. As they drew close, she stepped forward removing her goggles and her rubbery cowl revealing her face. Annabelle Five looked pristine, like I remembered her. She smiled slightly, her lips curling back to reveal perfect teeth.

"Mr. Silverstein, Ezra One, and Taylor. You've been gone for a long time, we thought we'd never see you again," Annabelle Five said, her voice smooth as usual, her unidentifiable accent only adding to her allure.

"Why are the tunnels all sealed up?" Ezra asked.

"I think you can probably guess that for yourself," Annabelle replied.

"People from above started coming down here. You narrowed the means of egress to better defend our territory. Fought them off?" Ezra stated, looking down at the ground.

I could tell Ezra was purposefully avoiding her gaze. It didn't strike me at the time, but I did feel a slight tingle every time I met her gaze, like she was looking right through me. Taylor stepped up from between the two of us and put her hands on her hips.

"Nice welcome wagon, by the way. We come down here to make sure you're okay and these guys try to work us over. We're pretty sure someone has a chemical weapon stashed down here to wipe you out and you want to play 'underground gladiators'? Are you crazy?" Taylor said, obviously irritated.

Annabelle adopted an expression of deep hurt and anger, if just for a moment, her eyes dropping to the floor. Something was wrong, and she'd spent a long time trying to keep her tribe calm. She'd spent a long time being brave when her courage had run out. I wasn't sure how I recognized that look, but it was plain and familiar to me.

"We're grateful you came to check on us," Annabelle replied, sounding absolutely genuine.

"Yeah, right," Taylor said, shaking her head.

"Taylor, cut her some slack. What's wrong, Annabelle?" I asked.

Taylor glared at me for a moment, but the look quickly vanished as Annabelle started to explain.

"We found it about a month ago. It's tamper resistant and in a place only a handful of the smallest of us can reach. Most of us can't stand being above ground under the sky, or even in a place with a high ceiling. There is no escape, nowhere for us to go. If the weapon goes off, and the agent is bad enough, we'll all die," Annabelle explained, her smile fading to a look of real concern.

It was bad. There's only one reason Madmar, or whoever had done this, would set things up this way. I felt a sickening chill in my gut as the numbers of the situation began to appear before my eyes. The variables were coming together, but there were too many unknowns, too many things that could skew my calculations.

"I bet it's in a place where only you and Taylor can get to it," I said, already seeing Ezra.

"Madmar set this all up, to draw us somewhere specific?" Taylor asked, looking up at me.

"Apparently, he thought I would try to stop him heading into orbit while you two came down here. Last time we split up, that's how it went. You and Ezra, me by myself," I said nodding.

"We have a bigger problem," Ezra whispered.

"What's that?" Taylor asked.

"There is no way Madmar got this bomb down here on his own. He's got Drones on his payroll, under his thumb, something," Ezra said, shaking his head.

"You mean one or more of these guys and gals might be in on the whole thing?" Taylor asked.

"Don't see how he'd have got it down here otherwise, put it somewhere tight," Ezra said.

"It's going to be like trying to solve the murder on the Orient Express," Taylor said excitedly.

CHAPTER 5

HERMANOS SERDÁN INTERNATIONAL AIRPORT

Puebla, Mexico
3:36 PM, January 25th, 2200 – Three Days Previous

Perfidy leaned back on the ancient automobile and watched passively as his granddaughter and her son ascended the steps to the airport. It was three hours until the next public commercial flight and there were few people in the loading zone this time of day. It was unseasonably warm, but the sky still tried to rain sending down a drop or two as the sun shone harshly down as if to spite the precipitation.

They were almost inside when a trio of slate grey transports suddenly appeared above the skyline darting between buildings and coming in low. They were sporting sound suppressed engines and jamming equipment, but Perfidy could see them clearly with his enhanced optics. Gritting his teeth he walked purposefully to the rear of the car and produced a single key to open the trunk. Inside was an array of weapons, including two surface to air missiles.

The transports were gaining speed as they approached the airport ruining the sound dampening abilities of their special engines. They were in a hurry, and time was running out. Perfidy produced one of the SAMs and took careful aim waiting for the guiding system to wirelessly sync with his own internal targeting computer. It took an extra second to account for the special countermeasures possessed by the aircraft before he could fire.

The missile struck the lead vehicle in the nose, sending it down into the road ahead flattening unfortified buildings and foliage in the wake of the wreckage. The other two transports began to deploy their passengers via anti-gravitational slip lines that slowed the enhanced mercenaries' descent just enough to prevent injury. A couple hit the ground at the wrong angle and didn't get up, but the remainder brought rifles up to their shoulders and opened fire.

They didn't care who they hit as they unleashed Hell on anything that moved in front of the airport terminal. Perfidy pulled out a case and set it down on the car in front of him as sub-sonic ammunition ground into everything nearby and cut the air with a cacophonous roar. It took him a moment to mount the barrel on his twenty millimeter rifle and drop the bipod so he could take aim. The first pull of the trigger blew out every car window in front of him.

The bullet struck one of the enhanced mercenaries down range in graphic fashion, sending his comrades scurrying for cover. Perfidy pulled the trigger two more times hitting targets behind hard cover using telemetry from an aerial drone he'd deployed earlier. Every time one of the mercs broke cover, Perfidy would pull the trigger, they would die, and their comrades would fall back even further. The two transports began to circle back around, coming at him perpendicular to their original approach and putting the airport in their line of fire.

Perfidy set his rifle down carefully on the hood of the car he was using as a firing position and walked casually over to the trunk and retrieved the second SAM. He took his time, letting the transports close to an optimal range before firing the missile. Not waiting for it to make contact he returned to his rifle. The mercs hadn't broken cover but Mexican emergency services was beginning to respond. Through the scope he could see blue flashing lights in the distance.

The missile struck one of the transports sending it down hard across the road between Perfidy and the remaining mercs. He swore, pulling a duffle from the trunk and heading toward the flaming wreckage. It was at least another ten minutes before the private flight carrying his family could get clear, and they would need all the time he could give them. The third transport flew over his position, a wing gunner firing at the ground in his direction. Perfidy ignored the transport for now, knowing he was too small a target and the transport was flying too fast for all but the best marksman to land a shot on him. Automatic fire tore up the pavement around him as he stepped over several innocent people having already been caught in the crossfire.

There was nothing he could do for them now but avenge them and protect his family. Perfidy held the twenty millimeter rifle in his off hand and looked down the road past the flaming wreckage. They were moving on his position now and there were more than enough of them to kill him. He set down the duffle and unzipped it. Inside were a trio of submachine guns loaded with armor piercing caseless ammunition. He grabbed up the first in his gun hand and set down his rifle.

The transport was turning in a wide arc over the airport, as if it was looking for a secondary target. Perfidy put it out of his mind for now and focused on the enhanced mercenaries rushing his position. The first came vaulting over the flaming wreckage, her augmented legs propelling her forward at preternatural velocity. She leveled her assault rifle in Perfidy's direction and unleashed a salvo of suppression fire.

Perfidy stood in the path of the onslaught taking careful aim with his own weapon. She missed; he didn't. The mercenary came skidding on her face at Perfidy's feet as the second mercenary rounded the wreckage, taking the time to drop to one knee. It would be the last mistake he ever made as Perfidy turned expertly and gunned him down with a controlled burst. The transport was high in the sky now, gunning its engines as it turned toward something at the far end of the runway.

"No," Perfidy hissed, letting the submachine gun fall from his hands and dangle from a strap over his right shoulder.

He stooped down and picked up his rifle. His enhanced hearing could detect the mercs closing behind him but he had to try to take a shot at the transport. Before he could draw a bead, there was a shimmering in the air over the terminal as something moved quickly across the roof. Whatever it was, it had countermeasures advanced enough to fool even Perfidy's enhanced senses. There was an audible hiss followed by several bolts of visual displacement that arced from the roof of the terminal to the transport.

Perfidy watched in awe as the transport shuddered and lost power before falling into pieces and hurtling toward the tarmac. The wreckage vanished behind the terminal building giving contrast to whatever was in the sky for a split second. It was small, just slightly larger than a man. Perfidy didn't get a chance to marvel at the sight for long as several bullets slammed into his back just below his left shoulder blade. Even with his augmented epidermis, the rounds hit deep and hard throwing him to the ground in a spray of blood.

Rolling with the blow, he turned quickly and drew a bead on one of the three mercs that had closed the distance. Perfidy opened fire, but his aim was askew due to the injury. His arm no longer responding like it should. Even the light recoil from the caseless ammunition made his whole left side hurt. He coughed, and fell to one knee unable to catch his breath.

It should have been over as several armed individuals gathered to gun him down as he tried to stand. The mercs never got a chance to finish him off as an unseen force quickly and quietly cut them down. Their bodies glinted with monofilament wire as they collapsed to the ground in pieces. There was an almost inaudible hydraulic hiss behind him as something mechanical drew close.

Fighting through the agony, Perfidy emptied the last of his magazine across the top of the flaming wreckage hoping to drive them back. Dropping the submachine gun he staggered over to the duffle and retrieved the second of three weapons. He could hear booted feet only getting further away, meaning they were fleeing the field for now.

Turning back toward the terminal he could see a suit of Aquiline power armor slowly descending to the street nearby. It was painted entirely black and had no identifying colors or insignias. It had a sinister but familiar look to it, not unlike the armor Matthias employed. The pilot seemed to stagger slightly as the suit touched down.

"Damned thing," Dr. Helmet muttered over the suit's loudspeaker.

Perfidy breathed heavily, staring angrily at the power armor.

"Ah, are you Perfidy?" Dr. Helmet asked, taking a few awkward steps forward.

"That's what I'm called, yes. First time flying?" Perfidy asked, keeping his submachine gun handy.

"I was assured this thing could fly itself, but never mind that. The Syndicate will be waiting for your family on the other end of their flight," Dr. Helmet said, holding up gauntleted hands in a non-threatening manner.

Perfidy's shoulder sank.

"I've made arrangements for their safety, but…"

"You want something from me?" Perfidy interrupted, angry again.

"No small thing I'm afraid, but I will help your family regardless of what you decide."

"What do you need?"

"Dr. Madmar is trying to move his operational timetable up, and take his resources to the Lunar Colony. He's taken significant steps to delay a mutual friend of ours from…"

"What do you need me to do?" Perfidy interrupted again, almost yelling.

"I need you to make sure a craft he has loaded with his research and certain materials never makes it to the moon. Timing is crucial and there are several precautions we must take to ensure he is unaware of our meddling," Dr. Helmet explained.

"I don't understand. Why don't you just…"

"He has countermeasures. I don't want him to use them," Dr. Helmet said, looking past Perfidy to the approaching emergency services vehicles.

"What kind of countermeasures?"

"Nanotechnological, among others."

"Liability?"

Dr. Helmet hesitated for a moment, letting the arms of the suit drop down to his sides.

"I have to die," Perfidy stated, suddenly understanding the dire nature of the situation.

"We both know that Madmar will come after everything you love if you're alive," Dr. Helmet stated sadly.

"What about the Cabal, the umbrella, and all the agents still beneath it?"

"All operational protocols must remain intact, and the IA must be allowed to return home now. It is simply an inevitability at this point. Also, I've every reason to believe that someone dropped an apple on Eden, and things are going to change very soon. I did my best to prevent all this, but with our mutual employer being somewhat indisposed…"

"I understand. Do you have transport arranged, and the details of the target?" Perfidy replied, walking past the doctor toward his car.

"Go to the old local safe house, everything you need is hidden under an oil barrel out back."

Dr. Helmet turned clumsily, doing his best to will the power armor to walk over to Perfidy's bullet riddled vehicle. Slicking back his greying hair, Perfidy rested his arms on the top of the vehicle and took a deep breath. He couldn't see the transport carrying his family anymore, as it had finally reached the horizon and vanished.

"I hope this will all be worth it."

"I've no way of knowing at this point. All we can do is carry out the rest of the plan now, try to get those close to us out of harm's way," Dr. Helmet replied.

"Vance Uroboros… I heard he's a little more than indisposed," Perfidy said, sitting down in his ancient car and starting the engine.

"He's not dead," Dr. Helmet replied.

"Then the work is not complete. Vaya con dios, whoever you are," Perfidy said, speeding away.

CHAPTER 6

PORT MONTAIGNE, LOWER WATER TREATMENT AND FILTRATION TUNNELS

3:11 PM, January 28th, 2200

Ezra's War Journal Part 7

It was bad to be home. I'd already had to choke out Senegal outside my tribe and the person they claimed to be in charge, comes from my own tribe. Last time I'd been home, the Sodality was trying to pull all the tribes together through intimidation and violence. I left to follow Silverstein to the sunlit world in a vain attempt to save the world when my tribe needed me most.

"Ezra, please talk to me," Annabelle said in our shared language, as we walked down the tunnel.

"How could you just invite members of the Sodality into our home?" I replied.

"We were scared, and they were desperate after losing their homes to encroaching surface dwellers," she explained.

"They are dangerous and unstable. I wonder how many lost Drones he's turned away or killed," I replied.

"None, Senegal isn't as bad as you think. Not many Drones travel with humans like you do, the sort that destroyed Senegal's home," she asked.

"I hope you know what you're doing," I said calmly.

"So do I. Our Elder Ezekiel has never seen the divisions in Drone society following the fall of the Republic. He built most of the tunnels we lived in. The Sodality is as old as the Drones. Ezekiel just wanted to try to keep us safe," Annabelle whispered, looking up at Silverstein and Taylor walking ahead of us.

There was chemistry between Silverstein and Taylor. Their hands would occasionally brush up against one another as they talked, they maintained eye-contact with each other a moment after they'd said their last word, and walked close to each other. They had a connection, probably from the first time they met. I knew how they felt, except the person I had that connection with was always distant, and reluctant to let me in. My own stupid mouth didn't help matters.

"Not doing a lot to dispel the rumors that Type Fives are conniving turncoats still working for the Factory," I whispered.

Annabelle looked pained for a moment, as if she were going to cry. She dropped her goggles so no one could see her eyes and donned her trademark smile. I'd pushed to come back to the tunnels, but now all I wanted to do was go back up to the wide open sky. I let myself drift back to the snow covered forests of Finland and the weeks following the Shutdown. I wanted to feel the cold open sky over me again.

"Annabelle, where are we going?" Silverstein asked.

"Same place you visited before, our tribe's home," Annabelle replied, in English this time.

"Who is this guy?" Taylor asked, pointing to our other escort.

"Senegal is a refugee. We had warning, time to prepare, and a group of warriors trained by a capable Type One Drone. The other tribes, particularly those under the Sodality flag, didn't do so well when desperate people from the surface began looking for shelter underground."

"Was it really that bad up top?" Silverstein asked.

Annabelle just lowered her head.

"Fatalities?" Taylor asked.

"From what we could see from the drains, the corporate security forces were firing at will on angry crowds of people. I think more people died being trampled by the crowds than from gunfire, though. We were dragging bodies from the ditches to the incinerators for weeks," Annabelle said, lowering her voice.

Silverstein stopped dead in his tracks and turned around in the tunnel to face Annabelle.

"What did you do with the people who managed to make it down here?" Silverstein asked.

"Maybe you want to discuss why they were trying to force their way into our domain in the first place?" Annabelle said defiantly.

"No. No, I don't," Silverstein replied, heading back down the tunnel.

Silverstein and Annabelle being at each other's throats wasn't going to help anything. This was uncharted territory for everyone involved. As a Drone, I watched the humans above ground living out their lives for decades, their brutality and heartlessness stopped surprising me a long time ago. Nevertheless, everything that had happened in the last few months was on a level no one could have foreseen.

Psychics can only gain insight into the individual. Their powers are lost when it comes to predicting the mob. Ezekiel and the others couldn't have foreseen all this. I wondered where Chelsea Six was.

The rest of the walk back through the tunnels was as I remembered it. When we got to the outside lid that separated my tribe's territory from everything else, Annabelle stopped and waited for a moment. The rest of the Drones spread out and did a quick search to make sure we weren't followed. I stayed where I was. I already knew we were secure, and if there were hostiles around, they were with us, or waiting for us inside already.

The lid opened up slowly, a cadre of heavily armed Drones waiting inside. It was just one of a host of things I wasn't used to. I missed my peaceful home, and it was setting in quickly that my old reality was going to be replaced by a new one. It wasn't like taking off my old Factory rubber suit and putting on the jacket and pants Taylor made for me. It was uncomfortable.

The interior of the tribe home was still colorfully decorated, Taylor's decorations hanging prominently everywhere. It still felt like home, but there were a lot more guns and unfamiliar faces. Objectively, the tribe home wasn't crowded, but even a couple extra bodies made it feel that way.

Senegal stumbled in behind us with his crew, just ahead of the lid closing. He looked up at me, goggles off, his eyes bloodshot. I could tell from his look that it wasn't over between us. More trouble I didn't need.

The tribe's elder, Ezekiel, only a few years younger than me, sat atop a horizontal pipe in the central gathering area. He seemed like a shadow of his former self. He'd done his best to hold the tribe together, but being a Type Six Drone, he'd started showing his age. Type Sixes were not designed to have a lifespan beyond that of a regular human. Things were going to fall apart with the last of the Elders passing, and the factory not making any more. Or, things would have to change.

"How long do you think Ezekiel has?" I said, speaking to Annabelle in our own language again.

"Think you could say that a little bit louder?" Annabelle hissed, looking around nervously.

"Listen, the time for games is over. Taylor and I are going to crawl into a tight place to try and disarm a bomb and it might not matter anyway," I said, looking at her out of the corner of my eye.

She shook her head and pulled me into an alcove while everyone else got in the soup line. I went grudgingly, my stomach grumbling at the smell of the mushroom stew. It'd been so long since I'd walked through the soup line for my favorite dish.

"Look, we all got handed a role by the Factory when we were made. Most of us liked what we were, and were suited to it. I have a special empathy and my tailored pheromones allow me to manipulate others. Because I'm nice to look at, people tend to listen, but all that doesn't add up to being a real leader," Annabelle said, sliding down to a sitting position, and hugging her legs.

"Annabelle, have you ever met another Type Five? A Drone with that Factory designation?" I asked her, looking over at the soup line.

"No, I haven't," Annabelle said, resting her forehead on her knees.

"Neither have I. You're the only Drone I've ever known with that designation. You are beautiful, but you're also utterly unique among our kind and as much as I don't trust the Factory, the Factory does not make mistakes," I said, leaning up against the wall and folding my arms.

"You think I'm beautiful?" she said, looking up, her face streaked with tears.

"Yeah. Can I get something to eat now?" I said pointing over to the soup line.

"In a minute. After you've eaten and rested yourselves, you and your friends should go. Our best engineers couldn't disarm the device. The device is magnetically shielded, set in concrete, and suspended in a fluid-filled canister. I won't have you guys going down there for nothing," Annabelle said, wiping her eyes with a bit of gray cloth.

"Good luck convincing Taylor. She decorated this place, it's like a work of art with her name on it. She won't abandon her work. Silverstein feels deeply responsible for everything that's happened. He's not going anywhere," I said.

"What about you?" Annabelle asked.

"I just came for the food," I said walking out of the alcove to the soup line.

There were a lot of familiar faces in the soup line. Most everyone in the tribe was a Type Three, a Drone designed for hazardous or heavy labor. I was the only Type One, and as far as I knew, Annabelle was the only Type Five, and our elder the only Type Six. All the others had gone or been killed. All the refugees were Type Three, and mean enough to survive a long time in the tunnels after their tribe homes were compromised. Whether this was a good thing or a bad thing would be put to the test of time.

There was talk of humans building communities underground because there was still power, steam, and other means of surviving. No one seemed to know what to do about it. The few Type Three Drones I'd trained to fight were like me, loathe to do so. Still, everyone knew that taking a defensive stance underground was the same as losing the war, if there was going to be a war.

I waited patiently in line then found my way over to where Silverstein and Taylor sat. They were at the end of a long picnic table scavenged from the surface, the blue plastic seats smooth with wear and dimpled from the work tools carried by the other Drones. I sat down with my steaming bowl of mushroom chowder and took in the fragrance.

"You like that soup?" Taylor asked.

"Fully ninety-seven percent of why I came back in the first place. No one makes a stew like Brook," I replied, just enjoying the aroma.

"What's the other three percent?" Silverstein asked.

"It is home. You always go home when things are bad, and right now, things are bad," I replied, taking a spoonful of the delicious stew up to my mouth.

"You and Annabelle seemed to be having a pretty intense conversation over there. Everything cool?" Taylor asked.

"She told me a little bit about the bomb," I replied.

"Can you disarm it?" Silverstein asked.

"I know only a little about bombs of this nature. I'm hoping Taylor will be able to commune with it and shut it down," I stated, looking over at Taylor.

"Weren't we already a little suspicious about it being put somewhere only you and I can fit?" Taylor asked.

"More than a little, I'd say," Silverstein muttered.

"Yeah, but with you being here we might be able to relay information to you about the bomb, its placement relative to the tunnels and similar," I said, taking another spoonful up to my mouth.

"You think there might be a safe zone in the event the bomb detonates or the agent is dispersed?" Taylor asked.

"If I'm right, and Madmar has agents operating down here, they'll want certain assurances to do so," I replied.

"Madmar might just break his word or lie, though," Silverstein said.

"Maybe, but if the deal went down in person, that would be risky. Drones are very sensitive to sound and vibrations. Like I said before, many of us are good at knowing when someone is lying or being deceptive. All the soldiers I worked with in space were trained to speak with Drones using only the truth to avoid confusion or misunderstandings. To some of us, humans almost stink when they lie," I explained.

"Wow. What about folks like Taylor or Kale?" Silverstein asked.

"That I can detect, neither of them has ever lied to me," I replied.

"Why didn't you say something about this sooner? A lot of what you've done in the past makes a lot more sense," Taylor asked.

"Never really thought about it, it's always been natural, like breathing. I forget sometimes that humans don't have the same sensitivity. I did say

Kale had prevaricated with us less than anyone else, didn't I?" I remarked, eyeing Taylor's remaining stew covetously.

"True. What about Madmar? You're heard him say more than a few things," Taylor said. She pushed her bowl over to me. "What's your take on him?"

"Virtually everything he says is a lie, or part of the sum of a greater deception." I paused and thought for a moment. "I don't think he realizes he's even doing it most of the time."

Taylor pulled out some knitting, or needlepoint, or something and began working on one of her many hobbies while Silverstein pulled out his mobile and gazed at it. I finished Taylor's soup and closed my eyes as life-giving nutrients flooded my body. I hadn't wanted to admit to anyone else, but even going a day without food was pretty tough. My condition seemed to be getting more serious the more I pushed myself.

That was when my nose was assaulted by the smell of baked goods. Brook, a Pygmy Drone like myself, came into the eating hall carrying a pan of her bread. She dressed in child's clothes found in drainage tunnels near the surface and even had a pair of real shoes. We'd always shared a deep connection because of our stature, and like me, she was intensely private about her abilities and Factory designation. I might have been the only one that knew anything about her.

I walked up to Brook and asked for some of the black flat bread she'd baked. She handed me a half loaf and a knife so I could cut it up. I filled my pockets and my small satchel with the bread and thanked her. She looked over at me, her heavily hooded eyes filled with worry.

"Are you going to try to deactivate the device everyone is worried about?" she asked, using our shared language.

"You know how it is, one problem, one Pygmy Drone," I replied with a smile.

Being the only Pygmy Drones in the tribe, we shared many jokes at the expense of our larger kin. She was younger than I was, having been created only in the last thirty years or so. She was probably one of the last Drones the Factory produced before operations were suspended.

"Please don't die," Brook said quietly.

I shook my head and smiled, doing my best to reassure her. As I stood beside her, I could smell something over the stew. Brook was menstruating, like a human woman would, on what I understood to be a monthly basis. Previous to that moment, I'd never met a Drone female that had the ability to reproduce. A chill ran through me, as I looked around wondering who else knew about it.

I looked back over my shoulder at Senegal, sitting with his crew across the way. There were six of them, all Type Three, and sitting together. They stared over in our direction intently watching our interactions. They knew.

"You know Senegal?" I asked.

"Yeah. It's funny, but Type Three Drones like him seem to choose cities or mountains as names to make themselves feel even bigger," Brook said.

"They bother you yet?" I asked.

"Yeah, but I don't really want a mate or a boyfriend," Brook said, self-consciously flattening out the front of her skirt.

"What's Senegal's crew do? What's their rotation?" I whispered, pretending like we were having a normal conversation.

"They patrol the tunnels outside. They caused some trouble before, and the Elder felt like that was the best way to prevent it in the future. Keep them busy outside more of the time. It wasn't without merit, though. There has been a lot to do in the tunnels up until recently," Brook explained.

I frowned slightly and looked over at Silverstein and Taylor. Why couldn't everyone just be civil with each other? Senegal stood up and walked purposefully over to where we were standing, his bowl in hand.

"Seconds," he grunted.

"We're on rations. Everyone only gets what I give them," Brook replied, her voice trembling.

Senegal scowled at her.

"Let Senegal have a second bowl. I give him good odds he'll need his strength pretty soon," I said in English.

"Runt, you got lucky before. Next time, you might not be so lucky," Senegal said, helping himself to Brook's bowl.

I wanted it to be fifty years ago when the original Underground Republic was in power and the Sodality was just a social movement. Back then, I could have just clawed Senegal's throat out, might making right. Those were bloody days best forgotten, but it was a lot simpler when dealing with problem individuals.

Senegal walked back over to the table and ate the bowl of food in front of his still hungry cohorts. I watched every movement he made, making note of every moment he was a little weaker from an old injury, or distracted by something around him. Like most Type Three Drones, I could tell his eyesight wasn't the best and his peripheral vision was tight. He was every bit as strong as I was though, maybe stronger, and two hundred pounds heavier, which counted for something.

I walked over to where the engineers were sitting, a trio of Drones called Lem, Dubs, and Lush. They were like a bunch of mechanically inclined peas in a pod, perpetually together working in tandem to solve engineering issues for the tribe home. Each had a rigging harness and dozens of tools they displayed proudly. They looked up from their soup and smiled, each lifting their thick lensed welding goggles so I could see their eyes.

"How's the still coming along, Lush?" I asked.

"You'd be surprised how difficult it is to distill mushrooms for the purpose of making alcoholic beverages. Seems like all I make is a stink most of the time. I have been able to brew several different types of mushroom tea," Lush said, squinting at me.

"You want to ask us about the device, am I right?" Dubs squeaked.

"Yeah, I'm going to head down there with my friend and see what we can do," I replied.

"You'll be able to fit, but be careful in there," Dubs said.

"What about my friend?" I said pointing a thumb over my shoulder at Taylor.

"She should be able to. Lem was the only one of us small enough to fit and neither of the two scanners we have would fit through the gap in the wall. It clearly has a magnetic seal based on the configuration of the exterior, but it's sunk into concrete making us think it is fluid filled to prevent tampering. Too much vibration and BOOM!" Dubs tittered.

"Lem? You actually got in there? What are your thoughts on it?" I said, patting him on the arm.

"I'm not sure it's a bomb. It's located in a place that was designed to bear the weight of the surface. If it's an explosive, it might have been designed to bring down something upstairs as well as incinerate us all. It is not in an ideal spot for a standard biological agent. We could close the lid to the tribe home and probably be safe in that event. If it's nanoid or similar in nature, it would depend on how the little buggers were programmed," Lem said, his voice almost a whisper.

"Lem, you barely fit?" I asked.

"Yeah, it was me or Brook. It's at the end of a long drainage pipe that's only eighteen inches in diameter. I almost didn't get back out. Scariest crawl I've ever done," Lem replied.

"How did you know it was there?" I asked.

"It's off a district annex. Newer construction closer to the surface. One of Senegal's crew noticed a red LED light blinking down at the end of the pipe and told us about it a week ago," Dubs muttered, taking a bite of Brook's black bread.

"Brook left the tribe home lately?" I asked.

"Not in a long time. I think the last time she did, it was with you. Remember the lost human that wandered into the sub-tunnel in sector 10?" Lush said.

"Yeah, that older guy? Brook was the only one who could go with me because she wasn't afraid of the sky like the rest of the tribe," I replied, remembering the incident clearly.

"You think a Drone from the surface helped a surface dweller put the device there?" Lem inquired, somewhat worried.

"It's a possibility. The guy we're dealing with is capable of all sorts of different things, and he's got resources at his disposal we don't even know about. I'm nervous about Senegal and the other refugees. You trust them?" I said, lowering my voice almost to a whisper.

"They've pitched in a lot. The trouble they started before was because the Elder is a psychic," Lem explained.

"Yeah, but it was all smoothed over once it was made clear we weren't pawns of the Factory," Dubs added.

"Senegal wants to lead the tribe. He's always trying to get the Elder to give him more responsibilities. He's a good warrior and has deterred a lot of surface dwellers from getting even close to the tribe home," Lush said.

I looked over at Senegal. He was paying way more attention to Brook than I liked. He didn't have my senses, and it was possible he was oblivious to her new condition. From that perspective, he looked more interested in her because she was easy prey. The other Type Three females could hold their own against him and would band together to that end. Brook like me, was different enough that she just didn't fit in, a social dynamic that usually worked in my favor, but always seemed to work against her.

I resolved to let Senegal make his move. When he did, I'd make an example out of him, or at least try. I knew it would take Taylor a while to forgive me considering her stance on killing, but sometimes it's the best solution to a problem. Also, I really didn't like Senegal.

I walked back over to where Silverstein and Taylor were having a conversation. Silverstein was commenting on her needlepoint while making a foul expression toward his partially eaten piece of black bread. I snatched it from his bowl and put it in my pocket.

"I guess that solves that. I didn't want to be rude and not eat it. Brook seems really nice," Silverstein said.

"Don't worry, I got your back. I love her black bread, and yeah, she is really nice," I replied, looking over at Senegal across the room.

"You've got that look on your face," Taylor said, raising an eyebrow.

"What look is that?" I asked.

"That frigid look that comes across your face, right before you're going to kill someone," Taylor replied, raising both eyebrows.

"Am I that easy to read?" I asked, somewhat self-conscious.

"Only when you're about to make people dead. What's up?" Silverstein said.

"Senegal might be a problem," I said leaning in closer to my friends.

"I'll watch him while you and Taylor are taking a crawl down to look at the device," Silverstein said, patting the rifle he'd laid on the table.

"No matter what he does, don't react. Just tell me when I get back. Drones have their own sort of justice down here, and I can get away with things you can't," I explained.

"Like killing another Drone?" Taylor said disapprovingly.

"Yeah, like killing another Drone," I replied.

"Can Senegal and his friends lead us to the tunnel where the device is?" Taylor asked.

"Yeah, they're the ones who found it," I said, looking at her knowingly.

"Maybe we should have them guide us to the tunnel then? Have Silverstein stay with your tribe?" Taylor said, putting her needlepoint away.

"What if they decide to jump us in the tunnel?" I asked.

"You haven't taught me how to fight yet, but I think we could probably handle ourselves," Taylor replied.

"No. No splitting up, remember? I'm going with you guys, even if it's just to stand at the far end of the tunnel with those goons and wait," Silverstein replied adamantly.

Annabelle Five reentered the room and took a bowl of soup and a bit of black bread and walked over to sit with us. I scooted over to make room so she could sit between Taylor and me. She'd left her goggles and cowl in her quarters and sat with her long hair hanging down as she ate for a moment. She'd used some sort of pigment to dye her hair a purple color Taylor called lavender.

As much as she angered me sometimes, I could stare at Annabelle for hours.

"You want to head right back out again? Look at the device now that you have taken in some food and rest?" Annabelle asked.

"Yeah, I think so," Silverstein replied.

"I'll arrange to have the engineers show you the way," Annabelle said, eating her soup slowly.

"No, I think you and Senegal should show us the way," Taylor said leaning over and putting her elbow on the table.

Annabelle thought about it for a moment.

"The engineers do have a lot of work to do if we're to make the tribe home suitable for more Drones. That might be a better idea. Besides, I might be able to help, particularly with Silverstein being there," Annabelle replied, smiling in a sultry way that gave me chills.

Taylor frowned and leaned back in her seat to rummage about in her bag. Silverstein smiled and picked up his rifle. He checked it like I had taught him and shouldered a bag that we had loaded with rope and a few other things we thought we might need. Annabelle went over and talked for a moment with Senegal who gathered his cohorts and made for the lid.

Annabelle waited for Senegal to leave before walking back over to our table. "It's done. As soon as we're all gathered at the lid between the outside and our tribe home, we'll set out. I need to head back to my quarters for my cowl and goggles, and then I'll be ready."

"I like your hair," Taylor said grudgingly.

"I would never have thought to color it this way if I hadn't met you," Annabelle said, smiling warmly.

Taylor smiled in return, the purple in her own hair turning a lighter shade. We proceeded to the lid and waited for Lem to set the locks to cycle. A minute later the lid slowly swung open, the old hydraulic hinges groaning as they expanded to their full length. There was no opposition outside so we proceeded quickly into the tunnel beyond.

Senegal and his cohorts were completely silent and carrying only lengths of pipe, a sledge hammer, and a crowbar. I wondered why they didn't bring the few firearms they seemed to possess until we reached the annex tunnel. It smelled faintly of methane and chemical agents present in natural gas, not the sort of place one would want to discharge a firearm, but an excellent place for a bomb.

"Silverstein, you'll probably want to put your rifle away and use a brick, pipe, or something else in here," I said, helping Annabelle up onto the expanded metal platform spanning the bottom of the tunnel.

"Would have been nice to know that in advance," Silverstein said, shooting a dirty look toward Senegal.

"I thought you had enough guns for all of us. Too bad I didn't bring an extra length of pipe," Senegal said with a sneer.

I locked eyes with Senegal for a moment, almost sure this was when he'd make his move. Annabelle cleared her throat and proceeded on ahead of us. Senegal broke his gaze and grumbled as he followed along behind her. It wasn't more than seventy-five feet later that we found the small drainage pipe that led to the device. It was terrifyingly close to the tribe home.

It was as the engineers said, if you squinted down the pipe you could see a faint red light at the far end. Even a shortsighted moron like Senegal could see it. The pipe wasn't entirely dry, a faint glimmer of water in the bottom carrying the illumination of the LED light at the far end along the length. The light blinked off and on with no clear pattern.

"What do you think?" Silverstein said looking down the pipe.

"Light might be a movement indicator. It doesn't seem to blink relative to our movements, but there could be stuff in the room. I should've asked the engineers about the room," I said, lamenting my own carelessness.

"We'll be in there to check it out for ourselves in a second," Taylor said, handing Annabelle her shoulder bag.

"You're letting Annabelle hold your shoulder bag? That's a rare honor," Silverstein teased.

"You're always stealing my cigarettes and Ezra is always eating my food. Besides, I wouldn't want to mess with you looking all manly with your rifle there," Taylor said, slugging Silverstein in the arm playfully.

"I do feel honored," Annabelle said, putting Taylor's bag up on her own shoulder.

"Maybe we could make you one like mine," Taylor said.

"I wish I had enough stuff to fill a bag like this," Annabelle replied, hefting the shoulder bag for emphasis.

"We going to do this or what?" Senegal growled, looking around nervously.

"Yeah. We're going to do this," I said crawling into the pipe.

It was a tight squeeze, even for me. Taylor was taller, but more slender and seemed to do better. I could see why Lem barely fit down the pipe. I edged forward an inch at a time for ten very long minutes until I could poke my head into a solid concrete room. There was thick electrical conduit cable running vertically at the corners of the room and several cooling fans. Only half of them were running.

I slid into the room quietly, pulling my rifle in behind me. Taylor was still making her way up the pipe, about fifteen feet remaining. The floor was damp from some sort of condensation and the air was heavy with moisture. It wasn't the ideal environment for defusing a regular bomb, but I had a feeling it wouldn't matter.

As Taylor dropped in behind me, I could hear a click from the device sticking partially out of the floor. We both froze, the sound echoed in the chamber for only a moment before everything was quiet again. I let myself breath again and looked around.

"There's no pressure plate," I said, thinking out loud.

"What was that noise then?" Taylor asked, shining an illuminator around in the darkness of the room.

My mobile vibrated as the light on the device went solid, ceasing to blink. I reached into my pocket, and pulled out my mobile. I held it up and showed Taylor.

"Blocked call. How are you even getting reception way down here?" Taylor asked.

"The device must also be a relay," I said, tapping the touchscreen on my mobile and holding it up to my ear.

"Hello, is this Ezra One?" Madmar said, his voice coming across loud and clear.

CHAPTER 7

PORT MONTAIGNE, LOWER WATER TREATMENT AND FILTRATION TUNNELS

7:27 PM, January 28th, 2200

Ezra's War Journal Part 8

"Madmar," I replied, looking about nervously.

"I couldn't leave before I concluded certain business. I know where you and Taylor are, but I had expected Mr. Uroboros by now. You don't know where he is, do you?" Madmar said, his voice calm and businesslike.

"I don't, sorry. Where are you?" I replied, motioning for Taylor to come closer.

She crept over beside me and pressed her ear to the outside of my mobile so we could both listen. There was a long pause, and what sounded like Madmar gathering up some things in the background. Then he returned, his voice still as calm as before.

"I am still in town. However, there is no indication he left downtown Port Montaigne, and yet, there he is at Uroboros Financial. It looks like he doesn't care about my impending departure as much as pulling his finance company back together in a world devoid of a global economy," Madmar said.

"I guess so. Yeah, that is strange," I replied, deadpan.

"The device I placed down near where your tribe dwells is a wondrous contrivance. It acts as a cellular relay, but it's also set up to painlessly take and distribute biological and nanotechnological samples," Madmar stated plainly.

The device suddenly opened, its oval top splitting into four separate pieces and retracting to reveal a plate with an indentation shaped like a handprint. There were several, almost imperceptible, holes along the length of the plate. The device rose out of the concrete about a foot revealing cylindrical and heavily armored siding.

"All Taylor needs to do is put her hand on the plate. You can do the same if you like. I'm more of a cyberneticist than anything, but I might be able to do something about your diabetes," Madmar explained.

There was only a handful of ways Madmar could know about my condition. Every possibility filled my mind with the blackest ink of anxiety spreading out to darken every thought. I feared for the safety of those we crossed paths with in Finland. The other possibility lay with Dragos, because even at that late hour, we weren't sure where he'd stood through it all.

"Why would we agree to do this exactly? All I want to do is give you a fatal gut wound at this point," I replied, keeping an eye on the device.

"Let's keep it civil. Like I said, the device in front of you is designed to store and release samples as well. If something doesn't get put in, I might decide to release something instead. Don't worry about the samples, I'll keep whatever I find out regarding them private. I'm a doctor, you can trust me," Madmar said, his voice wavering slightly with mirth and anticipation.

I wondered if that was some sort of clue. I feared that Madmar had grabbed up the doctor who helped me in Finland. Maybe he was just being a jerk. Whatever the case, he'd backed us up against a wall.

He'd obviously spent some time setting the whole situation up. It was possible that Madmar had intended to capture Silverstein to use as a bargaining chip, and the biological agent was a bluff. It was just as likely he intended to kill everyone with a malicious cloud of nanoids, or a neurotoxin, after getting the sample.

"I'm going to need some assurances," I said.

"Such as?" Madmar cooed.

"How do I know you won't just release whatever you've got stored in your device here, after we're given you what you want?" I asked.

"Well, I'm assuming Taylor has garnered a higher degree of control relative to her nanoid body. I'll probably get my scan of her nanotechnological material right before she wrests control of the device from me," Madmar explained, nonchalant.

Taylor looked at me and shrugged. I'd seen what she could do before she took the catalyst, befriending machines with onboard A.I.s and similar. However, Madmar's device could have countermeasures similar to the type that injured Matthias at the CCG secure facility. It was a risk regardless.

"You'd counted on Silverstein coming to you while we were down here. What had you intended to do in that event?" I asked.

"Sounds like you've managed to figure out the game, you're just unaware of the prize. Enough stalling, have Taylor put her hand on the device where indicated. I'm on a tight schedule here," Madmar said, giggling gleefully.

Taylor looked worriedly over at the device, then at me. I didn't know what to do, and she was clearly in the same boat. There were several venting fans that weren't operable in the room making it slightly hotter than was comfortable. Then, the rest shut down.

"The quad-copters I used to set the device you see before you are still down there. They are equipped with all sorts of delightful armament. It's a simple matter to have them visit your friends nearby," Madmar said, his voice sounding a little more distant than before.

"We'll take our chances," I said, keeping an eye on the device.

"Suit yourself," Madmar replied, ending the conversation.

The device began to dispense an aerosol based agent of some sort into the air. I could feel my motor functions quickly beginning to freeze up, as if something was taking control of my body. Taylor stood up and held her hands out beside her, about six inches from her hips and closed her eyes. Her hair went stark white for a moment as the strange sensation that had afflicted me slowly faded.

For the record, it was terrifying to feel something invade you like that, take control of your limbs. It made me wonder about the state of the world and what other sorts of technology has managed to go rogue at the hands of people like Madmar. I couldn't tell if I was shaky from the thought of it, or the nanoid machines in my body shutting down thanks to Taylor's influence.

"Are you okay down there? Something weird just happened over here," Silverstein shouted.

"We're okay," Taylor said, collapsing to her knees, the color rapidly flowing back into her hair from the roots.

"What happened?" I asked, catching her as she fell.

"He used a nanoid based agent to try to gain control of everyone. I reached out with my own and set them to inert as opposed to active. They're still in your bodies though, it was the best I could do," Taylor explained.

"Here," I said, giving her a piece of my black bread.

She took it and began to eat is slowly, crust first. Once I was sure she was going to be okay I headed back over to the device and watched the small vents slowly close. There was a loud whirring sound followed by grinding gears and muffled alarms as the device went dark. The room was filled with the smell of burning electronics and hydraulic fluid as the red LED light on the side of the device blinked one last time.

"What happened?" Taylor asked.

"I'm not sure. Apparently this thing was designed to wreck itself after releasing the aerosol agent? I've no idea," I said, hesitant to touch the device.

"I might be able to tell if I touched it," she said, rising to her feet.

The sounds of fighting broke out from down the small drainage pipe we'd used to access the room. It sounded like metal on metal but the sound was quickly drowned out as several eighteen inch diameter quad-copters dropped into the room through the vents near the electrical conduits in the corners.

These weren't designed to just collect unmanned surveillance, they were mechanical devices designed to hunt and kill. The small quad-copters had onboard weapons that included air-propelled darts and tiny guided missiles. As soon as they dropped into the room they began firing blindly, as if by a preprogrammed sequence.

Taylor dropped flat to the ground as I leapt up clawing the belly out of one of the devices. The other three immediately turned and fired on that position giving me only a split second to relocate as small guided missiles homed in on the machine I'd just destroyed. I ran up the wall and grabbed the electrical conduit where it met with the ceiling and held on for dear life as the small automated devices commenced tearing up the room.

It was clear these devices had been given basic programing and only a few alternate actions based on specific events. It was sloppy and indicative of Madmar having to throw this together in a hurry. We'd clearly done something he hadn't anticipated. Taylor rolled across the floor to a corner beneath one of the quad-copters and made herself very small.

It was in the space of a few seconds the machines expended their pay-loads and then slowly descend to the ground and shut off. Other than bits of shattered concrete falling off rebar concealed in the walls, to the floor below, there was barely a sound. After a moment I could hear Annabelle calling out to us down the drainage pipe.

"Ezra, Taylor, are you alright?"

Taylor popped up and waved down the pipe in response. The device buried in concrete at the center of the room suffered several direct hits and was ruined. Madmar had clearly set this up to go differently based on Silverstein going to try to stop him from breaking orbit on his own. When that didn't happen, he was forced to improvise.

"He's one of the best cyberneticists in the world. He could have done a lot better considering all the time he had to prepare this," Taylor said, dusting herself off.

"I don't think he did have time. I bet he intended to have Silverstein as a bargaining chip when he called me on my mobile," I said.

"Or, maybe it was us he meant to use as the bargaining chip? Can you call him back, tell him he made a mistake thinking he could always predict what we'd do?" Taylor asked.

"You might be right," I replied. "I think the device was the relay. He clearly didn't set this up with it in mind that we'd be able to call and gloat after it all went wrong."

Taylor peered down at the wreckage of the device.

"If it had been a bomb, it would have gone boom having taken all that damage. Was he really just after a piece of me in the aftermath of taking the catalyst?" Taylor asked.

"I don't know much about it, but it seems to me that in making the nanoid bodies, there would have to be a slow evolution or progression as the A.I. continued to get more complex and learn," I said picking up my rifle.

"So, the catalyst might just be the first step. If Madmar misses a step and isn't able to understand the evolution, he might not be able to control the lunar or Martian intelligent agents?" Taylor asked, thinking out loud.

"If that is the case, he might have more to do on Earth before he breaks orbit, unless he's already got a dose of the catalyst and a terrestrial intelligent agent in his possession," I said, letting Taylor step on my back to access the drain pipe.

"I've never met any of my brothers and sisters. Hopefully Vance the Younger is as slippery as he seemed and has managed to evade Madmar as well," Taylor said, her feet disappearing into the pipe.

"Crap, I didn't even think about that. I guess that would be a possible contingency in the event Madmar couldn't lay hands on the real deal."

We slowly made our way back out of the room an inch at a time. The second time through, the pipe was making even me claustrophobic. When we dropped back out into the annex tunnel two of our escorts had been killed, including Senegal. I frowned at the sight of the big Drone laying on his side, his back torn apart by what looked to be tiny guided missiles and poison darts.

"You guys got some of what we got," Taylor said sadly, gesturing to the pile of inactive quad-copters lining the walls of the tunnel.

"Senegal threw himself on Annabelle while the rest of us ran like heck. This guy panicked and froze, taking a poison dart to the throat," Silverstein said, kneeling down beside the Drone's still form.

"He wasn't such a bad guy after all," Taylor said, looking somewhat weepy.

"I guess not. May all our deaths be so noble," I said putting my hand on Senegal's shoulder.

"Is the device taken care of?" Silverstein asked.

"It wasn't a bomb. It was designed to take control of us using nanoid machines, assuming he couldn't get a sample from me willingly. Madmar was counting on you going to stop him from breaking orbit. Ezra and I think he probably needs more from me before he can attempt to control the lunar intelligent agent," Taylor said.

"So, we've successfully done something Madmar couldn't anticipate," Silverstein stated with a smile.

"Madmar does think you're at the Uroboros Financial building. Apparently, Kale is doing an awesome job being you," Taylor reported mirthfully.

"We need to stop Madmar. If he thinks Kale is me, he could be in terrible danger," Silverstein said.

Senegal coughed, took a deep raspy breath, and opened his eyes. Everyone was startled as he turned over, winced and pulled himself up to a sitting position. I'd never seen anyone, even a Drone, take so much damage and survive.

"Annabelle okay?" Senegal asked, trying to wipe the blood and explosive residue from his eyes.

"Yeah, you saved her. You are one tough son of a gun," Silverstein said.

"Oh, good. Good," Senegal mumbled laying his head against the wall.

Taylor cleaned off his face with a rag, so he could see, and handed him his goggles. He looked at them and held them aloft to see if they were alright. One of the lenses was lost, knocked out in the fight. It was nowhere to be found.

"Damn. Lens probably slipped through the cracks, and down into the water." Senegal said, putting his goggles around his neck.

"Your friend got killed," Annabelle said kneeling down beside Senegal.

Senegal nodded somberly and stood up, his back still oozing blood from his shredded rubber suit, damaged from the explosive ammunition that struck him. Taylor and Silverstein winced at the sight of Senegal lumbering ahead, exposed muscle and bone beginning to slowly knit back together before our eyes.

"Ever seen anything like that?" I whispered to Annabelle as we walked.

"No, but a few of the Drones in the tribe have begun to exhibit abilities beyond those normally possessed by our race. Senegal's regenerative abilities are something new, as far as I know. I'm afraid to ask, lest he realize how badly hurt he really is and go into shock," Annabelle replied.

It felt like a long walk back to the tribe home. Senegal's wounds were far from healed by the time we got back, but they'd already scabbed over.

His cohorts had to help him walk the last few hundred yards as he got more and more sleepy. Once we were inside the tribe home, he laid down just inside the lid and fell fast asleep, his body expending all available energy to heal.

"I remember when I choked him out. His body immediately started trying to wake him up. Normal for a Drone, but in hindsight, it seemed to come on quicker," I said, looking down at Senegal.

His cohorts just shrugged and left him there.

"Do you know about Brook?" Annabelle asked.

"Yeah, I know about her," I replied.

"Brook and Senegal are only two of a handful I was talking about earlier. Has anything changed for you?" Annabelle said.

"I have a form of diabetes. Not exactly a new ability, and probably has more to do with my age than anything else," I said.

The engineers operating the lid finished locking things down and departed the entry chamber. I wondered at what we had just endured and if that was the only device Madmar had planted in the underground. I could see by the thoughtful expressions on Silverstein and Taylor's faces that they had some concerns of their own.

"Do you think Madmar has any other failsafe or backup plans in place in the underground? Is everyone really safe?" Silverstein asked.

"I wish I could simply sense if it were so," Taylor said wistfully.

"He can't employ those countermeasures if he's dead. We should find him and put him down like the dog he is," I said, handing my mobile to Taylor.

"Why are you giving me your mobile?" Taylor asked.

"Madmar said you could take control of machines. He called my mobile using his device as a relay. Can't you trace him using my mobile now?" I asked.

"It doesn't work that way. Maybe if you had him on the line and I was holding your mobile," Taylor said with a smile, handing back my mobile.

"The call would have been recorded by the CGG telecom routing stations in Port Montaigne. If we can get to a terminal with the right amount of access or computing power we might be able to get that information," Silverstein explained.

"What are we waiting for?" I said.

"Leaving so soon?" Annabelle asked.

It was an eerie sensation to want to leave my home. Things were changing down here in ways they never had before. Soon, it wouldn't feel like home anymore, and deep down I knew it. The trouble was that I could just leave, do as I pleased, and had no fear of the wide open spaces above ground. Everyone else would have to endure, adapt, and embrace the new things good or not so good.

I could expect no understanding from my fellow Drones in that regard and would eventfully be viewed as an outsider, if I wasn't already. I wanted to tell Annabelle how I felt, find a way for her to come with me, or to deliver the whole tribe from these circumstances. There wasn't much I could do except hope they would still open the lid when I did happen to visit. I was going to go back outside and continue experiencing the world as I had in the months previous.

"If Madmar isn't stopped, he will just continue hurting people," I explained, taking Annabelle's hand.

"Are you the one that has to stop him? He must have many enemies, let someone else be the end of him, you are needed here," Annabelle pleaded.

Brook appeared in the tunnel leading from the entry chamber back into the rest of the tribe home. She smiled weakly, her thin face creasing with relief at the sight of us.

"I saw the others had returned and wanted to make sure you were alright," she said, clasping her hands together.

"Most of us made it back in one piece. Senegal got pretty tore up and we lost one of his friends," Taylor said, gesturing to where Senegal lay.

"I saw them carrying the one that was killed. That's why I was worried," Brook said, wringing her hands shyly.

I expected Annabelle to say something comforting, comment on how our brother had done his duty. Instead, she just gazed at Brook, her eyes twitching as though she was deep in thought.

"Take her with you," Annabelle said at last.

"Pardon?" Silverstein said, looking over at me.

"If Ezra is to leave again, I want him to take Brook along," Annabelle said, putting her hand on Brook's shoulder.

"We are going to confront an extremely dangerous individual that delights in hurting people. The more innocent they are, the more he seems to like it," Taylor said, her eyebrows shooting upward.

"I have a sense that everything will work out. In fact, I think everyone will be better off if Brook goes with you," Annabelle said, looking to me for support.

"Is this you being funny, or are you worried about Brook staying here because of Senegal?" I asked.

"You said the Factory made me for a reason, and I am starting to come around to that notion. Like you, Brook isn't afraid of the surface world, and probably has a destiny somewhere up there," Annabelle said, frowning at me.

Silverstein sighed and shrugged, looking to Taylor who seemed impartial. I didn't want to bring Brook along. She was personable enough but seemed to possess no ability to survive the calamity we were likely to find up above. She did have incredibly enhanced senses, and she made decent food, something I couldn't discount given my condition. I had learned a long time ago not to go against Annabelle, she had an unnerving propensity for being right.

"Yeah, she can come with us," I said at last.

"Must I go? I like it here," Brook said, looking up at Annabelle.

"Yes, you've something important to do elsewhere. Don't worry, everything will be fine," Annabelle said, taking Brook by the shoulders.

"Okay," Brook replied, seemingly satisfied.

The engineers returned after we'd taken a few hours to rest and opened the lid for us. There was no grand farewell, just the sight of Annabelle raising her hand as the portal to my home closed behind us. Brook brought very little with her save a blanket, her ladle, and a small book of recipes she had written herself. Silverstein and Taylor walked along together behind us, chatting quietly for the first few hundred yards of tunnel. Brook didn't say a word along the first leg of the journey, matching my pace as she walked along beside me.

When we got to a place where there was a long climb, Silverstein took the lead. The tunnels were quiet, even the sounds of running water sounded as if they were far away. I lamented not taking more time to speak with Annabelle, and that my own frustration with her probably soured what might be the last time I would see her. She didn't deserve my anger anymore, and maybe she never did in the first place.

The upper tunnels were still dry and the streets above were quiet. I had grown accustomed to the sounds of the city above when walking there, and couldn't imagine them ever being quiet. It was just more evidence that my home and the world around it had changed. The enormity of the economic collapse didn't sink in until I was in the most familiar surroundings, even having seen so much first hand.

The climb up into the apartment building was delayed for a moment by Brook who hesitated on the rungs of the ladder. She began to breathe deeply, as if suddenly very afraid. She had only been above ground twice before, and the adrenaline of that situation probably carried her through.

"This is a very different set of circumstances, isn't it?" I said, standing just below her.

"Yes. I don't want to leave. My will, and certainly my heart, are not in this," Brook confessed.

"No one is making you do this. We can take you home right now and tell Annabelle she made a mistake," I replied.

"Are you sure? It is such a long walk back, and you've things to do," Brook said, her voice wavering.

"I've got nothing else to do. Silverstein?" Taylor said, extending her hand down to Brook.

"I'm good, we can take Brook back if she wants," Silverstein said, kneeling down on the floor and looking down the ladder at us.

Brook hadn't looked up yet, and I knew how she would feel if she did. Slowly, she cast her eyes upward as if to look at the clear blue sky we still couldn't see. I could almost see the memories of our other adventures together dance through her eyes. Her arm dropped slightly as if still carrying the abandoned human child we found long ago.

"No, I'm fine, let's go," Brook said, taking Taylor's hand.

We ascended the ladder into the basement and made our way up into the hallway. We ventured quietly out into the foyer and looked back up the stairs. There was no sign or scent that anyone had passed this way since we we'd been gone. We were almost to the door when Silverstein hesitated.

"Ever thought that maybe we should have a look around this place?" Silverstein asked, looking back up the stairs.

"You mean for other people living here?" Taylor said.

"I don't recall seeing a soul except for Russ since I've been coming here," Silverstein said, heading for the stairs.

"There are nine other apartments besides mine, all with tenants. You're right though, I haven't seen anyone since I brought you here," Taylor said, somewhat fearfully.

We went up the stairs behind Silverstein who lingered outside the apartment left of Taylor's. He dropped his head, took a deep breath, and kicked the door in. Brook let out a short screech in surprise at the loud noise.

Looking beyond the door, hanging by one hinge, we could see an array of sensors and equipment pressed in around the inner walls. Taylor burst into tears at the sight of it. One could only wonder how long someone had been violating her privacy, spying on her from just the other side of a bit of wood and drywall.

The scene inside was worse. The previous occupants were vacuum sealed inside a large plastic enclosure, naked, both shot in the head. They were executed then sealed in a plastic bag so the smell wouldn't bother the other neighbors, assuming there were any. The equipment looked expensive, far beyond what a private citizen could afford, and clearly military grade.

"Why would someone do this?" Taylor asked.

"Someone in the CGG found out what I was doing, and that I'd entrusted you, unknowingly, with sensitive code? I don't honestly know," Silverstein replied sadly.

"It would be easier to just blame Madmar. You think any part of the CGG survived the financial collapse?" I asked.

"The equipment has been here for quite a while. Do you think it would have been hard to flip one of my rogue imprinted clones a few weeks ago? Information in exchange for safe refuge following the economic collapse. This could be Dick's work," Silverstein stated grimly.

Taylor was inconsolable. She couldn't even look at Silverstein at that moment returning to the hallway to sit on the stairs. I looked around for Brook, but she'd vanished. I felt a moment of panic until I saw her coming back around the hallway. She shook her head sadly at me clutching at her small rucksack.

"If you didn't like that apartment, you won't like any of the others. I sniffed at each of the doors. There are dead people inside them all," Brook said, her face even paler than normal.

Silverstein stood there and stared at the couple in the plastic enclosure, huddled in the corner, their eyes and skin completely grey. It was a ghastly sight, one I'm not sure how Silverstein could stand to look at for a moment, let alone a few. The two humans had been holding each other when they died, terror still etched on their faces.

"Hard to imagine that Madmar might be just the tip of the iceberg. It stands to reason that in order for my original plan to work, I would have needed contacts in government, in the military, secret police, and within every criminal organization and cartel," Silverstein said. He started heading back to the hallway.

"Was turning the lights back on part of the plan?" I asked.

Brook sat down beside Taylor and leaned into her. It was strange to see them sitting there together, and Taylor seemed a little better for the opportunity to comfort Brook. There was nothing that would comfort Silverstein. The realization of what he'd done kept coming, and the consequences of his actions were slowly unfolding with each new discovery.

"I sought to tell a lie. I wanted to create a monster so big the world would take notice and change for the better. Many selfless people became monsters to confront the lie I told, losing their humanity to battle against, or be victimized by it. In the end, the monster wasn't a lie. I am the monster they all feared," Silverstein said, lowering his head.

"You're not making sense," I said, grabbing Silverstein by the arm.

"I'm seeing this clearly for the first time. As far as I know, this all happened because of me," Silverstein said, sinking down to rest against the wall of the hallway.

He let out a loud sigh and shifted the rifle over his shoulder off and onto the ground.

"Complain," I stated plainly.

"What?" Silverstein said.

"It's all humans seem to do," I said, meeting Silverstein's gaze. "They make messes then complain about it, create tailored life forms to deal with it, and then complain some more."

Silverstein laughed, shaking his head and looking down at his shoes. Taylor and Brook turned around and looked at him, startled. I checked my rifle and ignored the pity parade on display in front of me. I meant every word of what I said. I liked Silverstein, but sometimes I think humans are the worst thing that ever happened to the world.

"You're right, Ezra. You are totally right," Silverstein said, sounding utterly defeated.

"I don't need you to tell me that. What I need right now is to know what you're going to do about it. Are you Vance Uroboros, the flawed idealist, or Silverstein, a person reborn in the wake of a terrible set of circumstances? I've followed you halfway around the globe on the pretense this was about saving that world. What do you have to say now?" I said, growing angrier.

"Ezra, it's okay. I think he probably feels really badly," Taylor said putting an arm around me, wiping the tears from her eyes.

Silverstein stood, meeting my angry gaze with more words. "I can see it clearly. The hubris that comes with being able to calculate things so precisely and an understanding of the world that lacked empathy for the people in it. Someone saw what I was doing, and could see how it would all end. They thought hitting me across the head and dumping me in an alley would give me perspective. They were right."

CHAPTER 8

PORT MONTAIGNE, TAYLOR'S APARTMENT, DOWNTOWN

4:17 AM, January 29th, 2200

Ezra's War Journal Part 9

We walked away from the apartments where Taylor had lived far more burdened than when we went in. I think the strain of the last few weeks had begun to set into us all, Silverstein particularly. I'd seen my share of awful things, but I was extra weary of chasing Dr. Madmar's agenda around the globe and bearing witness to his depravity.

Downtown wasn't completely empty that morning. I could see a few people pushing ancient shopping carts through the recently cleaned streets, looking for recyclables in vain. For many, the global Shutdown was probably just another brief smudge in the history of Port Montaigne. Taylor walked along beside me, almost bumping into things as she gazed down at my mobile, and hers, one in each hand.

"Any luck?" I asked.

"Telecom is pretty much down around the globe, or at least segregated from Port Montaigne. I'm bewildered that this place even has power and running water considering the rate at which infrastructure seems to be deteriorating," Taylor said, scrolling through a long block of text on her own mobile.

Brook jogged along beside Silverstein, her childlike wonder spurring her on around each new corner and up each new flight of concrete stairs.

We weren't counting on there being a train running in the tubes and a decent vehicle wasn't to be found. Walking all the way to uptown didn't sound like fun, but we didn't want to ruin the advantage we had. Still it was only good for us that Madmar thought Taylor and I were still underground while Silverstein was at Uroboros Financial. I worried about Kale.

We made it through the commercial district into the slums at the base of midtown. Large cargo cranes loomed overhead just beneath the underbelly of uptown, the hum of a few commercial air conditioning units spun overhead. We walked an extra mile just to avoid the warehouse district for fear that Madmar might still have agents there and found an old unused access.

It was a concrete stair that ascended the side of midtown, going up more than a dozen stories. Before the harbor was devoid of life, construction workers used to take the stair from midtown to the water to fish. I couldn't imagine walking up and down the stair all in the same day as my legs ached terribly on the climb up. All that we'd seen made me think about Port Montaigne's origins as well.

"Starting to get a better signal the closer we get to midtown," Taylor reported while we rested on a landing.

"Do you think we'll find somewhere to eat when we get there?" I asked.

"No idea. I hope so, that mushroom stew was a long time ago," Silverstein said.

I handed Silverstein a hunk of bread from my pocket.

"Wow, thanks. Never thought I'd be glad to see that bread," Silverstein said, winking at Brook.

We shared a little bread and some slightly brackish water that Brook brought with her. The sun began to appear across the horizon to the East over the ocean. I'd only seen it from this vantage a few times but it was obviously a first for Brook. She pulled at my sleeve and pointed down toward the water.

"Pretty, isn't it?" I said.

"Yeah, but look down there," Brook said, pointing far below the horizon.

Below us was a steady stream of people trudging slowly out of the slums to the stair. I couldn't tell what they were doing from that height but many of them were carrying what looked like lunch boxes or small packs. They walked somberly waiting their turn to ascend the stair below, like they were just heading to another workday.

When we reached the top of the midtown stairs, it was clear that midtown had changed as well. Old factories had been restored, forgotten markets were busy with lights, and there were people moving about with purpose. There were manufacturing representatives holding bundles of time cards and preparing to meet the day laborers that were probably ascending the stairs behind us.

I turned and looked back toward the downtown area. From this height it just looked like a smudge of grey spreading out beneath the jagged underside of uptown with concrete supports reaching down toward the ground below. My own quiet contemplation was suddenly broken by one of the factory reps.

"Looking for work? I've got time cards for the linen district. You two smaller folks look a little pale, but you can probably make double working the machine shops. If you aren't sick that is. I hear they intend to get the cranes running soon," he said.

The factory rep was a younger man, probably in his twenties, with red hair and freckles wearing a worn pair of trousers and a button up shirt that looked a size too big. His shoes and hat looked to have been made of the same canvas and he wore a wide grin. The time cards in his hands looked well-used, like they'd passed through many hands to be used over and over again.

"We're not looking for work, but can I ask you a question?" Silverstein said.

"Shoot."

"Are there ships running in and out of the port? There any sign that global commerce is resuming?" Silverstein asked.

"When the lights went out a few weeks ago, there were still ships out at sea. Most of them have autonomous systems that only communicate with a satellite every day or so to track their position. Most of the shipping companies continued to run. I know the Port Montaigne shipping companies just converted a tanker to act as a floating office so they'd have power and the ability to communicate with their boats," the rep replied.

"Life goes on?" Taylor asked.

"There are still radios, a few freighters in the sky, and just enough local government to keep things going around here. You guys talk like you've been out in darker areas. I guess the further you are from a coastline the worse things are. Times are hard around here, but we're getting by. I'm John Clark, what's your name?" John said extending his hand.

"Silverstein, and this is Taylor, Ezra, and Brook," Silverstein replied.

"Nice to meet you. If you're going to stay in midtown, you can usually find me here in the morning if you need work," John said, turning to go.

"Wait, I know you've got work to do, but we could really use some directions," Taylor asked.

"Oh, sure. I got a minute before the workers come up from downtown," John said turning on his heel to face us.

"There a decent place to get a bite to eat around here?" Taylor asked.

"Salvatore's, it's a place over in the open air market just below the lifts to uptown," John said and pointed into the distance. "It's pretty much the only operating restaurant."

Brook, still a little winded from the climb, took off her goggles and pulled back her cowl revealing her snow white hair. She turned and looked up at John with her big grey eyes, startling him somewhat. There was a moment of panic, as I was certain he recognized her as a drone.

"Are you sick? You're not sick are you?" John said taking a step back.

"No, I've always looked this way," Brook said, innocently.

"Hah, never seen an albino before?" Taylor said, pulling Brook's cowl back over her head.

"Oh, no I haven't. It's gotten really hard to find medicine. Everyone's afraid of getting sick," John said.

"Hey, thanks for the help. Looks like your workers are starting to show up," Silverstein said, pointing over to the people congregating toward the top of the stair.

"Oh, yep. Have a good day," John said, waving at us over his shoulder.

I breathed a deep sigh of relief as he walked away.

"Brook, you have to keep yourself covered up. From the sound of things, humans tried to go below and were repelled by Drones with mixed results. We may not have been welcomed above ground before, and the chances of that now are even less," I explained.

Brook nodded somberly and sulked.

"Let's see if that restaurant is open," Silverstein said, beckoning for us to follow.

"It's this way, fearless leader," Taylor said, pointing back the other direction.

"Oh. I've only been here a couple of times that I can remember, and everything looks so different," Silverstein said with a laugh.

We followed along behind Taylor as she wove her way through the ever-burgeoning crowd of people trying to push their way into midtown. We saw as many signs of hope as we did the contrary. It was clear that the human traffickers were still working their corners, pushers of a cheap high still peddled their wares, and gangs still marked their turf and there wasn't a police officer in sight.

I was surprised at how well people seemed to police themselves. I had pictured humans resorting to all sorts of barbarism in the wake of the Shutdown, and maybe that had occurred to some extent. Many people wore guns openly, carried on their hips like in the Wild West picture books I'd seen, and the more established factories and merchants all had armed guards, many with gang tattoos I didn't recognize.

The restaurant was busy. A dark haired man I presumed to be Salvatore was in an open air kitchen with several grills running at once. He was shouting and waving a butcher's knife at the other cooks, telling them to hurry. He wore a stained apron, t-shirt, a pair of nice slacks, loafers, and his fingers glittered with a handful of gold rings.

The menu looked to change daily depending on what was available and there were only a few open tables. Silverstein approached one of the wait staff. They chatted for a moment and Silverstein returned, putting the few bills he had on him back in his pocket.

"They don't take any sort of currency. There is a rumor that a shakeup in the local Port Montaigne government recently might yield such a thing, but for now they barter with people for meals," Silverstein said.

"That works, I'll be right back," Taylor said, heading off toward the kitchen.

Taylor went over to the open air kitchen and walked right up to the knife wielding chef. The taciturn man went from being hostile with his workers to what I would describe as sweet and accommodating the more he talked to Taylor. She handed him two cigarettes in exchange for a table tent and four menus.

"Over here," Taylor called out, beckoning to us.

We wove through the crowd of people to the head of the line and over to a table beneath an umbrella. I chose a seat with a good view of the restaurant. Silverstein waited until everyone else had seated themselves before taking the remaining seat.

"You scored us this sweet table with two cigarettes?" Silverstein asked.

"I did better than that. I got us credit with those and I offered Brook and myself as dishwashers after we've eaten," Taylor replied.

"Wow, you didn't have to do that," Silverstein said humbly.

"I wanted to. I kind of miss doing dishes at the Strip and Waffle. I hope it's alright with you, Brook, that I offered your services," Taylor asked.

"It could be fun," Brook said, holding the menu upside down.

"Can you not read?" I asked, putting the menu right side up.

"Yeah, I can read. Upside down, backwards and forwards. I don't even notice the orientation of the text anymore," Brook said, turning the menu back the way she'd had it.

"I didn't see any books down in the tribe home," Silverstein said.

"We have a library, but it only has about ninety books. I've read them all so many times I have them memorized," Brook said, folding the menu.

The waitress took our order. We had potato cakes that were too salty, fried flatbread, some kind of fish, and a weak beer that had no label and was likely bottled in someone's basement. I longed for some greens, but there were none to be had. I was just grateful for something to eat. I tucked some of the flatbread into my pockets for later and helped Taylor carry our dishes to a soaking tub behind the kitchen.

Taylor and Brook commenced making short work of the dirty dishes amidst splashing water and laughter. I envied them for being able to find some joy in what was a dismal situation. It seemed like the sights in midtown had taken their minds off the task at hand. Maybe it was the life I'd led up to that point, or something to do with being a Drone, but my mind rarely wandered from the mission.

"What do you want to do when we find him?" I asked Silverstein as we stood off to the side and observed the crowd.

"Madmar? I don't think there's any use in trying to question him. He seems to just lie and deceive those around him," Silverstein replied.

"In every lie, there is usually a grain of truth," I said, checking my rifle.

"Look there," Silverstein said pointing to the kitchen.

Several armed individuals had walked up to the kitchen. Salvatore was waving his knife at them and pointing back over their shoulders. It looked as though they were trying to make some sort of demands, of which Salvatore was unwilling to comply.

I was pretty sure I was going to have to intervene when virtually everyone in the restaurant stood up and began to close in around the armed thugs. I couldn't make out gang tattoos at that distance, but the thugs seemed indignant even as the fork-wielding crowd began to hurl insults and fried flatbread. After a few moments, the men left, unwilling to test the patience of the crowd.

Then, just as quickly as they'd stood, everyone went back to their plates like nothing had happened. Silverstein and I walked quickly over to the soak tub where Taylor and Brook were just finishing up. They both seemed to have missed the entire thing from their vantage.

"Thanks for the help," Salvatore said, coming over to start moving clean plates back over.

"Here, let us help, too," Silverstein said, grabbing a handful of plates.

"Oh sure, thanks," Salvatore said walking through the open air kitchen back to the front of the line.

"Who were those guys?" Silverstein asked.

"New blood. Seems like we get a new gang every time a ship manages to make it into port," Salvatore said, grunting as he put the plates down.

"Seems like you've got protection, but what about tonight when the restaurant closes?" I asked.

"My sons will be back from working at the docks. I should be fine. Why do you ask? Looking for work as a bodyguard?" Salvatore said, pointing to my rifle.

"Just for a night until we move on," I replied.

"You don't think we should push on to uptown today?" Silverstein said, grabbing more plates.

"I'm pretty tired, and this place is fun," Taylor said with a smile.

"Yeah, this place is fun," Brook said, echoing Taylor's tone of voice almost perfectly.

"Besides, they won't just let anyone walk into uptown anymore," Salvatore said. "You'll need to put together a bribe or find a way to get smuggled in. They closed the tunnels and the corporate security forces have checkpoints everywhere now."

"Thanks again, Sal," Taylor said, patting him on the arm.

"Sure, come back anytime. You'd be surprised how hard it is to find a good dishwasher. Bye now," Salvatore said, turning back to the grill.

We walked back down the edge of the concrete wall behind the restaurant. Sure enough the lifts were all closed. Also, both the tubes we checked that led up to street level in uptown had heavily armed corporate security guarding a checkpoint.

"Maybe we should try to determine where Madmar is exactly before going through all the trouble of getting into uptown. It's possible he's operating out of midtown," Silverstein said, pulling out his mobile.

"How are you going to do that?" Taylor asked.

"It probably isn't a good idea, but I'm going to call Kale," Silverstein said, tapping his thumb on the touchscreen of his mobile.

"Here, let me," Taylor said, taking Silverstein's mobile and holding it up to his ear for him.

We all crowded around so we could hear.

"Hello?" Kale said somewhat fearfully on the other end.

"It's Silverstein, I need your help."

"Oh, I was worried. This call is being routed in some way that our systems here can't break the encryption. Usually when I get calls like that, it isn't anyone I'd like to talk to," Kale said, followed by what sounded like a closing door.

"Taylor is holding the phone for me," Silverstein explained.

"Ah, clever girl," Kale said, the sounds of his footfalls echoing across the receiver.

"We need to find Dr. Madmar. Can you use his previous communications with you and the other imprinted clones that went through the Uroboros Financial to track down some possible locations in Port Montaigne?" Silverstein said.

"I think so. There's a meeting of the city council tonight to make some decisions about the governance of the region. Some of the larger cities along the East Coast have gone 'lights on' recently thanks to local mechanics," Kale said.

"Mechanics. You mean like Matthias?" Taylor asked.

"I don't know any names, but several CGG district offices were forced open allowing the cities to restore partial services even up to a week following the Shutdown. There's evidence that the Shutdown wasn't total and that there are two dozen of the larger cities worldwide that were able to continue operating or resume operation," Kale said.

"How can you explain that?" Silverstein asked.

"Someone intervened at the Finnish server farm where the CGG financial databases were stored," Kale said.

Taylor smiled quietly as an expression of deep relief crossed Silverstein's face.

"The world has a chance of recovering from this then?" Silverstein asked.

"Hard to say. If I hadn't been able to manipulate global food supplies far in advance of the Shutdown, things would have been far worse. As it is, there are only a few freighters in the sky and less than a hundred seagoing transports known to be in operation. That will need to change, and soon, if food is to reach the parts of the world where it is needed. It won't mean anything to have the lights on if there is nothing to eat," Kale said.

"What can we do about it?" Silverstein asked.

"I'm doing what I can. I've already assured the shipping companies that they'll be compensated. CGG currency is still circulating except where a barter economy became necessary due to the availability of supplies, or a lack of surplus. Dr. Madmar has agents everywhere though, and if he's allowed to continue operating unfettered, he could slow or halt the process of rebuilding of necessary infrastructure," Kale said.

"There any evidence that's part of his agenda?" I asked.

"Ah, hello, Ezra. No, but I do think he intends to try to gain control of what little global commerce there is. Many of the freighter captains I've talked to have reported attempts to extort them into transporting goods and performing services for a single individual calling himself—"

"Vance Uroboros," Silverstein interrupted, sounding frustrated.

"Correct. I'll try to get you the information you need and send it to Taylor's mobile as soon as I do. I'll make the transmission from your transport so it's as secure as possible. I don't suppose you'll be needing your transport?" Kale asked.

"Not yet. It depends on where Dr. Madmar is relative to our current location. It's better off with you for the time being. Madmar thinks you're me, and that could be dangerous. If you even get a bad feeling, you get out of there," Silverstein said.

"Very well. Talk with you soon," Kale said, ending the transmission.

Silverstein put his mobile back in his pocket and leaned up against the wall.

"Got any more of those cigarettes," he asked, extending an open hand to Taylor.

"I gave yours to Salvatore," Taylor said laughing.

"Dr. Madmar isn't the only person we should be trying to find," I said.

"Dr. Helmet?" Taylor said, lighting one of her fragrant cigarettes.

"Who is that?" Brook asked, pulling out her small cookbook.

We all hesitated at the question. The truth was that none of us really knew that much about him other than that he was a geneticist involved with the secret MDC program funded by the Central Global Government. I wondered if the man I talked to beneath the clinic in downtown was the real Dr. Helmet or just another imprinted clone sent to mislead or harm us.

"Is he even alive? We've heard some things that would cast some doubt on that," Silverstein asked.

"The most genuine article seems to be the man we met at the clinic," Taylor replied.

Brook began writing down the food she'd eaten at Salvatore's, including the ingredients and methods of preparation. I watched her tiny hand work the pencil back and forth on the page as she hummed to herself. She looked up at me, startled that I was even paying attention.

"Records. Dr. Helmet used his real name to run that clinic and probably generated records that would be submitted to the CGG database. We need to contact Matthias and see if he got that sentience core we liberated from the CGG secure facility hooked up," I said, nodding to Brook.

"You think the A.I. in the sentience core will remember those records?" Silverstein asked.

"If he doesn't, he'd know where to look and might even be able to access them remotely if they have power," Taylor said.

"How do you know that?" Brook asked.

"I'm not really sure, I just do. I learned a lot about that particular A.I. and myself from our brief contact. I couldn't even write a single line of code, but once I've got my hands on the terminal, everything just seems to open up to me," Taylor explained.

Taylor pulled out her mobile and tapped out a text message. She waited for several moment before putting her mobile away, somewhat frustrated.

"I couldn't get through. We'll need radio equipment to reach Matthias. There must not be an operational cellular tower anywhere near his workshop," Taylor said, wrinkling her nose slightly.

"Well, what are we going to do with our day? I'm sure it'll take some time for Kale to get back to us?" I asked.

"Teach me to fight," Silverstein said, after a moment.

"He's supposed to teach me first," Taylor said, shoving Silverstein playfully.

"Oh, me too!" Brook said grabbing me by the arm.

"Alright, let's find somewhere a little more private," I said.

Taylor led us around the concrete barriers and busy streets to an old fish market that had been boarded up long ago. There weren't any fresh gang tags or sign that anyone had passed through here recently. It sat just below uptown, some once-colorful flags on a string running down from the railing above, to the top of the closed market below.

I showed them a few moves, mostly how to block from a variety of angles and how to fall or roll with a blow to minimize getting hurt. Taylor was an impatient student while Brook seemed to mimic what I did perfectly. It made me think about how she was able to mimic Taylor's voice so perfectly before. Maybe she had a skill or two after all.

Silverstein seemed to catch on quickly, almost too quickly. It was as if he'd received training before and was remembering rather than learning. After a couple of hours we were all tired and in desperate need of some lunch. I broke out the fried flatbread from my pockets and passed it out. Taylor produced one of the home brews from the restaurant to share and we made the best of it.

We passed the afternoon walking around midtown to get the lay of the land, so to speak. Enough had changed, that even Taylor got lost once or twice. There were thousands of people working, traveling, and attempting to sell or trade what they had for what they needed. Brook and I kept to the shadows mostly, following along behind Taylor and Silverstein while they questioned the locals and took in the sights.

It was almost evening by the time Kale's text reached Taylor's mobile. We were in the linen district, just as the workers were gathering to collect an extra shirt, pair of shoes, or other garment they could either wear or trade. I was suddenly thankful for the clothes Taylor had made me, being far nicer than any I'd seen all day.

"Kale says there is a machine shop on the north side of midtown that looks to have been the source of several transmissions and deliveries connected with Madmar's activities. There are a couple of places in uptown, but none with the volume of traffic thought to be associated with Madmar's known movements in Port Montaigne," Taylor reported, putting her mobile back in her pocket.

"When it gets dark, we'll go check it out," Silverstein said.

"You want to walk by it during the daylight?" I asked.

"Not sure, what do you think?" Silverstein said, folding his arms.

"I'd really like to get some surveillance on the place before we go, but I don't want to blow our advantage," I said.

"What advantage is that?" Taylor asked.

"Surprise, hopefully. I think our day would have gone differently if he knew we were in midtown," I said.

"Agreed. The only one of us he doesn't know is Brook," Silverstein said.

"Me?" Brook said, looking up from her cookbook.

"You alright with walking past a building near here? All you have to do is walk past it and then come back and tell us what you saw," I said, patting Brook on the back.

"I don't know," Brook said fearfully.

"You don't have to. We could probably just ask around instead," Taylor said.

Brook fidgeted for a moment.

"I can walk past it," she said at last.

We walked through the rest of what little of midtown was abandoned to within view of a corrugated and sheet metal building. It had only a few windows on the upper floor that I could see from our vantage point and no one else seemed to be around. There were a few week-old gang tags, but I couldn't smell or hear anyone else within a block of us. We pointed out the building and then found a walkway between two buildings to wait.

Brook was gone so long I almost went out looking for her. When she returned, she was carrying a can of spray paint. Taylor went over and hugged her, relieved she was alright.

"Where did you find that?" Silverstein asked.

"Next to a dead person. He'd been electrocuted trying to climb the fence around the building you wanted me to walk past. The building smells of humans, men mostly, and all sorts of things that go on, or with, machines. Someone is still there, doing some sort of work," Brook said, turning the can of paint over in her small hands.

"Electrified fence? That is definitely a place I'd like to see the inside of," I said.

"Agreed. It should be dark soon. In an hour or so, we can head over and try to figure out a way to get inside," Silverstein replied, tapping a finger on the rifle strap over his left shoulder.

"Oh, there's a way in. There's a crane on the docks below. It smells like it's been used recently. If it is not too loud we could move the arm over the fence and climb down the cable," Brook said, putting the spray paint in her rucksack.

"Sounds better than any idea I had," I said, smiling at Brook.

We took the long way around and walked down to the docks. There were several spaces conspicuously empty, but there was a large seagoing freighter parked in the water beside the crane Brook told us about. Dock workers were just beginning to gather up their things to go home, and it was clear that none of them worked aboard the freighter.

"This is a perfect set up for a hideout. It's just enough out of the way you don't see a lot of foot traffic, a freighter to hide supplies, and easy access to uptown if you've got the equipment to climb up the concrete embankment. There's even a garage large enough to hide a flight-capable commercial transport around the back of the machine shop," Silverstein said pointing.

"You think Madmar is in there somewhere?" Taylor asked.

"If I were him, even if this wasn't where I was hanging my hat, I'd certainly store important stuff here," Silverstein replied.

"Let's grab some rest in one of these supply sheds along the quayside here until it gets dark. I have a feeling we'll need our strength," I said, pointing down the quay.

We found one that was unlocked and stepped inside. It looked to have been set up as a shelter for when a storm came through and the dock workers needed to take a break. There were a couple of benches and a stack of old magazines, most of them not fit for children, and an ashtray. I sat down beside the doorway and kept a lookout while Brook found a cozy corner where she instantly fell asleep.

"I wish I could do that," Silverstein remarked, pointing at Brook.

"I'm too nervous to sleep. Want to play some cards while we wait for sundown?" Taylor said, pulling a deck from her handbag.

"I nearly lost my shirt last time," Silverstein laughed, sitting cross-legged on the floor.

"That was only after I caught you counting cards. Play fair now," Taylor replied, dealing me a hand as well.

The next couple of hours passed slowly with the only notable event being the arrival of a cruise ship with a couple hundred refugees aboard. Most of them were dark haired and olive-skinned, and their loose-fitting clothing was different from what I'd seen people wear locally. I didn't wonder so much about where they'd come from as much as I worried about where I was going next.

CHAPTER 9

PORTMONTAIGNE, PORTER'S DISTRICT, DOWNTOWN

5:02 AM, May 15th, 2178 – 21 years previous to Shutdown

"Are you Brook?" Ezra asked, slowly standing up.

She nodded, looking about the darkened service road. Her reflective eyes glinted with the dim street lighting then vanished as she lowered her head. Ezra approached cautiously, holding up his hands in a non-threatening manner. The small Drone kept her hands at her sides, but she seemed to tense with every step Ezra took.

"The missive we received said you've come straight from manufacturing, one of the last to be created by the Factory?"

"Yes," Brook replied, her voice heavily laden with the accent all Drones possess immediately after leaving manufacturing.

She was a pygmy like Ezra, but just slightly broader, her boots betraying slightly larger feet. She was dressed in thrift store clothing, and wore a kerchief on her head. She'd come a long way, her footwear and leggings dressed in many layers of dirt and grime from passing through innumerable tunnels and passages. She also had a tan cooking apron with pockets laden with several objects. She smelled slightly of the sea, probably having traveled up the coast by boat.

"Why Port Montaigne? There are closer tribe homes to manufacturing," Ezra asked.

"You make it sounds like I had a choice. The Factory told me to come here. There were arrangements for my journey. I didn't think to ask why," Brook replied, tugging at her kerchief.

"That's odd, but manufacturing has been sending us out further as production shuts down," Ezra commented thoughtfully.

"Why is the Factory closing?" Brook asked.

"It is a mystery. It was funded by the human's central government and is about to run out of money. Instead of procuring more funds, they are letting it lapse for whatever reason," Ezra said, shrugging slightly.

"I don't know why, but that makes me feel a little sad. There may be no more of us?" Brook asked.

"Unless some of us suddenly cease being sterile, yeah, no more Drones."

Ezra turned on his heel, and beckoned for her to follow him. They walked into the downtown region of Port Montaigne, keeping their heads down and following a trail of shadows. Few Drones could tread above ground, and those who did kept the same routes. Ezra worried that it might make such movement predictable, but no one downtown seemed to ever notice or care.

There were to be new jobs for the humans, but the shipbuilding contract negotiations failed. Downtown was flush with those who had traveled far for those jobs and had nowhere to go now. How humans persisted without a home of some sort, or why they didn't take each other in was baffling to Ezra. Even if the Sodality came knocking, his tribe elder would give them shelter.

"Is it far?" Brook inquired.

"Yes, after a fashion. We only use a handful of access points to limit our exposure. You may see underground access every block or so, but a lot of it is locked down tight to prevent the humans trafficking narcotics, or each other," Ezra explained.

"Oh."

The tangled array of pipes and venting shafts above them got denser as they went west with midtown access getting further away. Brook's eyes widened as they neared the central downtown area. There were hundreds of neon signs decorating every establishment and walkways lit with string lighting.

It was warm and humid here, the exhaust from thousands of overhead air conditioning units constantly sending down droplets of condensation and hot air. The tempered glass awnings that covered the walkways beside the streets were continually streaked with water and dripping down into the road.

Brook watched the water run from above, then to the street, and finally down the gutters into the underground. Ezra paused to watch her take in the sights, suddenly remembering his first visit to Port Montaigne. She seemed to be studying the path of the water, as if it was of intense interest.

"Looking for something?" Ezra asked.

"How is the tribe home not flooded?" Brook asked.

"There are large pumps that pull the water back up to a filtration plant. Some of what we do down there is keep the cisterns and lids that separate them from pipes and aqueducts open. I think the humans have either forgotten that we're down there or don't care as long as things work. There hasn't been an inspection for a couple of decades," Ezra explained.

"What if we weren't there? Fixing things?" Brook asked, dangling a small hand in the water as it passed by in the gutter at her feet.

"Downtown would probably flood and drinking water would be less available. I'm not sure that the folks in the highest echelons of uptown would notice, but we aren't the only tribe working below ground. Including the Sodality, there are three or four tribes I think. C'mon, we should go," Ezra said, taking Brook's hand and pulling her down the street.

Form workers were heading home now, the concrete dust falling off of them turning to mud as they waited for transports to pick them up. Ezra and Brook huddled together under a window sill garden box and shared some bread while they waited for the area to clear. When the air conditioning units far overhead would cut out for a moment, one could hear a clamor of human voices, a gunshot or two, and the passing of water underground. The quiet was not to last, as uptown needed cool air almost year round.

"So many of these humans seem destitute. If there are jobs to be done underground, why aren't they being employed to do them? Why manufacture Drones at all?" Brook asked, pausing to gaze at a row of homeless folks prepping makeshift shelters in a vacant lot.

"Very little of what I see humans do makes any sense. I know that they would probably struggle to do what we do for long, and they wouldn't work for just living accommodations as we do. They believe they are entitled to more than just a home with their families and something to eat," Ezra replied, motioning for Brook to follow him.

"Why do they feel that way?"

"Brook, I really don't know, or care."

Brook stopped in her tracks. Ezra sighed for a moment and doubled back to apologize for his curt tone, but she seemed to look past him, her eyes slowly turning skyward.

"Are you alright, I..."

"Quiet, do you hear that?" Brook said, hushing Ezra with a finger pressed to her lips.

The shriek of expanding ventilation ducts built to a strange and distant crescendo. Light shown through the tangle above before a large private transport burst through the uptown bulwark. It fell a hundred feet to the downtown street below impacting with a deafening crash.

Even being a private transport, it was big, commercial grade, and outfitted similarly to a luxury yacht. Ezra put his arm around Brook and forced her down as debris and hot air rushed past them. Screams of panic rose up as portions of the large vehicle broke into pieces and caught fire spreading propellant to nearby businesses and tenements.

"Is that normal?" Brook asked, covering her mouth with a rag.

"No, decidedly not," Ezra replied, pulling his goggles down over his eyes.

Before Ezra could stop her, Brook dashed off into the chaos, her short legs carrying her quickly through the debris field. Ezra gave chase, hesitating for a moment to gaze fearfully upward at girders and support beams hanging precariously overhead by frayed cables and crumbling concrete forms. The whole area suddenly went dark as the power failed, sending up a clamor of panic. The dim emergency lighting was woefully inadequate to illuminate the area, but it didn't seem to hinder Brook.

"Wait!" Ezra hissed, grabbing Brook by the arm. She yanked free and turned toward the wreckage.

"People could be hurt, we should help."

Ezra watched Brook stop next to each blackened corpse she found and check for life before moving on. He wondered as to her training and what sort of instinct was driving her, but it was clear this was something she had been prepared for in the Factory. He caught up to her as she lingered beside a stasis pod. Ezra had seen the devices before, but this one was too small for an adult. He gazed into the empty pod, but saw only an empty place where a small child had likely been moments ago.

"It smells odd. People who weren't in the crash have been here," Brook remarked, sniffing the air.

"And, there are more coming," Ezra said, pointing to a man walking purposefully toward the wreckage.

"There," Brooke whispered, pointing to a pair of men in vinyl red coats, one carrying a bundle in his arms.

"Traffickers," Ezra spat, breaking into a dead run.

Brook wasn't as fast as Ezra, falling behind as he vaulted over trash bins and chain link fences in pursuit. He rounded a corner just west of the old power and gas district. It was a tangled maze of huge pipes that languished beneath the bulk of the shipping district above. A distant concrete dyke kept the ocean at bay but the ground was perpetually wet and sandy. Brook caught up just as Ezra stooped down to look for tracks.

"There's a man following us. He has robot eyes," Brook reported breathlessly.

"Our secondary epidermis should keep us concealed from his thermal range, but he'll sense our movements if he can close the distance. He must be after the child," Ezra concluded standing up.

"Maybe he's trying to help?" Brook speculated, looking back the way they came.

"Folks with bionic replacement are almost always mercenaries working for whoever has the most money. I've never met someone with those enhancements who was up to anything good. This is going to be dangerous, and there's no reason for you to endanger yourself further. Sneak back to the rendezvous point and I'll double back and pick you up when I'm finished," Ezra ordered.

"No," Brook replied.

Ezra looked at her, angry for a moment before considering the cold logic of the situation. She had a sense of smell that far surpassed his own and could navigate in total darkness somehow. Even if she would be a liability in a fight, she could track the child better than he could. Resigned to the situation, Ezra beckoned for her to follow.

"Be careful. If there's a fight, get to cover," Ezra pleaded.

"Kay."

Several times, the red coats would make a handoff, garner a third member to the operation then split off with a pair. They knew they were being tracked and had accounted for it. What they hadn't accounted for was Brook being there and getting the scent of the child. No number of countermeasures or amount of tradecraft could thwart her as she navigated the darkness. Brook paused for a moment and looked back.

"The man with the robot eyes, he's taking the wrong path. He's following decoys," Brook remarked, looking back into the darkness.

"Good, let's keep moving."

They crept along as quickly as they could for several hundred yards past huge concrete forms and pillars designed to suspend the enormous oil rigs and pumping stations above. The sound of the ocean and the deep harbor grew louder the further east they went. There were old building supplies, piping, rusting equipment, and dark makeshift shelters everywhere. Brook never hesitated though, moving quickly ahead as if the path were obvious to her.

The dyke was just in sight when gunfire broke out, catching the steel siding nearby as they approached a maintenance shed up against the dyke. Ezra ducked down, pulling Brook down with him. They froze, listening intently to the ocean beyond the concrete barrier for a moment. It was quiet, and continued to be so for several moments.

"They were firing blind. They must have caught sight of us and fired to scare us off. Let's give it a couple minutes before we move ahead," Ezra said, gazing at the sheet metal shack.

Brook made herself small in the shadow of a stack of corrugated metal piping. "I'll stay here."

"What is it the Factory trained you to do?" Ezra whispered, picking up a handful of small stones and putting them in his pocket.

"I'm a Type 3 ES."

"ES? I've never heard of a Type 3 having a special designation like that. What did the training consist of?" Ezra whispered.

"They had me memorize mazes and then run through them to find things, scented things. Sometimes I'd have to move things out of the way or squeeze through tiny places. The Factory would try to confuse me with smoke and loud noises, but it was kind of fun," Brook explained.

"Odd, I wonder what the Factory intended for you to do."

"Do you think they will hurt the baby?" Brook replied, clasping her hands together worriedly.

"No."

Brook watched Ezra quietly disappear into the shadows beneath the loading dock above and then lost sight of him. Ezra moved slowly and deliberately. These traffickers had gone to great, even extraordinary, lengths to avoid being followed and were heavily armed. Ezra took his time getting up next to the maintenance shed, waiting for the waves battering the dyke, or the creaking of support forms above to cover the sound of his movements. He could hear at least three individuals inside, each speaking quietly to one another.

"Whoever they were, I think we scared them off."

Ezra pulled himself up slowly by the window sill, ducking through a tattered screen and down into a boiler room. It was dark, but he could see a dim light coming in from under the only exit.

"We better have. Our buyer is supposed to send someone by to pick up the package soon, and any detection will cancel the arrangements."

Lowering himself slowly, Ezra gazed under the door and counted the pairs of feet in the room. There were only three voices, but four sets of feet. One of these folks was probably in charge, and far deadlier than the others. Ezra wagered it was the quiet guy standing at the corner near the window facing the exterior door.

"What's so special about this kid?"

Ezra waited until he saw nothing but heels and the backs of shoes before pulling out a small tin of lubricant from his toolkit. He placed a single drop on the hinges of the door and rubbed it in with his thumb. Slowly, he opened the door, gathering a collection of small stones from his pocket.

"Special enough to be worth eight figures? I don't think I want to even know the answer."

Brook watched from outside as the figures passed back and forth in front of the windows. She wanted desperately to get closer, but she was afraid that she would compromise whatever Ezra was attempting to do inside. She clenched her fists and tucked into a ball as gunfire broke out inside the shed. There was shouting and screaming as one of the men wearing a red coat fell from a window to a bloody heap below.

Silence and the gentle thrum of the ocean quickly took the place of firearms as things became still and peaceful once more. It was quiet for several moments before Ezra appeared at the shed's front entrance and beckoned Brook over to the shed. She tucked her arms in at her sides and sprinted for the door, crossing the threshold into the shed. Ezra grabbed the body lying outside and dragged it through the door pushing it to one side.

Brook hurriedly looked about the interior for the child. Amidst the corpses on the floor was a small and technologically sophisticated capsule, but it was dark and spattered with blood, wet sand, and oil. One of the corpses had a small stone lodged in an eye socket, throat ripped out. She winced and turned away grabbing her knees for a moment to steady herself.

"Did you have to... hurt them so badly?" Brook asked.

"They were each rigged with a chemical harness so they could fight even when close to death, or badly injured. I didn't have a choice, Brook," Ezra said, looking vigilantly through a window. "I'm sorry, we haven't much time. Check to make sure the baby is okay and let's get out of here."

Brook nodded, placing a hand on the capsule. It lit up at her touch, making a panel measuring biometric input turn from red to green. With a hydraulic hiss the capsule opened to reveal a small girl inside, barely two years old from her size. Brook wiped her hands off on her apron and gathered the child up in her arms. She was asleep and unharmed, breathing peacefully.

"I don't think the baby heard a thing in there," Brook said, looking inquisitively at the interior of the device.

"How'd you open it?" Ezra asked, looking back.

"Oh, it was easy," Brook remarked, cradling the child in her arms.

They went west, traveling beneath the midtown sprawl and shipping cranes until they broke through into downtown. Ezra worried that they took too direct of a route, but he wanted to be underground before the tracker with robot eyes or the red coats figured out what had happened. The crowds had moved on now, but emergency vehicles still buzzed by overhead going back and forth from the wreckage. They paused on a rooftop to catch their breath, not far from where the transport had torn a path downward through the uptown bulwark above.

Fire response had the conflagration under control and Central Global Government officials were already surveying the area. Brook sat down beside Ezra and looked worriedly down at the child in her arms. For the first time in her life, she didn't know what to do.

"She can't come with us," Brook said.

"No, but there is a place we can take her," Ezra replied, pushing his goggles up onto his forehead.

"What if her parents are down there, looking for her?" Brook asked.

"Someone sold this little girl, and for a lot of money. There's no one down there looking for this child that isn't looking to profit by her," Ezra stated with a frown.

Brook looked dismayed, clearly unable to comprehend the cruel situation the child had become entangled in. Ezra patted her as reassuringly as he could, watching as individuals wearing black coats mixed with the white of emergency services personnel. They were heavily armed under those coats and they had a legion of individuals gathering up every piece of the wreckage.

"There's no media," Ezra said at last, helping Brook to her feet.

"Media?" Brook said, squinting down at the crowd.

"Humans who report news to other humans. This is getting hushed up and every effort to erase that it even happened is going to be ongoing. They'll kill us if they find out we have this child, and would probably try to do the same to our tribe," Ezra explained, heading for the fire escape.

"Who is it that would come after us? Come after a child?" Brook asked.

"I don't plan to find out, but it'll be best if we get the child somewhere safe and ourselves back underground as quickly as possible. Look, Port Montaigne is a special place, but strange things happen here. There are forces at work here that I've only just caught a glimpse of," Ezra said, making his way down to the street.

"Okay, let's go."

Brook followed Ezra west to a strange structure lit from the ground below, but with a roof that met high in the form of spires and other strange decoration. Ezra beckoned for Brook to hand him the child, which she did reluctantly, then headed for the building. Brook watched him leave the child by a side door where a light shone through a window to the street. He knocked loudly, then ran back to the darkness of the alley.

After a few moments a woman dressed like no other Brook had seen stepped out. She was covered in black with only a stripe of white across the hood over her head. She had a silver ornament at her neck that she grasped tightly upon seeing the child. The woman stooped down and picked up the child barely giving the streets around her a glance before stepping back inside and shutting the door.

"Who are these people?" Brook said, gesturing to the spires atop the building.

"Adherents of one of the many gods humans worship," Ezra explained already heading down the alley.

"Oh."

"This is a place of lost children, an orphanage. When we find them in the tunnels below, lost or abandoned, we bring them here. I've known of the place for years, and the humans here genuinely try to help others," Ezra explained.

"Like us? Like Drones?"

"I don't think they'd help us," Ezra laughed.

"No, I mean they help people like Drones do. Just because," Brook giggled, looking up at the high spires of the orphanage.

"I guess so."

They made their way toward the old row of concrete factories on the darkest side of downtown Port Montaigne. Humans tread here only to engage in the most shadowy of activities and Drones took this route only when absolutely necessary. Ezra led Brook past abandoned cement mixers, through empty warehouses, and amidst large piles of gravel before finally reaching a lonely grating covered with a dirty tarp. Whisking the canvas to the side, Ezra bowed and gestured to a pair of bent bars that would just barely allow them access to the underground.

"Will we always use this entrance?" Brook asked, looking warily around.

"No, probably just today. Decided to take the extremely paranoid route home after all that nonsense with the traffickers," Ezra replied, wearily.

They descended into the underground past trash dangling from pipes and shadows wavering against feeble emergency lighting. The metal ladder groaned in protest with each step, each rung covered in rust and corrosion. Brook paused to look up at the black gap obscured by bent metal bars wondering if she'd made a mistake. Maybe the Factory had been wrong in sending her here.

Meanwhile, at the orphanage, the sister checked the simple garment the baby was dressed in, and the blanket wrapped around her. There was nothing identifying the baby save a plastic wristband that she had to cut off with a pair of scissors. She gazed at the only word on the wristband amidst a collection of numbers that read "tailored". She gazed at the letters for a moment, English not being her first language. After a moment of contemplation, she entered the baby's name into the ledger as best as she could in her native Slovak as "Taylor".

CHAPTER 10

PORT MONTAIGNE, MIDTOWN

11:32 PM, January 29th, 2200

Taylor's Diary, Part 7

The crane on the dock was, thankfully, pretty quiet in operation. It took a moment for it to build up enough of a charge to start, being all electric and the municipal power grid already being taxed. Once it was up and running, Silverstein guided the long arm up over the concrete embankment and above the electrified fence. As we climbed up the arm, all I could do was wish I'd worn more sensible shoes.

The interior of the yard was filled with rusty scrap metal, oil drums, and pallets stacked up against each other around the outside of the machine shop. Silverstein wore a pair of gloves, and the metal cable didn't seem to bother Ezra or Brook. When it was my turn to climb down I used a scarf wrapped around one hand to slowly slide down the steel cable at the end of the crane arm.

Once inside the fence, I felt an almost giddy anxiety as we crept over to the garage out back. The high grass in the back brushed against my legs as I kept an eye out for broken glass, rusted metal, and other hazards. I wondered if I could even get tetanus.

Ezra stood on Silverstein's shoulders and wiped the film off one of the windows to have a look inside. He dropped silently to the ground beside me and motioned for us to gather around. Brook dropped to her hands and knees and sniffed the ground instead.

"There's a pursuit class military transport parked in there," Ezra whispered.

"Can it break orbit?" Silverstein asked.

"Easily," Ezra replied.

"Someone lost a lot of blood out here. Right here in fact," Brook said, regaining her feet.

There was no exterior surveillance to speak of, no cameras, motion sensors or similar. It was as if Madmar never expected anyone but the locals to stray too close to his hideout, or he hadn't planned on being here too long. Ezra looked at the padlock around the handles of the huge garage doors examining it closely.

"New, and recently oiled to resist corrosion," Ezra reported.

"Let's see if we can get a look inside the machine shop," I said, creeping toward the back door.

"Wait," Ezra said, taking me by the shoulder.

Ezra dropped down on all fours and looked around the length of the warehouse. Brook did the same, almost comically mimicking his stern expression. I couldn't help but smile, even being as nervous as I was.

"Tripwires," they said, almost in unison.

"How do we get past them?" I asked.

"Do you have a bit of ribbon in your handbag?" Ezra asked.

"Do I? Red, purple, gold, or pink?" I replied.

"What, no blue?" Silverstein teased.

I stuck my tongue out at him and handed Ezra a bit of the gold. He used it to mark a length of tripwire running between two heaps of scrap, and another just in front of the back service door. We stepped carefully, trying to go only where Ezra went until we were all by the back door.

"I marked the tripwires in case we have to leave in a hurry. We need to remember to take the ribbon with us after we leave," Ezra whispered, looking at the lock on the back door.

"Problem?" Silverstein asked.

"This is a pretty good lock. Been a while since I've picked one like this, don't see them much below ground," Ezra said, fishing around in his pockets.

"I can pick it," Brook said shyly.

Ezra stepped aside. From her sleeve, Brook produced a cloth roll that when unfurled contained an array of picks, probes, and a small selection of silverware. She selected three probes and with two in one hand, one in the other, deftly picked the lock in under thirty seconds. She then made her small kit vanish.

"Where did you learn to do that?" Silverstein asked.

"The engineers. The Drones refugees from disbanded tribes picked on me a lot. Sometimes the best place to be alone was behind a locked door or a sub-basement of a building downtown. Getting into those places..." Brook stopped mid-sentence and looked about nervously.

Ezra did the same. His ears twitched back and forth. He motioned for us to quickly move away from the door. Silverstein dropped behind an oil drum while I went to a stack of pallets. Ezra and Brook seemed to just vanish as the back door swung open.

Two burly paramilitary types walked out into the yard, one handing the other a cigarette. From my hiding place, all I could do was pray they didn't notice the gold ribbon wrapped around the tripwires. They stepped over the first, not even noticing like it was habit, lighting up as they did.

One was clearly augmented, his right hand an obvious mechanical replacement. The other had eyes that looked to have been replaced by sensors. I could only guess at what sort of visual augmentation he had, but the heat coming off the end of his cigarette must have been enough interference that he didn't see us.

They were both dressed in urban camouflage, black combat boots, caps, and web belts with ammunition, knives, and the usual stuff you'd see military types carrying. Each had a rifle of some kind and a pistol. I couldn't believe they didn't notice the ribbon.

"Did he tell you why we were packing up?" mechanical arm said in a gruff voice.

"No. Why are you always asking questions? It all pays the same," Mechanical Eyes complained, turning his gaze up at the sky.

"I hear the imprinted clones got the kill switch the other day. You ever wonder if we're just another liability to this guy?" Mechanical Arm asked in a low tone.

"No matter what sort of ambition in life you've got, you rise high enough on the food chain... you're going to need guys with guns. We're those guys," Mechanical Eyes said, pushing his assault rifle around behind his back and putting one hand in his pocket.

"You better be right. We've got a lot riding on this," Mechanical Arm said, stepping back over the tripwire to head back inside.

Mechanical Eyes dropped what remained of his cigarette on the ground and looked about the yard. His accomplice hesitated at the door for a moment, looked over his shoulder then ducked inside.

"You coming?" Mechanical Arm said from inside.

"Yeah, I'll be there in a minute," Mechanical Eyes said, turning to look directly at me.

I stood up slowly from my hiding place, knowing he'd caught me. Silverstein started to stand as well, but I shook my head. Mechanical Eyes ground out his cigarette with his boot while straightening his cap. Then he raised his hand out at about waist level and lowered it slowly, like he wanted me to stay where I was.

Needless to say, I was baffled.

"Taylor, right? Have you ever been to Mexico?" Mechanical Eyes asked quietly.

"No," I said, trying to see where Ezra or Brook was.

"A lot of it was off the grid before the Shutdown. Compared to most of the rest of the world, it is a nice place. There's food, running water, and lots of job opportunities for enterprising individuals," he said, looking back out at the ocean.

"That sounds nice," I replied. "Are you going to go?"

"Go back you mean? I don't think so."

"How do you know my name?" I asked.

"Dr. Madmar is paying us good money to detain you, in the event we run across you. Every mercenary on the Eastern seaboard knows your face," Mechanical Eyes said calmly.

I swallowed loudly.

"What are you going to do now?"

"Don't worry, you're protected. Everyone working under the umbrella knows better, which puts me in a rather compromising position," Mechanical Eyes said.

Mechanical Arm suddenly returned, stepping out over the first tripwire.

"Hey, c'mon, we've got work to do in here," Mechanical Arm said, stepping up to Mechanical Eyes, just on the other side of the pallets I was hiding behind.

He turned in one fluid motion, driving a long combat knife into Mechanical Arm's throat, just under the chin. Mechanical Arm didn't struggle, he just stopped moving as his attacker cradled him in his arms before placing him gently on the ground. I stood up, and began to step away from him.

Ezra rose from his hiding place as Silverstein brought up his rifle, the time for subtlety appeared to be at an end. Mechanical Eyes produced a detonator, holding it out at arm's length for everyone to see. We froze, waiting to see what mechanical eyes was going to do next.

"How are you, Mr. Uroboros?" Mechanical Eyes asked.

"I'm okay. You planning on blowing something up?" Silverstein looked intently at the detonator.

Mechanical Eyes nodded.

"Should we leave?" Silverstein said, pointing over to the crane cable at the far end of the yard.

"The kill switch went out, so I'm assuming you're the real deal, yet you don't seem to recognize me. Tell me why you are here, sir," Mechanical Eyes said, cocking his head to one side.

"To confront Dr. Madmar. To stop him," Silverstein said, moving his finger from the trigger guard on his rifle to the trigger itself.

"He's leaving in an hour or so, from a different location, according to the schedule you'd calculated. We are supposed to follow along with the bulk of his resources and equipment," Mechanical Eyes said.

"What's your name?" I asked stepping between him and Silverstein.

"My code name is Perfidy," he replied, still holding the detonator.

"Why are you doing this?" I asked.

"Because I was asked to. I'm a little confused as to why Mr. Uroboros is acting like he doesn't know why I'm here," Perfidy said, gazing intently at Silverstein.

"He lost his memory. Tell us why he should know you, or why he should know the reasons behind your actions," I replied, holding up my hands.

"Vance Uroboros was a high ranking member of the Cabal before he stepped away," Perfidy said, slowly stepping back over the tripwire to stand inside the backdoor.

"The Cabal? The Cabal of what?" Silverstein asked.

"You should all go, now. I'm on a tight schedule, and if Dr. Madmar finds out that we are meddling in his affairs, he may engage certain countermeasures that will prevent me from completing my mission," Perfidy said with a slight smile.

"We?" Silverstein asked, exasperated.

Perfidy turned on his heel and went back into the building. Silverstein looked as though he was going to pursue, but Ezra and I grabbed him. He fought us for a moment, but he seemed to see reason as his shoulders slumped and we began making our way quickly toward the back fence. Brook was already at the crane cable waiting for us.

"Cabal? What the hell was that guy talking about?" Silverstein said, helping me up the first few feet of cable.

"I don't know, but I've seen that look before. He's going to blow this whole place up, with him in it. We need to be somewhere else," Ezra whispered, obviously disappointed.

"Look?" Brook said.

"The look on a soldier's face right before they leave on a mission they don't expect to come back from," Ezra said, climbing the cable.

"I thought he looked kind of peaceful," Brook said, climbing up onto the crane arm.

We made it down the crane arm about the time the place went up. I had seen an explosion like it on video, but never in real life. The heat from it blew past us in the wind with smoke and debris. My ears ached from the noise and my lungs burned from the fumes. We made our way down to the edge of the dock beside the freighter moored there to consider our next move.

"There's no way we'll find Madmar in an hour, but maybe he's left something behind that Perfidy didn't blow up? We haven't looked on board the freighter. Assuming it isn't going to blow up, we should probably check it out," I said, pointing to the gangplank.

"Ship looks like it is probably empty," Silverstein said pointing to the water lines etched into the side of the hull.

The ship was riding high in the water, like the hold was almost empty.

"Let's look anyway," Ezra said, taking the lead.

We all followed him up the rickety gangplank. Ezra and Silverstein leapt up, like commandos, and pointed their rifles around, but there was no one on deck. The freighter was large, almost a hundred and fifty feet in length, but there were only a few cargo containers on the top.

"I smell people. People were here recently," Brook whispered.

"Anyone you know?" I asked.

She shook her head. Ezra opened the door to the deck cabins and stepped into the long corridor beyond. We followed along as he wove his way forward, taking a right into what looked like the bridge. There were several sets of controls with swivel seating and a view out the front of the boat set aglow by the burning machine shop. A man stood at the far end of the room, bent over, his arms leaning heavily on the railing.

"Dr. Helmet," Ezra said, raising his rifle.

He wore a pair of beige slacks, a tweed suit coat, hat, and carried a medical bag. He looked genuinely surprised to see us. The spectacle of the explosion must have distracted him from seeing our approach across the dock. Dr. Helmet looked as we did, tired, and lacking a night's sleep in a decent bed.

"Hello again," Dr. Helmet said, turning around and leaning back on the railing, his back to the window.

"Come to make sure everything went as planned?" Silverstein asked.

"After a fashion. You appear to be in two places at once. An impressive feat, even for you," the doctor remarked coolly.

Ezra leapt over the controls and landed gracefully on the railing beside the doctor. He grabbed him by the throat and pressed him back over the railing, his face mashed against the window at an odd angle. Silverstein closed the distance, with us in tow, and stooped over to look Dr. Helmet in the eyes.

"How did I lose my memory?" Silverstein demanded, doing nothing to deter Ezra.

"We really aren't certain. I can only assume you did it to yourself, and then instinctively sought out Taylor. I did follow you to downtown Port Montaigne in an attempt to answer that same question," he gasped, struggling to take a breath.

"We?" Silverstein asked, taking hold of Dr. Helmet's suit coat.

"Indeed," Dr. Helmet replied hoarsely, adjusting his glasses with his free hand.

Ezra loosened his grip.

"Why would he have instinctively sought me out?" I asked.

Dr. Helmet straightened his crumpled collar and looked down at Brook.

"Who is this? You need to stop involving the Drones in your affairs, as they've endured enough already," Dr. Helmet asked.

"Answer Taylor's question," Ezra said, putting a clawed hand on the side of Dr. Helmet's face.

"You are the only terrestrial A.I. we have been able to identify, and integral to our long range plans as a consequence. Even bereft of most of his memories, Vance Uroboros would have known you by virtue of having been your steward during the last twenty years," Dr. Helmet explained.

"No one was my steward. I was abandoned at the downtown mission and I raised myself on those streets, made my own way. No one helped me," I said indignantly.

"That is because Vance made sure no one tried to add you to their portfolio, manipulating you from afar. He wanted you to have a choice and make your own way. He traded away a lot to make sure that happened," Dr. Helmet said.

"Portfolio?" Silverstein asked.

"It's what members of the Cabal call those they have gathered under their influence," Dr. Helmet explained.

"What's the Cabal?" Brook asked.

"It's an ancient global organization that has been manipulating world affairs, governments, and powerful individuals toward a particular agenda. Vance Uroboros was one of the oldest living members of the Cabal before he left," Dr. Helmet explained.

"Why did I leave?" Silverstein said, shaking his head.

"There were things about the Shutdown that you had to manage personally. I think you had become aware of outsiders meddling with your design," the doctor answered, polishing the lenses of his glasses with a cloth.

"How do you know about the Cabal, and what else do you know about them?" Silverstein asked.

"Only that it exists, and little else. Matthias had begun to suspect he was being manipulated and his work used for some purpose other than what he'd been told. I think you may have wanted to reassure him without revealing yourself. Madmar's own desires have always been an enigma, but I'm fairly certain he was aware of the Cabal," Dr. Helmet said shaking his head sadly.

"Matthias was in on this?" I asked.

"Not really. He was just an asset, and knew nothing of the Cabal. Silverstein's meeting with him following the loss of his memory was probably the first time they'd met face to face. He probably has no idea you've been guiding him for decades," Dr. Helmet explained.

"Decades? How old is Silverstein, err… Vance Uroboros?" I asked, extremely weirded out now.

"I'm not sure. My knowledge of the Cabal has been limited, being only Vance's asset," Dr. Helmet said, his voice going all spooky.

"This just more lies?" Ezra asked, looking back at Silverstein.

"You're the one that's good at telling the difference, you tell me," Silverstein replied, looking to Ezra and then to Brook.

"Hard to say. This guy stinks of deception, but I think that's more a lifestyle choice than the words he speaks," Ezra said, folding his arms.

Silverstein walked around the control console and sat in one of the swiveling chairs, his face in his hands. I knew how he felt. I can remember when Dr. Helmet told me what I was, taking away the reality I'd known all my life.

"When you ran those tests on me before, and told me I was a terrestrial A.I., did you already know what I was?" I asked.

Dr. Helmet looked genuinely embarrassed by my question, turning a rosy hue.

"Yes. The truth is, I didn't have the equipment to run the tests, and I already knew the catalyst on sight. I needed you to believe that I was only just discovering what you were to further my own agenda, and to honor Vance Uroboros' wishes. Vance, before losing his memory, would have been furious with me for telling you," Dr. Helmet said.

"Then why did you?" Ezra asked, somewhat annoyed.

"Because Vance wanted to tell you himself right before taking you back to the Lunar Colony. It didn't seem likely that was going to happen, so I took the liberty when I could," Dr. Helmet replied, looking over at Silverstein mournfully.

"I can only wonder where else you've deceived us," Ezra said, shaking his head.

"Brook, is this guy a man? Does he smell right to you?" I asked.

"Yeah, he smells like a man. An old stinky man," Brook said wrinkling her nose.

"What about me?" I asked.

"You smell pretty, but you aren't a woman... not like other women anyway. Strange, you have always smelled familiar to me for some reason," she replied, smiling shyly.

"Brook, is it? Would you like to know what *you* were designed to do?" Dr. Helmet said, bending over to talk to her, like she was a child.

"My friends think you're a liar," Brook said, wrinkling her nose again.

"Hear him out," Ezra said reluctantly.

"Only a few of you were ever meant to be born in the Factory. I wished there could have been more, especially during these very dark times. You were meant to rescue people. Your small stature would allow you to make your way through rubble, and your nose would lead you to those trapped beneath. The ES in your designation is for Emergency Services," Dr. Helmet explained.

"Like in an earthquake?" Brook asked innocently.

"Exactly. I would wager you are extremely strong too," Dr. Helmet said sweetly.

Brook nodded, which surprised us all because of how gentle she seemed.

"Why weren't more like her made?" I asked.

"What I told you, and what you probably heard about my being expelled from the MDC project was mostly true. There were other interested parties that possessed different ideas about how Drones and Metasapients would be used," Dr. Helmet said quietly marveling at the sight of Brook.

"This guy is like our dad?" Brook asked.

"Unfortunately, it seems that way," Ezra said, glowering over by Silverstein.

"I like him better than the Factory. The Factory only ever told us how, but never why," Brook said walking over behind me to play with my hair.

Silverstein stood up and walked down the corridor and out to the deck. If I'd heard the doctor unload all that at once, I would have needed a moment as well. Ezra followed him out, lingering at the doorway for a moment.

"I'm going to go have a look around," Ezra said, disappearing down the corridor.

"Silverstein is going to have some more questions, I'm sure," I said, deciding to stick around and keep an eye on Dr. Helmet.

"I won't be of much use I'm afraid. Each member of the Cabal had their own methods and autonomy. Vance... Silverstein was one of the most mysterious. I don't know if he is merely the successor in a long line of individuals to hold the name Vance Uroboros, or if he really did find a way to greatly extend his lifespan," Dr. Helmet admitted.

"What do you know?" I asked.

"I thought you would have far more questions about yourself than anyone else," Dr. Helmet said, smiling wearily.

"I'll get my questions answered when we visit the Lunar Colony I think," I said.

"Indeed. Vance Uroboros was one of an ancient order called the Amnestic Monks. They used a technique that would allow them to manipulate the memories of other people. It's unknown how they did this, but it was the means Vance used to collect his portfolio of influences and join the Cabal," Dr. Helmet said.

"Tell me about these monks," I said, curious almost beyond the threshold of my willpower.

"I know very little I'm afraid. They were celibate, reclusive, and there are no recorded female members of the order. The few texts that I have been able to catch a glimpse of in the Cabal archives spoke of a woman, or women, that had something to do with the order. The legend was that they were inviolable and immune to the memory manipulation of the order. It wasn't clear, from what I read, whether these women were allies, founders, or rivals of the Amnestic Monks," Dr. Helmet said, adopting a professorial tone.

"A woman like me," I said, beginning to understand Silverstein's fascination with me before losing his memory.

"I don't know how the Amnestic Monks manipulate the memories of others, but from what I understand, terrestrial A.I.s have redundant systems that prevent their minds from being tampered with. I didn't think about it before, but you would make a valuable asset in the event of a schism among the Amnestic Monks," Dr. Helmet said.

"Or, if one among them just needed a friend or someone to hang out with," I said, looking out the window at Silverstein.

He was leaning against the railing out on the deck, clearly distraught, talking to Ezra.

"What was your plan after Perfidy blew up the machine shop? How do you sleep at night knowing you sent those people to their deaths?" I asked, turning my attention back to Dr. Helmet.

Brook fidgeted nervously beside me as he sat down at the control console to rest himself.

"Each of those men had received cybernetic enhancements from Dr. Madmar. Their lives were on a timer, and most had no idea. I approached the one called Perfidy for a number of reasons, but mostly because he had family he was trying to support and protect. I made arrangements for their protection in Mexico," Dr. Helmet said sadly.

"How screwed is Dr. Madmar now?" I asked.

"Given the difficulty of building redundancy into his plans? I think that he will reach the Lunar Colony with none of his research, resources, or mercenaries, mostly thanks to Silverstein, Ezra, and yourself. You distracted and delayed him greatly, which allowed me to make my own move. He, like myself, thought Vance was at Uroboros Financial and that you were probably out of reach in the underground," Dr. Helmet replied, meeting my gaze and smiling.

"I'm hungry," Brook said, tugging on my arm.

"I am, too. We need to find something to eat and a place to crash, we're all tired," I said.

"My transportation doesn't arrive until the morning. I was going to just sleep in a cabin on board the ship," Dr. Helmet stated.

Brook's keen nose was able to find some canned food supplies in the galley, and there were a few beds that hadn't been stripped of linens. We had a hot stew with green beans, corn, lentils, and chicken from a can. Brook gleefully stirred the stew with her ladle, glad to have someone to cook for. Silverstein sullenly ate his food while Ezra took his to the deck to keep a lookout.

"Where are you going tomorrow morning?" I asked.

"Mexico. I have an old freighter pilot on retainer that takes me around where I need to go. I'd already be gone if he wasn't on another errand already," Dr. Helmet replied, mouth full of food.

"Perfidy's family?" I inquired.

"I need to see they are safe with my own eyes," Dr. Helmet said.

After dinner, the doctor retired to a cabin and closed the door. Brook and I did the dishes, although I'm not sure why. We were probably going to leave tomorrow. Silverstein hung out in the kitchen, and listened to Brook sing hymns while she washed. I doubted she even knew who or what God was, but the hymnal was evidently one of her favorite books in the library back home.

Silverstein leaned up against the prep table in the galley and tried in vain to smooth his hair out of his face. When I finished putting the last plate away Brook was nowhere to be found, gone to find her own place to sleep. Silverstein sighed loudly and looked up at me, his eyes full of weary and worry.

"Do I need to get Ezra down here and have him yell at you again for feeling sorry for yourself?" I said, only pretending to be stern.

"No. I don't suppose you know how to cut hair?" Silverstein said, jumping up to sit on the prep table.

I stood on the table behind him and cut his hair with a comb and a pair of fabric shears from my bag. It wasn't ideal, but he looked so good afterward, even though he needed a shave like I needed sleep. Afterward, we walked back to the first empty cabin, made sure it wasn't horrible, and went in.

"Think we're safe here?" he asked, flopping down onto one of the cots.

"Ezra hasn't gotten to kill anyone for a while. I think I would be almost afraid to come aboard knowing he was here," I said smiling at him from the doorway.

Silverstein laughed and turned over on his back, kicking off his shoes. He turned over on his side to face the wall, the mirth on his face draining away as whatever was troubling him returned to pollute his mind. I laid down beside him and threw my arm over him.

"Before I lost my memory, do you think I was trying to hurt or use you?" Silverstein asked.

"No, I think you wanted a friend. You were afraid to get close because of the business you were involved in, and tried to protect me above and beyond your own desires," I said, snuggling up beside him.

"What is it you think I desire?" Silverstein asked.

"Now? I don't know. You should make a decision though," I replied hugging him.

"Thanks," he said putting his arm on mine.

"For what?"

"Believing in me, even when I haven't been able to lately. The more I learn about who I was, the less I want that to influence who I am now," Silverstein whispered, turning to face me.

"That makes sense. Dr. Helmet thinks your memory loss might be self-inflicted. Maybe you wanted to start over," I said, continuing to hug him.

"Maybe."

"It sounds like you used to be an important and powerful guy. Aren't you the least bit interested in exploring your past? We could look for the Cabal and try to get in touch with your other assets," I suggested.

"No, everything I want in life is pretty much already in the room with me. I just want to be with you. I think that is the only thing that has made any sense throughout all of this. I want you to be safe," Silverstein said, with the certitude that usually accompanied his voice.

I know I probably blushed. I really liked Silverstein, and he hadn't seemed like himself lately. I wanted to help him the way he had probably helped me.

We laid there for a while, looking into each other's eyes, until fatigue finally robbed us of consciousness. I slept peacefully in his arms through the night, dreaming of the moon, my mind trying to conjure what the colony would look like. Even though I couldn't remember ever being there, I longed to go home.

CHAPTER 11

PORT MONTAIGNE, HARBOR, MIDTOWN

7:51 AM, January 30th, 2200

Taylor's Diary, Part 8

When I woke up, Silverstein was already awake. Apparently the boat still had power so he had plugged our mobiles in to charge. I rubbed my eyes and smiled at the sun coming in through the porthole.

"I don't know why we carry these things," Silverstein said, gesturing to our mobiles sitting beside one another on the cot.

"Probably in the hope that we'll be living in a world where we'll need them again someday? Also, I have a bunch of cute patterns saved on mine," I replied looking for my shoes.

I put the shoes I'd worn the day before in my bag and fished around until I found a pair of flip-flops. Silverstein left the room so I could change, since I actually had a change of clothes with me. When I came out, I could smell Brook's cooking from down the hall as it wafted in with a breeze.

Ezra was already at the prep table in the galley cradling a stainless steel cup of instant coffee. I yearned for the same and looked about until Brook pointed out the cupboard that had a box of the stuff. Fortunately, Brook already had water boiling and I made both Silverstein and myself a cup of java.

"Thank you," he said as I handed him one of the two cups I was carrying.

"Where's Dr. Helmet?" I asked.

"Left on a freighter about an hour ago. A Mark III freighter hauler, a lot like the one Tullia owns and everyone on board had the same accent," Ezra said.

"Romani?" Silverstein asked.

"Pretty sure," Ezra replied.

"I wonder what that's like, to go from being the underdog, almost squeezed out by the large corporations, to providing one of the most valuable services in the world," Silverstein said.

"Busy," Brook said, not intending for it to sound funny.

We chuckled anyway. She was probably right, I bet they couldn't keep up with the demand to move goods and people right now. They could probably barter for whatever they wanted or needed, but I was certain after our recent experiences that their lives were infinitely more dangerous too. In that I could certainly empathize.

"Dr. Helmet says Madmar went to the moon, but without his resources or personnel. I think we should calculate a new time to break orbit and chase him down," Ezra said.

"You just want to go to the moon," I teased.

"You don't?" He smiled.

"We need to go and stop him from hurting anyone. He'll get there, realize he's bereft of his resources, and do something dangerous. I can't bear the thought of another person being harmed by him," Silverstein said, the determination we'd come to know him for obviously having made a return.

"He sounds pretty bad," Brook said, packing up her meager possessions.

"He is. How are we going to get there? The military transport probably went up with the machine shop. Does the transport you lent Kale have the capability to get us to the moon?" Ezra asked.

"No. We might need Matthias and Tullia to help us," Silverstein replied.

"There's probably a radio on this boat," Ezra said, hoping off the stool to the floor.

"I'll help you look. It is Silverstein's turn to do dishes," I said with a wink, following him out.

We located the radio and began to transmit on the last frequency known to be used by Tullia when we got to North America. It took almost thirty minutes but she eventually answered and replied using Morse code. Ezra replied and then shut the radio down.

"She'll come get us," Ezra said.

Silverstein and Brook came onto the bridge a moment later.

"Just got a call from Kale," Silverstein said, putting his mobile into his pocket.

"What did he say?" I asked.

"That everything was fine and we didn't need to come to the meeting today," Silverstein said worriedly.

If it were even possible, the blood in my veins dropped several degrees as soon as the words came out of Silverstein's mouth.

"What meeting?" Brook said.

"There isn't one, he's in some kind of trouble," Silverstein said.

"We have to get there and help," Ezra said, checking his rifle.

"It'll be an hour before Tullia gets here, at least, if she's coming from Matthias' workshop," I said, wringing my hands in worry.

"Then I guess we'll have to wait," Silverstein said.

We waited as patiently as we could until Tullia's transport appeared on the northern horizon out over the water. It had only been thirty minutes since we'd called, and it was clear the freighter was moving far faster than it had right to. It was whisper quiet as it approached, setting down on the quay just a few yards from the ship we were on.

We raced down the dock to the waiting transport and inside the waiting cargo hold. Tullia was there, dressed in a new flight suit she looked to have made herself. Her hair was up in a neat bun off to one side and she had earrings on, something I hadn't seen her wear before. The cuffs of her flight suit were rolled up and she was wearing some minimalist looking sandals.

"Oh, those are nice!" I said pointing to the sandals.

"Using cargo runs as a means to barter has perks," Tullia said with a smile.

"We have to hurry," Ezra said, taking up a spot in the hold.

"What's wrong?" Tullia asked.

"I'll explain on the way. We need to get to Uroboros Financial as fast as possible," I said breathlessly.

"Good thing Matthias made some upgrades," Tullia said running to the cockpit.

That was evident by the interior of the cargo hold. Some of it was taken up by housings for new equipment and undoubtedly more powerful engines. There were new ports that looked like they were meant to eject shell casings and the whole ship sat a little lower on the landing gear for the weight it was carrying. There was also a ceiling mounted air conditioning unit, but its flow was directed at the housing where the A.I. sentience core was housed toward the center wall between the cargo area and crew quarters.

We followed Tullia up to the cockpit and grabbed a spot on the benches along the corridor.

"Please take your seats and strap in," a familiar voice came over the intercom.

"He hooked up the CGG A.I.? Nice," Ezra said.

"We call him Lucius," Tullia said, flipping a line of switches along the console in front of him.

"Hello, Lucius!" Brook yelled up at the ceiling as she struggled with her seatbelt.

"Greetings," Lucius said, his voice seeming to come from everywhere at once.

The freighter hauler powered back up, but not like I remembered. Where it felt like it struggled to get airborne before, it felt powerful, almost burly now. It effortlessly responded to Tullia as she worked the controls, hurtling up into the sky at a speed that was almost uncomfortable. I shut my eyes.

"Amazing what Matthias has been able to do with just a few days," Silverstein said, holding on for dear life.

"So what's going on at Uroboros Financial?" Tullia asked, leveling the freighter hauler out so the horizon appeared once more through the windshield.

"Kale's in some kind of trouble. I don't understand, isn't Dr. Madmar supposed to be gone by now?" I said, taking a deep breath as the freighter started to accelerate to cruising speed.

"That's what Perfidy said," Ezra replied.

"We'll be there in two minutes," Tullia said.

Some kind of alarm went off in the cockpit, and Tullia swore in her own language. She pushed the controls forward and down. I felt weightless for a moment and we dropped altitude.

"CGG interceptors are airborne. Just got issued a warning that I was in their airspace and instructions to land," Tullia shouted over the sound of wind rushing past outside.

"How is that even possible?" Silverstein hollered back, gripping the restraints at his shoulders tightly.

"Mobile command and control aboard a larger ship," Ezra shouted, pointing.

As we broke through the clouds a large warship came into view. It looked to have sustained damage recently, but it still looked more than functional enough to deploy unmanned craft and take shots at us. It was hovering just above Port Montaigne's uptown area right beside the Uroboros Financial tower. There was a military shuttle already parked on the landing area. Tullia put her hand up to her headset and listened intently as interceptor craft dropped down beside us, their gun turrets training on us.

"This thing have guns?" Ezra asked.

"Yeah, but not enough to mix it up with a Malleus Class cruiser with a full complement of unmanned interceptors," Tullia said.

"The people in the city below us would be put at risk, we have to comply with whatever they want, at least for now," I said.

Tullia pulled back on the controls causing the freighter hauler to decelerate. The unmanned craft accompanied us to a second landing pad on the other side of the Uroboros Financial tower. Ezra unbuckled first while the rest of us caught our breath. He began hurriedly working to remove the scope on his rifle and reset the sights fixed on the barrel.

"What are you doing?" I asked.

"The CGG cruiser is sporting replica colors. Its designation and tag-ging is all wrong. I don't think they are really government soldiers aboard," Ezra said, moving magazines of ammunition around to the front of his belt.

"What do you want me to do?" Tullia said, turning around in the cockpit.

"Stay here with Taylor," Silverstein said standing up.

"What? I should go with you?" I protested.

"Try to work with Lucius to contact the A.I. aboard the cruiser. See if it's happy with its current assignment," Silverstein said, readying his own rifle.

"Brook, try to escape as soon as the cargo bay door opens. If it's like the other landing pad, there should be access to the air conditioning unit on the left. Use your ladle to jam the fan and drop in," Ezra said, putting his clawed hand on Brook's shoulder.

"Then what?" she asked.

"Get away. Just run and don't look back," Ezra said.

I pulled out my mobile and willed it to access Lucius directly. I followed them to the cargo bay and ducked behind some crates while I formed a telemechanical confluence with Lucius. He felt constrained within the freighter hauler, being capable of controlling a much larger network of systems and devices.

It only took me a moment to gain access to his external surveillance and look out beyond the ship. I could see every infrared beam and radio signal floating through the air around us. I could also see Ezra and Silver-stein step out onto the landing pad where a handful of augmented merce-naries waited, and I could see Brook's tiny form sprinting for a rooftop air conditioning unit.

Everything seemed to slow down. My mind reached out, pressing against the firewalls surrounding the A.I. aboard the ship floating just fifty yards away, touching the almost frighteningly powerful intelligence just beyond. Whatever was aboard the Malleus Class, it was an extremely pow-erful A.I. that had remotely taken possession. When our minds touched, all I could hear was melodic death metal and an ominous voice growling somewhere behind it.

"Hello?" I intoned empathically across the digital interface.

"Hey, little sister." The voice growled in time with the metal music being transmitted over the stream.

Ezra took his first step off the loading ramp as the mercenaries began to reach for their weapons.

"I'm Taylor, a terrestrial A.I.,"

"...begat of the Omegas, Moon and Mars?" the voice reverberated, as if it could be heard through the furthest reaches of space.

"I think so. I'm not really sure," I replied honestly.

The high tech weapons carried by the mercenaries, those connected to the Malleus Class cruiser, and the voice I was conversing with went status red and locked up. Only I seemed to have access. Ezra took his second step, waiting for the mercenaries to fire. Silverstein was a step and a half behind, and I could see through the freighter hauler's sensors his heart rate increase.

"I'd made an arrangement. I'm capable of hurting people, but my program still dictates that there must be a benefit to the people I was put in place to protect," the voice keened, it's dirge-like voice swaying to the thrum of the music transmitted with it.

Silverstein's rifle came up to his shoulder as Ezra's mouth opened slowly as if to say something. I couldn't hear, there was no auditory input outside the freighter hauler, and it was all I could do to receive the voice from somewhere beyond even the moon's own faint radio transmissions.

"You must have some prowess to be able to collect enough wattage and influence to transmit out this far," the voice continued, the music in the background diminishing somewhat.

Silverstein let off a single round from his rifle that traveled through the air at a painfully slow rate of speed. The mercenaries, only just realizing their weapons wouldn't fire, took a step toward cover. Ezra was yelling now, his rifle still raised.

"Tell me how you're mixed up in all this?" the dirge-like voice said.

"My friends and I are trying to stop a man from hurting any more innocent people. He already killed my landlord and who knows else. I just wanted to work a job, have a little apartment, and make my own clothes. Everything has gone off the rails because of this man," I said.

The round Silverstein fired hits one of the mercenaries in the shoulder, lifting him up off his feet. The other mercs started to let go of their weapons, falling to their knees for cover. Tullia must have hit the ramp control, as it was slowly ascending to seal the cargo hold for the freighter.

"This man, what does he call himself?" the voice growled.

"His real name is Dr. Madmar, but he's been using my friend's name, Vance Uroboros, to further his murderous agenda," I replied.

Ezra took a second step out of the cargo hold, the ramp rising slowly behind him. Silverstein was a step behind, dropping down onto the landing pad below. The world ground to a halt as the voice reached down through me to the Malleus Class cruiser, issuing a recall order for all personnel and unmanned craft.

The radios carried by the mercenaries lit up, even as they were still slowly running for cover. In that moment, it all returned to real time, my forced perspective abruptly returning to the interior of the cargo hold where I was. I stood and ran for the rapidly closing cargo bay door and leapt through.

Ezra was screaming for the mercenaries to stay down as Silverstein stepped forward and looked up. Unmanned craft flew by overhead, on a course for the Malleus Class cruiser. I rolled to the ground, skinning my knee on the rough surface of the landing pad.

"You were supposed to stay behind, contact the A.I. aboard the Malleus over there," Silverstein said, helping me up.

"It's already done," I said.

"Dang, that was quick," he replied with a laugh.

"You've no idea," I said, following them into the lift past several mercenaries still lying face down on the ground.

The lift doors closed, blotting out the noise of engines and the warbling of radios out on the landing pad. Silverstein dropped the clip on his rifle and threaded a bullet into it, replacing the one he'd fired. I looked down at my scuffed up knee and frowned. It really hurt.

I held up my mobile, trying to see if there was any remnant or record of my conversation I'd just had with my "brother." There was a notification that I'd downloaded several hundred new music tracks. I thumbed through the playlist and found nothing but melodic death metal, thrash, and hard rock from dozens of different artists.

"He likes metal. All kinds," I said, holding up my mobile.

"Who?" Silverstein asked.

"The intelligent agent controlling the CGG cruiser from space. He called me his sister. Even so, I don't think he and I are the same," I said.

"Ezra?" Silverstein said, looking down.

"When I did EVA for the CGG military, there were rumors of ships that hung around at the edge of the solar system. They called them Eclipse Class Interdictors, ships large enough to repel an invasion on their own. It was rumored that they had A.I.s on board that could control dozens of ships, drones and coordinate thousands of marines. I, and everyone else, pretty much assumed it was propaganda," Ezra explained, watching the indicator lights on the elevator's control panel.

"There's at least one out there. Had to be. He was so large... it was like talking to someone who was fifty feet tall," I said, failing to find the right words to describe what I'd experienced.

"Wow, what did he have to say?" Silverstein asked.

"I told him what we were trying to do, and he issued a recall order to the cruiser outside," I replied, my voice shaking a little.

"That's why they couldn't fire at us?" Ezra said.

"We were lucky. They'd have torn us apart otherwise," Silverstein said.

"Why did you guys do that then?" I said, half shouting.

"The game ends as soon as he gets his hands on you. We didn't see another option," Silverstein said.

They had gone out there, ready to die to keep Tullia and me safe. More than that, they were counting on me saving them before it got that far. We'd been traveling together long enough that we knew each other that well. It wasn't until that moment, talking in the elevator, that it really sank in.

"What if they'd killed you?" I asked.

"Tullia would have had to try to pull both of you out of there, and Brook would hopefully have gotten away," Ezra said.

"Silverstein fired before you did, what's up with that?" I teased.

"None of them had their fingers on the triggers. They were there to take us alive," Ezra said.

The lift doors opened, letting us out into a maze of cubicles. We headed quickly for the executive offices, stopping just outside the door. Ezra stooped down and closed his eyes, listening at the threshold. He held up two fingers, then put his shoulder to the door. Silverstein followed quickly behind as we stepped into the lavishly adorned offices.

All of the glass doors were open, and every office was dark. Silverstein and Ezra checked each one as we went further toward Vance's old office, the most likely place to find Kale. The doors opened on their own at our approach, sliding to the sides.

The office was as I remembered it, except the doors out to the balcony were open and a man stood outside. Kale was laying on the floor, his hand clasped over a wound in his belly. I knelt beside him and felt for a pulse. He was still alive, but unconscious.

"Get in here," Ezra shouted, raising his rifle.

The man turned around, a pistol still in his hand. He was tall and youthful looking, wearing a white suit and matching leather shoes. His sapphire blue tie was loose and the top button of his shirt undone. Dr. Madmar's hair wasn't wild like the last time I saw him. It was straight, and had grown a bit longer dangling about the collar of his shirt.

"You must be Vance Uroboros," Dr. Madmar said, putting the handgun down on the desk.

"Don't recognize us, Dr. Madmar?" I asked, willing the nanoid machines that made up my body to help Kale.

"I don't, I'm sorry. I'm really just a cunning replica of Dr. Madmar, and I don't possess all his memories," the man in white said, walking around the desk toward us.

Silverstein moved forward, within reach of the Madmar clone when he abruptly turned, and with one fluid motion, disarmed Silverstein and knocked him down. Ezra leapt forward, claws out, and the two tumbled to the floor. He gave Ezra two savage blows to the head before tossing his limp form to one side. Fear, no, terror ripped through my mind as the Madmar replica slowly rose to his feet again.

By the time I drew the pistol I had in my handbag, he'd closed the distance and batted it from my hand. He smiled and took hold of my wrist with his right hand. Silverstein lunged at him from behind, but the Madmar clone turned, bringing his left elbow into Silverstein's jaw. Something clicked in my brain.

"You're him, aren't you? You aren't a replica," I said, looking at the cufflink sticking out from his jacket sleeve.

"You're half right, how could you tell?" He smiled wickedly.

"I read a lot about clothes, and those cufflinks are too expensive to hand off to an imprinted clone or artificial replica of yourself. You are the real Dr. Madmar," I said, looking up into his eyes.

I'd hoped the comment would get him talking, but stalling for time wasn't all I was trying to do. If he was really a replica, and I honestly couldn't tell, finding out who he was really loyal to was pretty much paramount. It seemed to work, for a moment, as he cocked his head to one side, his smile fading slightly.

"Does it really matter? Think what you like," he said, looking back at Ezra who had begun to twitch, his body trying to wake him up.

"What do you want?" I said, struggling against his grip while he dragged me toward the door.

"The same thing Vance Uroboros wanted, a companion and friend. Someone to share things with. Once I've figured out how to bypass the redundant systems that safeguard your personality, I can make you into anything, or anyone, I want," Dr. Madmar said, the wickedness from his face fading to what I could only describe as serenity.

"You're that lonely? Is this why you wrecked the world economy and murdered all those people?" I asked, still trying to slow him down.

He stopped and laughed out loud.

"Don't flatter yourself. You've no idea what your real role in all this has been, and you're personality won't survive long enough for it to matter. Save your questions, we've got a shuttle to catch."

"There is no shuttle. The A.I. you were colluding with sent them away. Besides, we're past the window Silverstein plotted anyway," I said breaking free.

He backhanded me, harder than any normal man had right to. I spun around almost losing consciousness as I fell to the ground. I looked across the floor, under the desk in the office adjoining the hallway we were in. There was a letter opener laying there, only a few feet away.

"You talked to C.O.N.? That was very naughty. I want you to call Tullia aboard the freighter hauler, tell her everything is okay and you want to be picked up," Madmar said, straightening his tie.

"She'll see you on the landing pad," I said, crawling toward the office.

"Not if you convince the onboard A.I. to send false visual data to her headset," Madmar said, grabbing me by the leg and dragging me back into the hallway.

My head swam with nausea as he picked me up and set me back down on my feet. I looked past him into the executive office where Silverstein and Ezra lay beside Kale, and wept. I was exhausted. Communicating with C.O.N. took a lot more out of me than I'd previously thought. Even the data load that carried his voice was more than I'd ever experienced.

"Let's go," Madmar said, dragging me roughly toward the lift.

We were almost there when a small form swept passed me. Madmar's grasp was wrenched from my arm and we both tumbled to the floor. I looked up to see Brook, wielding her ladle in both hands. She was completely covered in dust, presumably from crawling around in the air conditioning system. She battered Madmar ruthlessly, her ladle getting bend up and dented from every swing.

"Leave us alone!" Brook cried out.

Madmar took a swing of his own, but Brook parried the blow, expertly mimicking the defensive moves Ezra had shown her while we were in Midtown. She was easily as strong as he was, but he had size and leverage on her. I crawled backward as quickly as I could, rooting around in my handbag for anything that looked like a weapon. Madmar finally managed to get a hold of Brook just about the time I found a pair of sewing shears.

"Madmar! Stop!" I shouted.

He rolled over, and wrapped both hands around Brook's neck a split second before I came up behind him. I hesitated for a moment, as if some part of me was vehemently against what I was about to do. I could hear Brook choking, and see her small legs kicking feebly from beneath Madmar as he did his best to choke the life out of her.

I plunged the shears into his back, over and over again screaming as I did. I didn't want to hurt anyone, but my hate for him overcame my restraint. Each swing of my shears that bit down into his flesh a little easier than the last. He cried out, and swept his arm back, knocking me to the floor. Brook pulled spray paint from her sack and sprayed Madmar in the eyes.

"Really? I would have shown you a measure of mercy before, but now..." Madmar said, flinging Brook against a wall so hard she split the drywall.

He loomed over me, wiping paint from his eyes as shots rang out behind me. His pure white suit suddenly spattered with red as the force of the bullets caused him to stumble backwards. I rolled over and covered my head with my hands as Silverstein stepped into the hallway, the barrel of his rifle filling the narrow corridor with noise and bullets.

Silverstein stopped firing only after he reached me, his breathing ragged, almost wet. Ezra stumbled into the hallway behind him, holding the side of his head with one hand. They were both really messed up, and Silverstein's jaw was hanging at an odd angle. I winced at the awful laceration extending from Ezra's hair line down to the middle of his right cheek.

"Wasn't supposed to be like this," Madmar said, clutching at several bullet wounds in his chest.

"How was it supposed to play out?" I asked, my ears still ringing from the gunfire.

"Oh, this will do I suppose. This is only a minor setback, after all, and I've lots of time. Still, taking you should have been far easier," Madmar said, blood oozing down from the corner of his mouth.

"EASIER?!" I screamed, feeling as angry as I can ever remember.

"Indeed. I would grab you, depart aboard the Malleus Class cruiser, take a few more shots from the orbital defense relays, and then... we could be together," Madmar admitted, looking down at his wounded torso.

"When did you think you could take me? Why wasn't I supposed to ever find out about, what did you call him, C.O.N.?" I asked.

Madmar didn't respond, the mirth on his face draining away instantly as he slumped to the floor. Something I said took the wind and fury straight out of him. It was like the words hit him harder than the bullets. I don't know what realization took him in that moment, but it must have been profound.

"Brook! Are you okay?!" I called out, not wanting to step anywhere near Madmar.

Brook stepped back into the hallway, brushing drywall and paint chips from her shoulders and waved wearily. She looked about for her spindled ladle, and then ran over to hug me. I knelt down and returned the embrace, glad she'd had our back. Apparently, Annabelle Five did know what she was doing sending Brook along with us.

"I've got assets all over the city. They'll detonate several devices if I don't call them back in the next three minutes indicating I got away with what I came for," Madmar said, gesturing at me with his mobile.

"Man, that trick is getting old," I said, shaking my head in disappointment.

"No trick, you're just easily swayed by anything that prevents me killing lots of people you've never even met," Madmar said, the mirth returning to his face.

Brook walked up to Madmar and pushed him down roughly. Then, she rummaged in his coat pockets until she found his mobile and handed it to me. It was thin, made of high grade aluminum, and powder coated white, presumably to match the rest of his spooky villain ensemble. I looked at the call history and found that only a single number had been dialed over and over, every hour for the last three hours.

"Call his friends, I'll tell them to leave. I'm good at voices," Brook stated plainly.

I looked back at Ezra who just nodded, still dazed from the blows he took from Madmar. He walked over and sat on Madmar's chest, holding one clawed hand over his mouth. I dialed the number and held the mobile up to one of her ears. We all waited, wondering if she could pull it off.

"It's all over. You can pack your things and go home," Brook said, mimicking Madmar's voice perfectly.

There was a short pause as Brook listened to whoever was on the other end of the call.

"Yes, you can take the devices with you, I don't need them anymore," Brook replied, again sounding just like Madmar.

After she was done, Brook nodded to me and I ended the call.

"Wow, you are full of surprises," I said, patting Brook affectionately.

Ezra pulled Madmar up to a sitting position. He looked up at Ezra, and then over at me, a snide look on his face. He shook his head as if all we'd just done would be futile. Ezra gestured for me to step back drawing a pistol from his waistband.

"Does this all seem right to you?" Madmar said, looking at the barrel, then back over to me.

"You were supposed to be on the moon by now, right? Maybe you are just a replica like you claimed, but I really don't care at this point," Ezra replied, pulling the trigger twice in rapid succession.

Brook screamed as Madmar's head snapped back and he went limp across the office floor. We sat there in stunned silence as Ezra put the handgun back in his waistband and turned to look at Brook.

"This guy smell like a man?" Ezra asked, looking at Brook.

"Smells more like a really big baby with mechanical parts inside him, and chemicals," Brook replied, hiding her face inside my jacket.

I wrapped my left arm around her while she cried.

"But still a man?" Ezra asked.

"Yeah, I guess," Brook said faintly, still weeping bitterly.

Silverstein sat down, leaning back against the wall in the hallway. His jaw was broken and the perimeter of both his eyes were swelling and rapidly going black. He let out a loud sigh as he dropped his rifle, smoke still wafting up from the barrel.

"Oh my God, Silverstein..." I said, kneeling down in front of him.

Silverstein looked down at the bloody shears still held in a death grip by my right hand, then up into my eyes. From the nose down, he was bloody, but his eyes said it all. This isn't how any of us imagined our last encounter with Madmar would be. I ran my hand through his freshly cut hair and pressed my forehead against his.

Ezra fished around in Madmar's pockets, eventually finding what looked like a small, spiral-bound journal. He only glanced inside for a moment before putting it in his pocket.

"We need to get Kale, and then get out of here," Ezra said, throwing his rifle over his shoulder and heading back to the executive office.

Silverstein leaned heavily on me while Ezra and Brook did their best to carry Kale. We dragged ourselves to the lift, then out onto the launch pad where the freighter hauler was waiting. The cargo hold opened slowly as we approached and we stepped up and into the inside just as soon as we could.

"Good God, what happened to you guys?" Tullia said over the intercom.

"Dr. Madmar maybe. I think we killed him. Ezra, Kale, and Silverstein are all tore up, we need medical aid," I said, hitting the intercom button.

"Anywhere in town that isn't compromised potentially?" Tullia asked.

"I doubt it," I said.

"I can have us at Matthias' workshop in twenty-five minutes. There is a medical kit back in the hold, but no auto-doc," Tullia replied. "Do what you can until we get there."

The freighter hauler gently lifted into the air and then gained speed as we tried desperately to help Kale.

CHAPTER 12

SOMEWHERE IN RURAL GEORGIA - MATTHIAS' HIDEOUT

10:28 AM, January 31st, 2200

Taylor's Diary, Part 9

Matthias was glad to see us, and even gladder to see Tullia. I could tell the old man had taken a liking to her, something beyond friendship. All those hours spent holding her hand in the cockpit of her freighter hauler probably. I thought it was cute.

Tullia was harder to read, and if she had any similar feelings, they were locked up tight with the rest of her emotions. The only time I saw her react with any feeling, was when we went into the makeshift infirmary where Truman lay, still in a coma.

"You get your mom?" I asked.

"Yeah, she's resting right now."

"Any chance he'll wake up?" I asked, lingering beside Truman and putting a hand on his arm.

"Matthias isn't a doctor, and the auto-doc he had installed is almost thirty years old. The readings are always inconclusive, and his status changes daily. I think the nanoid machines still working in his body are confusing it," Tullia said, taking a wet rag to Truman's arms and forehead.

"I could remove them," I said, somewhat uncertainly.

"Matthias didn't think you had that sort of minute control already," Tullia said softly, turning Truman over to check his back for bed sores.

That was pretty much true. Every time I tried something new, my body seemed to comply, the small nanoid machines doing their best to invisibly carry out my will. I had a sense of them, like I knew they were in the room when I came into the infirmary, but little else. It did little to diminish my desire to help Truman.

I suppose it was a sort of simple mercy. I would want to name each of my tiny minions, even though they likely replicated themselves and subsequently died every few days. The same redundant systems that kept my own personality safe from hacking or intrusion likely kept my tiny nanoid machines working external to my body stable as well. Even now, they were probably still trying to help Truman however they could.

"He loves you," Tullia said.

"Who? Truman?" I laughed.

"No, Silverstein," Tullia said.

"We're pretty close, but not sure I would go that far," I replied, a little annoyed at Tullia's intruding into my affairs. Tullia could tell I was annoyed and lowered her head.

"He could have died back there. I understand why Ezra would do something like that, he's a Drone, it is part of his DNA," Tullia said.

"Yeah, if I hadn't gotten through to C.O.N. or whatever it's called," I replied.

"When are you going to protect him, like he's tried to protect you?" Tullia asked, meeting my gaze.

Her eyes were cold, like I'd never seen them before.

"Informally, we all decided that this was more important than any one of us individually, or our feelings for each other. I think Ezra did a lot of things because of who he is, not just because he's a Drone," I replied.

"You've done all you can. If Dr. Madmar is truly dead, then you can go wherever you want, do whatever you want. I think you should," Tullia said, folding her arms.

"Right now, all I want to do is look at the patterns you made for the flight suit you're wearing. It's lovely, and you always have a way with making grays and greens look so good together," I said, smiling.

Tullia blushed, and looked down at the garment.

"Would you like one?" she asked.

"I don't hope to fly as much as you do, but I would like a new coat. The one I'm wearing is bloodstained and smells of gunpowder, the underground, and a bunch places I'd like to forget," I replied, taking off my fuzzy multi-colored coat.

"Skirt and leggings to match I suppose?" Tullia said, as we walked from the infirmary to the hall.

Silverstein was in the hall, waiting. His jaw was swollen and his mouth was wired shut. I hugged him, feeling terrible that had happened to him. Tullia patted him on the shoulder and smiled, none of us wanting to say a word out of respect for the fact that Silverstein couldn't right now. He pulled out a pad and a pen and wrote something down.

"Matthias wants to talk to everyone," it read.

We went into the workshop proper, a place I hardly recognized with everything cleared out of it. The center was dominated by a large table with a full color display with an array of information scrolling out in a dozen different text frames. I only glanced at it for a moment before Matthias came in.

"About thirty minutes before you arrived, radio transmissions in and around the Lunar Colony ceased. There was only a three second interruption in service. According to Ezra, that happened right around the time Taylor and Brook used Madmar's mobile to call off a bomb attack," Matthias explained.

"You think it was some sort of failsafe? Something set up by Madmar in the event of his death?" I asked.

"Transmissions on the ground are extremely hard to trace right now. There is so little telecom service right now and with all the CGG installations in lockdown, none of it is being recorded," Matthias said.

"So, you don't know, is what you're saying," I said, taking Silverstein's hand.

"No, I don't know," Matthias replied, taking a sip of his coffee.

"The source of the disruption came from somewhere on the moon, that much Matthias was able to figure out," Ezra said, patting me on the arm.

"We can listen in to what's happening within the Lunar Colony, but they've no way to hear anything that comes up from earth. As long as the CGG telecoms are all down, there's no way to talk to the moon," Matthias said.

Silverstein held up a crudely drawn question mark.

"Why? It has to do with how the CGG used to monitor every electronic message across the globe. The moon will only receive and relay transmissions if they are tagged a certain way," Matthias said, using his hands to talk a little more than what was normal, even for him.

"I was able to talk to C.O.N. using the moon as a relay," I said.

Matthias looked genuinely surprised.

"How do you know it was C.O.N.?" Matthias asked.

"Something Madmar said, before Ezra shot him. He had that same look of surprise on his face that you do now," I explained.

"C.O.N. is a myth, a boogie-man among those of us who write code for artificial intelligences. I wouldn't trust what Madmar had to say was true," Matthias said.

"I used my mobile as a switch, or a focus I guess. After I got done talking with C.O.N., several audio files were uploaded to my mobile by way of the same transmission," I said, handing Matthias my mobile.

Matthias unlocked my mobile and simply held it in his hand. He closed his eyes as he communed with the small device, using his own psychic potential to review the contents. He opened his eyes and put my mobile back in hand.

"It's decades old death metal. There's something odd about the audio files, but I can't discern what exactly. They are recorded at a bit rate to not only include the tiniest audio detail, but a lot more as well. It is far in excess to what the human ear can even perceive. If there is something hidden in the music, you'd need some institution grade studio equipment to isolate it," Matthias said.

Silverstein held up his pad again. This time the page read, "Where?"

"Canada maybe, but I'm sure any place with that sort of equipment has been defunded and is in CGG lockdown. If the files did come from C.O.N., it's likely that they won't mean anything to anyone that isn't an intelligent agent themselves," Matthias said.

"What does C.O.N. even stand for?" Ezra asked.

"The N is for Nascence, I think. The term is old, relating to some out of use vernacular for intelligent agents, at least as they were understood a century ago," Matthias replied, scratching his head thoughtfully.

"So, you don't really know anything about it, yeah? I'm going to go find Brook," Ezra said, dropping down off the table to the floor.

"I don't know that anyone really does."

Ezra left the four of us in the workshop. Silverstein laid down on a work table and closed his eyes while Matthias scratched his chin thoughtfully. Tullia and I got the idea to leave about the same time, and did just that.

"You think if you listen to the music enough, something of it might start to make sense?" Tullia asked, closing the workshop door.

"Never really listened to a lot of music, except for the dozen or so songs they played at the Strip and Waffle when I worked there," I replied, heading down the hallway.

"I think Ezra is wrong, and that Matthias does know things," Tullia said after a few moments walking back toward the garage.

"He knows things, but they are probably the sum of rumors and myths surrounding C.O.N., and he's weighing whether or not it's all nonsense and whether to burden me with it," I stated, running my hand along the smoothly painted metal wall.

"Yeah," Tullia said nodding.

We got to the garage where Matthias stored all his vehicles, failed experiments in robotics and Tullia's transport. We went aboard and walked through the main cargo hold around to where she had her sewing room. It was as it was last time I visited, well stocked and well lit. I breathed a deep sigh of relief as I sat down on a stack of heavy fabric.

"All the rest of our troubles don't seem to matter in here, am I right?" Tullia said, sitting down at her sewing machine.

"No, they don't," I replied.

Silverstein appeared at the doorway, did his best to smile, and invaded the sewing room. I could tell he was sleepy from the drugs he'd been given to dull the pain of his broken jaw. I gestured over to the corner where a couple large trash bags full of poly fill sat. He laid down on them and closed his eyes, falling almost instantly to sleep.

"So much for continuing our previous conversation," Tullia said, frowning at Silverstein.

"I think we were done talking about that anyway. Message received and all that. Let's make some clothes?" I asked.

"Yes, lets," Tullia said with a smile.

We killed the afternoon in her sewing room making skirts, leggings, and a coat to replace the dirty and haphazard outfit I'd been wearing for days. We traded tips and went on like we'd been friends forever. I desperately wanted to ask her if she'd heard from Dragos, but it seemed like a shame to wreck a perfectly good afternoon.

It was toward dinner time I heard Brook and Ezra return to the workshop. I was in the galley of the freighter hauler making a lentil soup when they arrived, Brook carrying a handful of picked flowers. If it were possible, I'd have sworn they were rosy-cheeked and somewhat recharged from their excursion into the woods in the surrounding area.

"Have a nice time?" I asked, taking out my ear buds.

"Oh, yes. Ezra showed me around the grounds and we took a walk up a trail to look for bears, but there weren't any," Brook said, looking down at the flowers.

"I needed to get out. Matthias was making me paranoid," Ezra said, winking at me.

"Totally understand," I replied.

"What are you listening to?" Ezra asked, his ears aquiver.

"The music that C.O.N. sent me," I replied, offering an ear bud to Ezra.

He listened intently to the music for a few moments before whipping the ear bud off and handing it back to me.

"There is a strange echo about it, like there's a ghost or something singing in the background," Ezra said, standing on his tip-toes to look at the soup.

"That's kind of what I thought, but I haven't had enough time to listen to it all," I said, tapping the screen on my mobile to halt playback.

"We'll have time, when we get to the moon and take a year off from all this crap," Ezra said, sniffing the soup.

"You think we're still going to the moon?" I asked.

"Kale will be well enough to resume pretending to be Silverstein back at Uroboros Financial soon. There are odd happenings there, but most importantly, I think we'd all like to go anyway right?" Ezra said, rummaging for a bowl.

"I know I do," I said, using a ladle to fill Ezra's bowl.

"That's two votes, and since Silverstein can't talk, we could always turn in a proxy vote for him," Ezra said smiling.

"We'll still need to find a way to get there. We will need a ship. I don't want to take it for granted that Tullia will take us there, she might have other plans," I said.

"The only plans I have right now, is to try some of your soup," Tullia said, appearing at the doorway to the galley.

I took a step back to allow her enough room to squeeze past me to the stove. She served herself a bowl and leaned against the back wall of the cramped galley and sampled the soup tentatively. Brook appeared a moment later and looked mournfully into the galley, then up at the soup.

"We should probably eat in the hold, there's more room," Tullia said with a laugh.

"I'll meet you guys out there. I'm going to take a bowl and a straw to Silverstein," I said, heading back to the sewing room.

It took me a few minutes to wake Silverstein, but he eventually turned over and took the bowl. He stood up groggily and followed me back to the hold where everyone but Matthias sat eating. It was probably the most normal thing I'd done in a while, and it felt good, even if I couldn't talk to Silverstein like we usually did.

"I'll bet there are a lot of supplies, spare parts, and other items that would be of real value to the Lunar Colony. If Silverstein plotted a departure and a return course, I could probably jump up there, drop you guys off, turn a profit, and return with relative ease," Tullia said, finishing her soup.

"Getting back to earth might be tricky, since you can't send any sort of transmission up from Earth right now," Ezra said.

"You can listen in on the chatter from the moon though right? I bet I could use my mobile to send the transmission to Versa-013, the little A.I. we met in Finland, and use him as a relay," I said.

"Won't know for sure until you're up there, and we're able to gauge the amount of interference that can be generated by the CGG satellite web currently in orbit," Ezra said.

"Allegedly in orbit. Right, Silverstein?" Tullia said.

Silverstein nodded.

"Depending on when we calculated our windows of opportunity, I could probably stay at the Lunar Colony for a few days while you conducted your business," Tullia said as she collected empty bowls.

"You'll take us up?" I asked.

"Of course," she replied.

The next few days were filled with a great deal of debate. Matthias was hesitant to let Tullia take the risks associated with a quick trip to the lunar colonies. We were hesitant to make the attempt in a vessel, or with a pilot we didn't implicitly trust. In the end, Silverstein spent the next week or so calculating the next windows of opportunity for making the trip.

We still didn't know whether or not the CGG satellite web was real, operational, and what sort of countermeasures were in place to prevent signals from getting from Earth to the moon. Every piece of communications equipment manufactured in the last fifty years was set to use CGG telecoms, routing stations, satellites, and similar, as relays rather than employing direct communication.

I learned more about how the old global government had been using those relays to spy on people than I ever wanted to. In the aftermath of the CGG, along with everything else being shut down by the global banking system, much of the more modern communication system was rendered useless. Old radios aboard seagoing vessels, older model freighter haulers, and equipment possessed by hobbyists seemed to be the best way to communicate.

There were a very limited number of cellular towers and providers that weren't under the thumb of the Central Global Government, which explained why our mobiles still functioned in certain places. We had time to calculate all the angles and do some research, as the next opportunity to break orbit wouldn't come for another thirty-five days according to Silverstein's calculations.

We started loading Tullia's freighter right around the time Kale was well enough to return to Port Montaigne, and Silverstein was having his jaw unwired by the auto-doc. I was glad to hear his voice, more than I thought I would be. Even though we'd been texting each other constantly for the past four weeks, it just wasn't the same as hearing how he talked.

"Ezra, do you think Brook will come with us?" Silverstein asked, carrying a box up the ramp into the freighter.

"Not sure. She's been having a good time planting a garden outside the compound. I haven't asked her what she wants to do yet," Ezra said, walking back down the ramp into the garage.

"Why haven't you asked her?" I said, shaking my head.

"I figured if she wanted to go, she would have said something," Ezra said, shrugging.

"Hah, that's not how it works. Sometimes people want to feel wanted. We should ask her what she wants to do," I said, throwing some packing foam at Ezra.

Kale came into the room, looking strong and suave. He paused before descending the stairs into the garage where we were currently having a foam fight and sighed loudly. Silverstein responded by throwing a bit of foam at him, a mirthful gesture that Kale regarded wearily.

"I've kept in contact with the partners at the firm, and continuing to pretend I'm Vance Uroboros. They bought the story of how I'd arranged for us to put a transport up to the Lunar Colony for a look around," Kale said, inspecting his nails.

"We were just talking about Brook. No one's talked to her about what her plans might be," I said, tossing a handful of foam at Kale.

"I've already talked to her," Kale said, batting the foam out of the air, his sliver smile briefly appearing on his face.

"Oh?" Silverstein and Ezra said, almost in unison.

"She's a capable agent, and I offered her a job at Uroboros Financial, working for me," Kale said, brushing poly fibers off his coat sleeve.

"You think?" I asked.

"She's a skilled laborer and has an eidetic memory. Also, she can answer the phone and sound, quite convincingly, like me. I've already been able to quickly teach her all sorts of things where others have tested my patience. She can also spy on the other partners using the air conditioning system," Kale replied, deadpan.

"She's good with it?" Ezra asked.

"I had to explain the corporate dental plan in greater detail, but yes, she seems content."

We called a truce, ending the foam war, and finished loading the transport. We still had a couple of days before we were to make the journey, days that Matthias and Silverstein spent checking and rechecking equipment and calculations. Tullia was excited in equal measure to the anxiety that Matthias obviously felt.

It was hard to say goodbye to Brook, Kale, and Matthias. I don't know why it was such a big deal, the plan was to come back relatively soon, but everything was so uncertain. The ascent into orbit was nerve wracking as well, the freighter hauler breaking though each layer of the atmosphere, the outside of the ship aglow, and the awful turbulence. Ezra took it in from his seat with all the fascination of a child, smiling like crazy through the whole ordeal.

"So, are there satellites up here?" I asked, turning to look at Silverstein.

He was looking at a data slate Matthias had set up to remotely access the ship's systems and sensors. He tapped the touch screen diligently looking for the answer to my question. He turned the screen on the data slate toward me and pointed to dozens of objects slowly moving across a rendered representation of the globe.

"Yes, but there are fewer since several have collided with one another over time and as a result of their decaying orbits. Even in the heavens, everything isn't perfect or predictable," Silverstein said with a smirk.

"You predicted it," I said tilting my head toward the port looking out from the cockpit.

"I'm a mathematical pessimist is all, and entropy is always tugging downward at everything we do," Silverstein said, looking out at the star field.

We got clear of the satellite grid just as the fuel cores powering our ascent cut out and the normal means of propulsion kicked in. The whole ship lurched as it changed course, making us all cry out in panic. Even Tullia was a little startled.

"Lucius, status?" Tullia said nervously.

"All is well. Handles a little differently up here, doesn't it ma'am?" Lucius politely responded over the intercom.

We all had a hearty laugh about it except Ezra, who was pretty freaked out over the whole thing. The moon came quickly into view and the hundred thousand lights of the Lunar Colony blinking across the surface. It was beautiful, replete with elegant spires, faintly luminescent bio-domes, and an enclosed light rail running at tremendous speeds thanks in part to the low gravity.

There was also the old mining facility, and the CGG military installation, both dark and unused for years most likely. In spite of those blemishes, the whole of the Lunar Colony sparkled with wondrous mystery. I'd always wondered why it was such an alluring vacation spot, but never again.

"Isn't it beautiful? I can't wait to walk around every inch of it," I said grabbing Silverstein's hand.

"Once we've verified that Madmar's agenda ceased with his death, we will definitely have to take in the sights," Ezra said, reminding me for the twentieth time why we were really there.

"I'm sure we will see plenty in doing that as well. Do you think there are Drones and Metasapients living in the colony?" Silverstein asked.

"I know there are," Ezra said.

"You said you did EVA in space, but you act like this was your first time up. What did you really do up here, Ezra?" I asked.

"Just what I said. When we were brought up, it was in stasis tubes and we were only deployed when needed. Most of the time we were doing hazardous EVA rescue when things would go wrong at one colony or the other. Sometimes, we were deployed on the ground. That was always bad," Ezra said, his voice getting quieter the more he talked.

"We've got docking clearance. Should be on the station for a customs inspection in a few minutes. Once we go through that, we should be cleared to head to the colony," Tullia said over her shoulder.

"Customs?" Silverstein asked.

"Apparently, it's the only CGG facility in operation outside of Mars. Guy on the radio sounded friendly enough," Tullia said.

We proceeded to land in the hanger of a large orbital station that acted as a checkpoint for the Lunar Colony. Security was tight, but there were only a handful of marines on duty. The man in charge had a lengthy conversation with Tullia and Silverstein while we waited inside the freighter hauler. Old CGG currency credits exchanged hands, papers were signed, and, after a pointless one hour processing period, we were allowed to depart for the colony.

"Processing period?" I asked, as Silverstein returned to his seat.

"Apparently the guy that runs this is one of those that goes strictly by the book. Even though there is no one on the ground to receive our application or authorize us, he still sends it down. I guess he's afraid if things ever get back to normal, he'd be found in dereliction of his duties otherwise," Silverstein said, buckling himself in again.

"Nice guy, though, letting us take advantage of a tourism discount since you guys are here to sightsee," Tullia added, kicking back in the cockpit.

"He even counted the time we spent filling out the forms toward the one hour wait," Silverstein said, checking the data slate.

"Looking for a place to eat when we land?" Tullia asked.

"They have an impressive grid up here, faster and better regulated than the Internet back on Earth. If they had weather on the moon, I bet it would be really easy to check it," Silverstein said with a chuckle.

"What did you expect? The Lunar Colony is probably a technocracy, with an A.I. sitting somewhere at the top of the food chain," Ezra said, nudging me with his elbow.

"If it is like we suspect, and the lunar A.I. is one of the parent Omega systems of all the terrestrial artificial intelligences, what is the first thing you'll ask?" Silverstein asked.

"I don't know. I guess I would want to know why I was abandoned in Port Montaigne of all places. I might would want to know where my brother and sisters are. Heck, if we're just machines, why do we have a gender?" I mused.

"The only thing I want to know is whether or not Madmar or any of his agents have holdings or interests within the Lunar Colony. I dislike loose ends," Ezra said, scowling.

"What would you ask them, Silverstein?" Tullia asked.

"Not a thing," Silverstein replied, setting the data slate down.

"Not even a about the Cabal?" I asked.

"Last on my list of things I would ask, if I had anything to ask them about," Silverstein said, putting his hands up behind his head and leaning back.

I guess I couldn't blame him. Silverstein's past had haunted him since I met him and been the source of many hardships and perils. I couldn't help but wonder if the Cabal was still out there, and what they were up to.

The processing time passed uneventfully, and we were allowed to depart and make our way to the Lunar Colony. It was like Jonah and the whale as we approached, the huge hangar doors yawning wide open to allow us entry beside what were dozens of other ships. Most looked to have been in dock for some time.

It took another hour or so as engineers had to rig up an older umbilical to attach to the cargo hatch and allow us egress to the station. Once it was pressurized, we were clear to come aboard the station. I took my first steps and nearly stumbled at the sensation of artificial gravity coming on suddenly. I definitely felt lighter on the moon.

The passage beyond the umbilical was squalid, with the expanded metal walkways and insulated panels of the walls filthy and gouged by the movement of goods and people. Muck clung to the floor beneath our feet and there was strangely stylized graffiti across the blast doors leading to the ship across the corridor. There was no one to greet us. We stood there awkwardly for a moment trying to figure out our next move.

"I think I'll stay here with the ship until a port authority agent happens along. May I borrow your rifle, Silverstein?" Tullia asked.

"Yeah, I'll take my handgun and the data slate. We'll head up the corridor here and see if we can get acquainted with the locals," Silverstein said, heading off to the left.

"You know where you're going?" Ezra asked.

"No, but the data slate does. The colony has an interactive map that will take us to the nearest tourism office," Silverstein said, almost tripping over a heap of refuse.

"Hopefully it's cleaner than the port," I said, already wondering if we'd made a mistake.

CHAPTER 13

PORT OF PARIS, LUNAR COLONY

8:31 AM UTC/GMT March 6th, 2200

Telemetry

The port looked more like a homeless shelter than a glittering welcome mat laid out for the discerning tourist. People were huddled together around heating vents and wearing bubble wrap and synthetic sheeting for blankets. Ezra grabbed his duffle off the luggage cart, just to have his rifle a little closer at hand.

"It's kinda like home, isn't it?" Taylor asked, eyebrows raised.

"Yeah, it's a little slice of downtown Port Montaigne up here," Ezra said, letting out a deep sigh.

"This is supposed to be a tourist destination. With no tourists, I bet a lot of people found themselves out of work pretty quick," Silverstein said.

"Some of these guys have Mars Company Mining jackets and hats. That doesn't seem like a good sign, either," Ezra said, pointing at some of the locals.

The rest of the stroll through the port showcased the misery that hung about the colony like an unwanted shadow. People were selling themselves, each other, and whatever they had to survive, squatting in empty storefronts and in the drainage tunnels just below the promenade. It was as depressing a sight as anyone could see, and not the sort one would expect as a greeting to what was only months previous the premiere vacation destination.

Two CGG troopers stood guard at the entrance to the first colony zone, a bio-dome that looked to house all sorts of tourist traps, high-rise hotels, and family-safe attractions. Most of them were dark, and there were very few people in the streets. The two troopers looked like they hadn't shaved in weeks, wearily keeping a vigil at a gate that only the most downtrodden usually passed through.

"Got your clearance from the station?" One of them held out his hand.

"Yeah," Silverstein said, handing a printout to the soldier.

He looked at it for a moment, then handed it back.

"Earth? How the heck did you get up here past the satellite grid?" the soldier asked.

"And why'd you bring a kid? This is no place for a kid anymore," the other said, pointing at Ezra.

Ezra looked up at them, his grayscale Drone eyes narrowing slightly. The soldiers were startled, but said nothing, handing back Silverstein's paperwork. They passed through the checkpoint and into the Lunar Colony, their feet kicking at trash and empty plastic containers as they walked.

Most of the hotels were closed, and only a few bars were in operation. Taylor pointed to a place called 'The Cloud', a small bar with plenty of open tables and a kitchen. A neon blue sign with the lettering and a blue outline of a cloud flickered over the doors. Ezra shrugged and headed in.

"Oh my, what is that?" Taylor said, pointing to the Metasapient using pincers to juggle cooking implements back in the kitchen.

"Crustacea Type, designed for skilled labor in zero to low gravity environments," Ezra said, waving three fingers to the serving girl.

The serving girl was an Ichthyic Metasapient, wearing a globe filled with water and slender oxygenation tanks on her back. She was slim, brightly colored, and only about as tall as Taylor, in the five and a half foot range. Her eyes were bright gold and much larger than that of any other human or Metasapient they'd seen.

"Would you like to sit at the bar, in a booth, or at a table?" Her voice came across clearly through a small speaker beneath the glass globe over her head.

"Booth, please. Hey, do you really need that globe to breathe?" Taylor asked, her curiosity getting the better of her.

Ezra glared at Taylor, but the server just smiled.

"No, I can breathe fine in both environments, I wear this for the tourists. First time on the moon?" she replied.

"First we can remember," Silverstein said, grabbing a seat.

"There are only two places to stay in the dome, and I wouldn't recommend either one. Both are basically Syndicate fronts. If you've got a ship in port still, I'd stay there. Oh, and I recommend the seaweed," she said, pulling up a small data slate to take their order.

"What else do you have besides seaweed?" Ezra asked.

"Cucumber stew. For now, it's just whatever we can grow in the water filtration tanks," she replied.

"You grow things in the filtration tanks?" Silverstein asked.

"Don't worry, my sisters and I bathe before we go down to pick things from the garden. Now, what would you like?" the server asked.

"I think we're all having the stew," Taylor said.

The server wandered back to the kitchen where the big crab working the stove served up three bowls, and pushed them through the window. He rang the bell, even though the server was standing right there, causing her to roll her enormous eyes. She returned to the table and quickly arrayed the table with silverware, napkins, bowls of stew, and a short glass of water each, but only half full.

"This is pretty good," Ezra said, after hesitantly taking a first bite.

"I sat awake last night, almost all night trying to imagine what the Lunar Colony would be like. I mean, this is where I'm from right?" Taylor said, leaning back in the booth.

"Didn't imagine it would be anything like this? I had a feeling things would be bad, just looking at the numbers, but nothing like this," Silverstein said.

"There's something more than just the Earth's global economy collapsing at work here?" Ezra asked.

"Yep," Silverstein replied. "I spent my night calculating what sort of impact the Shutdown would have on colonies, and even at the worst, it wouldn't be anything like this. Something is definitely wrong."

"Everything tasting all right?" the server asked, coming back by the table.

"Is your name really Bubbles?" Silverstein asked, smiling broadly.

"No, my sisters and I share a name tag. None of us are actually named that. The food?" she said.

"The food's fine. I'm looking for a diversion. There a place around here to play some cards?" Silverstein asked.

"There is. What kind of odds and stakes are you looking for?" she asked.

Silverstein held both of his hands to display seven fingers total.

"I'll have to make a call, find out where that particular table will be tonight," she said, her smile diminishing slightly.

"What are you doing?" Taylor asked.

"I want to talk to the Syndicate. If I take enough of their money, I'll get to talk to someone in charge," Silverstein said, taking a bite of stew.

"You going to give the money back?" Ezra asked.

"We aren't here an hour and you guys are already trying to figure out how to get us into trouble?" Taylor snapped as she pushed the remainder of her stew away.

"You okay with someone doing this to what's probably your home-town?" Silverstein said, looking back over his shoulder.

"No."

"Okay then."

They finished their stew and waited for the server to come back. About fifteen minutes later, the cook and the server were nowhere to be seen. Ezra unzipped his duffle bag and set it down under the table. A long black limousine hovered up the narrow street coming to a stop outside the bar.

"Here we go," Silverstein said, watching as several men in business suits stepped out and headed for the bar.

There were three of them, two obviously there for security reasons. The third was an older gentleman who walked with a slight limp. He had curly white hair that hung down just above his collar, a cruel curl to his lip, and cane with a silver snake's head with jewels for eyes.

"I understand you're looking for a game," the man said as his two goons sat down at a table nearby.

"That's right," Silverstein said, standing up to face the man.

The old man looked at Silverstein intently, then gestured to his men. They stood up, somewhat confused.

"Wait for me in the car, it'll be alright," the old man insisted.

"I guess I'm not going to get a chair at the table?" Silverstein said, narrowing his eyes.

"You don't look like you've aged a day. If anything, you look younger. Where's that old jacket you always wore?" the old man asked.

"Do I know you?" Silverstein asked.

"It has been awhile. It's me, Henry. Henry Scarsdale," the old man said.

Silverstein willed his body to age about twenty years, making him look like he was nearly in his fifties.

"There you are, Vance, now you look like you. That's a neat trick. Who are your friends?" Henry asked as he pulled a chair up to the booth.

"Taylor, and this is Ezra," Silverstein said, sitting back down.

"I did what you wanted. Why didn't you just call me direct? I would have had someone pick you up instead of having to hoof it through the Port of Paris back there," Henry asked with a chuckle.

"Port of Paris?" Ezra asked.

"It's what we used to call it, yes," Henry replied.

"Henry, I need you to tell me what's going on here," Silverstein said, leaning in over the table.

"You act like you don't remember. I would think you'd know better than me," Henry replied, cocking his head to one side.

"Things went sideways on Earth, you're going to need to break it down for me. What may not seem off to you, might seem off to me," Silverstein bluffed.

"Okay, Vance. All the financials and reports waiting to be filed with management are there, in the encrypted folder," Henry said, sliding his mobile across the table.

Silverstein tapped the touchscreen with his thumb, easily accessing the encrypted data. It was all there, every move the Syndicate on the Lunar Colony made following the Shutdown. They had skimmed relief funds from CGG contracts, taken control of privatized resources, and done their best to create a Shutdown of their own. The Lunar Colony was crippled financially.

Silverstein uploaded the files wirelessly to his own data slate and then looked at the personnel files of every syndicate operative on the Lunar Colony, Henry included. The elderly gentleman sat there patiently for a few moments then walked back to the kitchen to get himself a drink. Ezra stood up in the booth and looked back at the limousine while Taylor leaned into Silverstein.

"What are you doing?" Taylor hissed.

"Playing a bluff. I'm clearly responsible for all this, I've got to untangle it," Silverstein said, typing out numbers into spreadsheets on his data slate.

"What makes you think you can do that here when you couldn't on Earth?" Taylor asked, calming a little.

"It's complicated, but I'll try to explain. Earth was defunded and completely shut down. The system locked out on the other side of all safe guards having been legislatively removed. Earth's global economy is dead. The economies on the Martian and Lunar Colonies were regulated by Omega class artificial intelligences sitting at the center of some of the most advanced fire walls ever constructed," Silverstein said.

"Their economies are just sleeping then?" Taylor asked.

"Yeah, that's a good way of putting it. They're like an appliance without power or a toy robot without batteries. All they need is money, safe shipping lanes through Earth's satellite web, and new management, and they'll come back to life," Silverstein said, typing on his data slate.

"You figured out what our next move will be, Numbers Man?" Henry quipped, returning with a small glass of apricot liquor.

"I think so. You've done well holding the fort. How's Dr. Madmar doing these days?" Silverstein asked.

"About the same. He's been working his own angles from the usual place," Henry said, sitting down casually.

"I need to see him," Silverstein said, looking wide-eyed over at Ezra and Taylor.

"Sure. It's not like he's hard to find, right?" Henry said with a chuckle, finishing off the liquor.

"Alright, give us a moment to confer?" Silverstein asked.

"I'll be in the car. I'll have my guys pull your luggage from the cart and put it in the trunk," Henry said, standing up and heading out to the limousine.

Ezra sank down in his seat and reached under for his duffle.

"What made you ask him about Madmar?" Ezra asked.

"The Syndicate has made several large purchases of biomedical and cybernetics supplies and materials. It all gets funneled to someone referred to in their financials as M," Silverstein replied grimly.

"What did he mean about Madmar being easy to find? I thought we killed him in back in Port Montaigne?" Taylor whispered.

"What we killed could have been a more traditional clone, augmented with cybernetics and controlled by Madmar using the Puppet Cage device we were told about. If Madmar is on the moon..." Ezra said, shaking his head.

"When I accused him of being the real Madmar to distract him, he did say I was half right," Taylor whispered fearfully.

"I don't know what it means, but something tells me that Madmar has been here all along, using imprinted intelligent agents and modified cyborgs to confuse us. Henry is firmly on our team though, it's pretty clear he's been in my portfolio from the beginning, from when I was with the Cabal," Silverstein said, standing up.

"How do you know?" Ezra asked.

"I guessed the password to his encrypted files on the first try, and he knew I could do it," Silverstein said with a smirk.

"So, before you lost your memory you had Madmar under surveillance? Sounds like a motive to see harm done to you if he found out," Ezra stated, sipping the last of his water.

"It's clear we had a relationship if he had access to these resources. The nature of that relationship is what's unclear. All I have is financials to look at," Silverstein said.

"Let's just go, I guess" Taylor said nervously.

"It'll be okay," Silverstein said, taking her by the hand.

They walked out and climbed into the limousine sitting across from Henry. His two bodyguards loaded their luggage into the trunk and sat up front. Moments later they were on their way.

"Did we just dine and dash? We gotta go back and pay," Taylor said, wrinkling her nose at Henry as he fumbled for a bottle at the minibar.

"I'll take care of it. They give you good service? I'll let them skip a week paying protection," Henry said, pouring himself a glass of bourbon.

"About that, I've got some new numbers to add to the equation," Silverstein said, pulling out his data slate.

"It is renewal time, right?" Henry said, nodding.

"After a fashion. What's gone on for weeks isn't sustainable, it was only supposed to go on for days," Silverstein said.

"When you went underground right before the Shutdown, I thought maybe you'd changed your mind. I just held course with what you'd given me so far. You guys want anything? Limousine service still has a decent minibar," Henry said taking a drink.

"We're good. How long until we get to Madmar?" Taylor asked.

"If you'd seen him recently, you wouldn't be in a huge hurry to get there. It's bad, Vance," Henry said, shaking his head.

"How so?" Ezra asked.

"Let's just say, unlike Vance here, he can't just make himself younger by wishing. How'd you get to be able to do that anyway? Implants? Chemical therapy?" Henry said with a chuckle.

"Monkey's paw," Silverstein replied, holding out an empty shot glass.

Henry laughed and filled Silverstein's glass. It was a short ride through the bio-dome to an enclosed freeway that led to an even larger enclosure, the top meeting up with upper floors of towers and high rise buildings. The streets were immaculately clean and the lights were on. People walked from venue to venue looking for a distraction along the side of every street as cabs and limousines hovered along slowly in line.

"Does the rest of the colony look this good?" Taylor asked.

"Nope, most of it looks like the slum you just came from. We shut down a lot of the business that supported the populace, trading credits back and forth to sustain. Thousands ended up in the streets outside empty apartment complexes that had to close the doors because they had no renters. It was pretty messed up," Henry said, taking another drink.

Taylor shook her head and looked out the limousine window, obviously dismayed.

"All part of the plan, young lady. You've been traveling around with Vance long enough, I figured you knew all this already," Henry said, as apologetically as he could.

"I'll never get used to seeing people without homes and subject to poverty," Taylor replied, pressing a hand to the window beside her.

The limousine turned into an underground parking garage and drove to the far end past several hundred empty spaces. The vehicle came to a stop near some service doors, lit only by a single light overhead. They stepped out into the garage and began to slowly make their way toward the doors.

"Stay with the car," Henry ordered the hired muscle, taking out a cigarette. They nodded in response, bringing the limousine to a halt across several empty parking places.

"No spots on the concrete, no skid marks, oil drips, nothing. No one has ever parked down here," Ezra whispered nervously to Taylor.

"I guess I shouldn't be surprised that Madmar picked the creepiest place possible to hide out," Taylor replied, keeping her voice low.

Henry fished a key ring out of his pocket and unlocked the door. He held it open while Silverstein, Ezra, and Taylor stepped through. After a quick glance in either direction, Henry stepped in and locked it behind them. The concrete hallway was unfinished, metal restraining bolts protruding out at regular intervals. Every few feet there was a stagnant pool of water or a puddle of dried blood. The place stunk of gunfire, urine, and industrial chemicals.

"Haven't been down here in a while. Wasn't this messed up down here last year when I came for a face to face," Henry said, shaking his head.

"Madmar's been busy," Silverstein said, picking up the pace a little. "It is part of the reason I want to see him."

"Yeah, well, you're the boss. We gave him a slice up here only because you said so. It was kind of unexpected, and the word came up through one of your own imprinted clones. It was legit, right?" Henry asked nervously.

"It doesn't matter now, Henry," Silverstein replied softly.

Fifty yards of corridor later, they reached the end of the hallway, passing at least a dozen other doors in the process. Henry pulled out his key ring again and opened a set of double industrial doors. Inside was what looked like a surgery theater, with a walkway above, and a large circular chamber below. Silverstein stepped to the edge and looked down into the operating floor.

Madmar was there, suspended upright in a tank of fluid and surrounded by an array of life support systems, servers, and data lines leading up through the ceiling. There were tubes running in and out of every orifice, a dozen of his veins tapped by intravenous plugs including two over his heart. There were augmented reality goggles strapped to his head and dozens of surveillance terminals throughout the room. Actuators attached to a harness about his torso kept him from drifting back into the various contrivances that shared space with him inside the enclosure.

"Hello, Dr. Madmar," Silverstein said, stepping down the steps to the operating floor.

"Vance, what an unexpected pleasure," Madmar said, his disembodied voice coming out over the intercom.

"The pleasure is all mine," Silverstein said, walking up to stand beside the tank holding Dr. Madmar.

The VR goggles disengaged and slowly rose up off of Madmar's head, revealing an ancient and wrinkled face. He'd once been much heavier, loose skin clinging around the back of his arms and across his belly and thighs. He was breathing the fluid, but his voice still came across clearly as though he was in the open air.

"I see you've brought our mutual colleague, Mr. Scarsdale, and our friends, Taylor and Ezra One," Madmar said, turning his head slightly in the tank.

"This isn't a social call, we're here to stop you," Silverstein said, knocking on the front of the tank.

"Oh, I think you know better than that. Do the math," Madmar replied, chuckling slightly.

"Pretty sure you've still got one of your strange cyborg clone things out there, and at least two of my imprinted intelligent agents are still wandering about," Silverstein said, nodding.

"I'm so close to what we both want. Between the two of us, we have all the pieces now," Madmar said, putting his hands on the glass inside the tank.

"You're the only one who wants to garner control of the Omega artificial intelligences. I'm good with letting them do whatever it is they want to do," Silverstein replied.

Madmar chuckled and shook his head.

"That's always been your problem, Vance. You don't quite dream big enough. Being born into the Cabal, I guess you couldn't understand my predicament or the wall I found my back up against."

"Enlighten us," Silverstein said, holding his hands out to his side and bowing sarcastically.

"What if you could do more than imprint a semblance of yourself on a regular blank slate nanoid body? What if one existed with almost perfect redundancy systems that could write and rewrite who you were and maintain the sum of everything you learned, even better than the human brain? These spontaneous intelligent agents created by the Omegas were designed to fail within a normal human life span. Who is to say that duration couldn't be altered, and extended to an almost indefinite amount of time?" Madmar explained excitedly.

"I don't understand how that has anything to do with me, or with the Cabal," Silverstein replied, shaking his head.

"The Cabal is an exclusive club to be sure," Madmar said, feebly clenching his fists. "The only way one gains access is by having a lifespan far beyond that of a normal human being. This gambit was my way in, and a means of escaping the decrepitude you now see ravaging my being. Mastering the understanding necessary to transfer my consciousness would also allow me to create others, alter others, and create my own intelligent agents. We could be Gods, Vance Uroboros."

"That's what your double was babbling about before, when he said he would have Taylor, alter her programming to make her something else entirely?" Silverstein said, eyes narrowing slightly.

"Yes! You and I could have each have a harem of exquisite women like Taylor, each one with a carefully contrived personality to make them more… agreeable. When I watched Taylor interact with the global grid in Finland, her interactions were effortless, instinctive, and emergent in a way that transcends a machine merely reacting to a set of programmed responses. She was literally feeling things across the grid. I recorded all 47 seconds of that interaction and could see what constituted her consciousness stretch out beyond the technological interface. When you and Ezra severed the link, something of her remained out in the grid," Madmar said, the last few words just shy of babbling incoherence.

"You're insane," Silverstein hissed, stepping away from the tank.

"Am I? The Cabal sets the standards for admittance fairly high, and I was finished being a pawn in their games. Becoming immortal when one wasn't born of a lost civilization? Or, as a sinister aberration of nature? Or, a student of a master alchemist? Getting into the Cabal is somewhat difficult, Vance. WHAT WOULD YOU HAVE ME DO?" Madmar bellowed, coughing fluid into fluid at the end.

"You can't move the essence of a person across a technological threshold, or escape the death that these machines have spared you from for so long," Silverstein replied, calmly looking up into Madmar's eyes. "Even the imprinted intelligent agents became their own beings with their own agency. In making assumptions about the agency of thinking creatures in this way, you are delving into the blackest of darkness."

"What of Kale then? If nothing of you persists there, is he just a soulless machine?" Madmar asked, anger polluting every word.

"Kale looks like me, but that's where the similarities end. If he didn't have a soul before, he's managed to grow one since you tried to corrupt him. He made a choice to stay loyal out of a dozen or more of my imprinted intelligent agents. That isn't a statement about the integrity of a programmed machine as much about the unpredictable human condition," Silverstein countered.

"Is that what you think of our dear Kale? Oh, Vance…"

"Shut your lying mouth," Ezra growled.

"Vance, I'm nearly to the next phase. Once I've rounded up enough Mechanics with the proper psychic potential, we just need Taylor and the equipment I'm in the process of having built. I can escape this decaying shell and you can build that utopia you've been dreaming of for centuries. Don't be a fool," Madmar chided, his face contorted into a venomous scowl.

"Your machines, your research, it's all gone," Taylor said, punctuating the sentence with her own rendition of how an explosion sounds.

"What about the catalyst? Don't we need that?" Silverstein asked, still calmly regarding Madmar.

Madmar paused for a moment, a crooked smile wreaking terrible havoc across his face. The operating theater was quiet for that moment, with only the sounds of the machines pumping and churning faintly from inside Madmar's support tank. Silverstein gestured to Taylor, who then pulled out the catalyst and placed it on a stainless steel table.

"Oh, I don't think we'll need it," Madmar said quietly.

"All the readings you took were from Taylor after she'd been exposed to only a very small quantity. Her ability to interact and feel machines is much greater now. Isn't that why you placed a chemical agent near Ezra's tribe home? To get new readings?" Silverstein asked.

"You've no idea the lengths I've gone to just to get a glimpse of her doing what she does. I think you're only just beginning to realize the value of such data. As I said, transferring one's consciousness is just the beginning. If it isn't me that pulls it off, it'll be someone else. As for the device I placed near Ezra's tribe home, it had fulfilled its primary purpose before you even arrived," Madmar replied with a cackle.

"We found all the surveillance gear and the bodies. I've got some idea of what you're capable of," Silverstein replied.

"What's he talking about? What did you do to my tribe home?" Ezra growled angrily.

"I've ushered them out of Eden, but that must have become apparent to you while you were there. After all, Gods need followers, creations that exalt and worship them," Madmar replied, his crooked smile only getting broader.

"What did you do?" Silverstein demanded angrily.

"Let's just say that Ezra's tribe will no longer require the Factory to replenish the underground, and that they'll be better equipped to defend their territory against interlopers," Madmar replied happily.

"Brook being no longer sterile, and Senegal's regenerative abilities… oh no," Ezra whispered, turning away from Madmar.

"Silverstein, what are we going to do with him?" Taylor asked, taking him by the arm.

"I've got a couple of ideas," Silverstein replied, turning his back to Madmar.

Silverstein turned around and leaned against the outside of the poly- carbonate shielding that housed Madmar, and pulled out his data slate. Ezra readied his rifle, dropping the duffle bag to the floor. Henry looked around nervously while Silverstein typed on the data slate for a few moments. They gathered by the entrance to converse for a moment, Silverstein gaz- ing calmly into Henry's eyes.

"When we get back into cell tower range, you'll get a message from me. It'll have everything you need to take us to the next phase," Silverstein said to Henry, placing a hand on his shoulder.

"Okay. So what now? I take a piss in Madmar's tank and then your man here shoots him?" Henry replied.

Taylor squeezed Silverstein's arm and shook her head.

"I'm not really certain. We can't leave him down here, and it feels wrong to just kill him. It's clear he's lost his mind," Silverstein remarked, shaking his head sadly.

"Ahem, perhaps a demonstration is in order," Madmar said with a wry grin.

A clear sheet of polycarbonate almost a foot thick dropped between Madmar's stasis tank and the gathering at the entrance cutting the room in half. The floor around the stasis tank fell away revealing six captives connected to a tangle of hoses, wires, and mechanical contrivances. They were alive and breathing, but in some sort of medically induced coma.

"I don't have all that I need to garner certitude, but these should be enough for an honest attempt," Madmar said, looking down at the captives.

"They are the Mechanics he said he'd need for the process," Ezra said, banging his fist on the polycarbonate in frustration.

"Don't do this, Madmar!" Silverstein called out angrily. "You said it yourself the machines aren't complete and we both know you do not have all the data necessary to attempt transference."

Taylor put her hands on the polycarbonate and looked in both directions for some sort of panel or switch that could lift the wall. She ran to the left hand wall past instrument panels as they went dark. She reached a control panel just as it lost power.

"No good, the entry points on this side are without power, and the polycarbonate was dead dropped. It's way too heavy to lift," Taylor said, looking back to Silverstein with wide eyes.

The circle of Mechanics awoke, struggling against the metal restraints that held them fast as some unseen platform lifted them so their heads were knee-high to Madmar in the stasis tank. Heavy machinery came to life as the chamber filled with a strange mist of photoluminescence, a sign that nanoid machines were beginning to overload and die. The Mechanics jerked as if they were being shocked, some of them crying out in anguish and terror.

Madmar smiled slightly, holding his hands out to his sides as the stasis tank began to slowly open.

"There's got to be something we can do," Silverstein said, looking around.

"The poly is too thick for even my rifle, we need something that can burn a hole through," Ezra said, looking around frantically.

Hazard lights turned slowly overhead as generators hidden beneath the chamber began to cycle. The sound was displaced by a strange flushing noise as the fluid in Madmar's stasis chamber quickly drained away. The whole contrivance split across the front allowing actuators to carry Madmar out to hang over the struggling Mechanics below. The photoluminescence began to spin around him creating a strange vortex of light mixed with the hazard lights turning overhead.

"I go to my new vessel now, whole of mind, my entire conscience transferred," Madmar said, looking upward.

Henry came back in with a fire ax and handed it off to Ezra who took a swing at the polycarbonate partition. It barely made a dent, breaking out a sliver sized chip of industrial plastic. Ezra swung harder the second time, breaking the haft of the axe. Cursing, he gave the wall a solid kick and looked on helplessly as the transference process went into a second phase.

Taylor looked mournfully down at the Mechanics as they began to seize and spasm from the nanoid machines invading their bodies. Fury seemed to overwhelm her at the sight of innocent people suffering so terribly, and her own nanoid form responded. Placing her hand against the polycarbonate she began to agitate the surface with the tiny machines that composed her physical form. Her hand grew white hot, setting the cuff of her shirt aflame as she slowly melted through the industrial plastic.

"Yes! Hurry! Just make a hole big enough for me to get through, I'll do the rest," Ezra pleaded.

Taylor fell back into Silverstein's arms, her right hand and forearm badly burned. Ezra scrambled through the tight opening, getting caught half way through. Henry gave him a hard shoulder to the bottom of his feet forcing him the rest of the way. Popping back up to his feet, Ezra jumped back using the hole in the wall to help get distance and elevation. He landed on the platform beneath Madmar and looked back into the stasis pod.

There were dozens of cables, and they all looked important. He brought his claws across the tubes and oxygen hoses that snaked up the actuators to Madmar. Red indicator lights began to blink quietly in the stasis chamber as Madmar gasped for breath. Clawing out the hydraulic hoses along the heavier actuators brought them and Madmar down to the platform where Ezra could reach him. Jumping the gap back to where Madmar now knelt, Ezra grabbed him by the temples and took a deep breath.

"You're too late," Madmar rasped, a strange turquoise fluid oozing from his nose and ears.

Ezra twisted hard, breaking Madmar's neck before letting his limp form drop to the ground. Looking up he could see Silverstein just nod from beyond the barrier as the machinery in the chamber slowed and went idle without Madmar's direction. Ezra turned and looked down at the captives. Two of them were gone, killed by the process. There were four that survived, and four empty harnesses that Madmar had not had a chance to fill with victims.

"Can you get the survivors out of there?" Silverstein asked, ducking to look through the hole in the polycarbonate.

"They are all unconscious now, and the machines might be keeping them alive. We need paramedics. Do you think the transference worked?" Ezra asked, passing his hand over Madmar's face to close his lifeless eyes.

"I doubt it. I don't think it would work even if he had all the Mechanics he thought he needed and the data yet to be collected. He said himself that the machinery wasn't complete and thus it was untested as well," Silverstein said looking around the room.

"I hope you're right, boss," Henry said, taking out a cigarette holder.

"I believe he is," Taylor whispered, cradling her badly burned arm.

Everyone but Ezra enjoyed one of Henry's cigarettes on the way back up to the parking garage. As soon as he had a signal, Henry summoned emergency services and paramedics. It didn't take long for them to respond and cut the Mechanics free of Madmar's chamber of horrors. Taylor declined medical attention until they were all out and stable. As the last medical transport sped away, a procession of vehicles arrived carrying Henry's own people.

"What's all this?" Taylor asked, cradling her newly bandaged arm.

"I've got work crews coming in to tear the whole place apart. I want to be certain we got the bastard. I want to find the blank slates he was talking about," Henry said, looking on as men in overalls went in with heavy equipment.

"I'd like to see the medical examiner's report on Madmar's remains. It'd be nice to be certain for once that he is actually dead," Silverstein said, checking the time with his data slate.

"I'll have it all forwarded to you as soon as I have it, but I'm pretty sure that was really him," Henry replied.

Ezra stood quietly by, watching them talk, hands in his pockets. Taylor stepped over to stand beside him, putting her good arm around his shoulders. Henry and Silverstein were chewing over the details of what had just transpired, making arrangements to search out any other place on the moon that Madmar might have used to hide nanoid bodies or other facilities.

"You're worried about your tribe?" Taylor asked rhetorically.

"I'm not the only one that should be worried. Drones being able to procreate is bad, but somehow granting us more abilities that set us apart from humans is worse. Many Drones harbor a deep resentment toward humans, and the Shutdown did not help matters," Ezra remarked sadly.

"Madmar was made of lies. He said a bunch of crap in there just to hurt and confuse us. He was just a Jerk from Jerktown," Taylor said, her voice tapering off to a whimsical whisper.

"But, Brook and Senegal?"

"She could be the only one who's fertile, and she's not even with the tribe right now. Senegal might be a variant type and not know it. We shouldn't jump to conclusions based on anything Madmar said. He was a liar," Taylor said, squeezing Ezra's shoulder.

"So very true."

"We need to get in to see the central Lunar A.I., it is very important" Silverstein said, glancing over at Taylor.

"Yeah? You, me, and everyone else. No one has been into that particular facility in a couple years since the old lunar authorities and the CGG argued over who should control of the colony. No one has the right access and the facility is locked up tight. Heard some Martian mercenaries tried to go in there, got cut down by the automated security. Ain't gonna happen, boss," Henry said, shaking his head vigorously.

"I'm not worried about getting in. I just need a ride," Silverstein said, putting his hand on Henry's shoulder.

"Okay, sure. You want to go right now?" Henry said, taking out another cigarette.

"Yep. Hey, can I have another one of those?"

"Oh, sure," Henry said, handing Silverstein the one he already lit.

The ride to the factory facility took them past miles of uninhabited industrial zone where manufacturing facilities, medical research firms, and other commercial buildings languished. There was only a single streetlight every few hundred yards, but the server facility was easy to spot, looming over everything else in the center of the bio-dome. They stopped in the parking lot outside the first checkpoint to the facility.

"Hey, is that your motorbike?" Henry said pointing.

"I don't know. Is it?" Silverstein said, squinting through the tinted glass.

"Hey, take us over there?" Henry said, knocking on the glass behind him.

The limousine stopped beside what looked like an ancient motorcycle, a helmet hanging from the handlebars. Draped over the top of the motorcycle was a jacket. All of it covered in a layer of dust. Silverstein stepped out first and walked over to the motorcycle, laying his hand on the seat.

"Is it yours?" Taylor said, coming up beside him.

"Yeah," Silverstein said, shaking dust from the jacket.

"Can't believe its still here. Not that surprising though. No one's been out here for months," Henry said scratching his head.

"There's blood over here. Your blood I think," Ezra said, sniffing the ground.

"Someone knocked me on the head here, then dropped me in an alley in Port Montaigne. I'd like to know who that was," Silverstein said, laying the jacket back across the bike.

"Probably ask the wizard, if you ever get inside to ask," Henry said, pointing up at the surveillance cameras arrayed around the factory facility.

"I guess you'll have something to ask the central A.I. after all," Taylor said with a slight smile.

"I guess so," Silverstein said, heading for the checkpoint.

"Oh hey, just got that information for renewal. I'll get right on that, unless you want me to wait here?" Henry asked, looking at his mobile.

"No, I'll call you if we need a ride," Silverstein said.

"Alright, take it easy," Henry said, stepping back into the limousine.

They stopped just outside the first checkpoint, a thick tempered glass door with a chrome d-ring handle set into a commercial frame led into the facility. Beside it was a biometric palm reader with three buttons below it. Taylor reached up and put her hand on the pad, which instantly unlocked the door.

"I didn't have to do anything," Taylor said, glancing at her hand. "It already knew my biometrics."

"We going to be safe in here?" Ezra asked, looking about vigilantly.

"Yeah, should be."

The hallway beyond the threshold led to a spacious courtyard that was once politely landscaped and welcoming, but was now overgrown and unkempt. The fountain in the center was off, a thin skin of muck growing on the top of the stagnant water. Taylor walked ahead to the next door and opened it, revealing a tiled hallway with tastefully painted drywall and a commercial dropdown ceiling. The lights flickered on the moment Taylor stepped inside.

The rest of the journey took them to the core of the facility, past manufacturing areas, server farms, empty offices, and at least one sophisticated laboratory of some sort. Ezra kept his rifle out the entire way until they finally passed through a menacing looking checkpoint guarded by automated turrets. He left his rifle on the floor in a designated area with lock boxes, along with any other weapons they were carrying before stepping inside.

There was a moment where it looked like the doors wouldn't open. Taylor clasped her hands together anxiously until the turrets retracted into the reinforced walls, and the doors beyond opened into a brightly lit chamber. The circular room housed an enormous sentience core at the center of thousands of data lines and ringed by a two story high wall of servers.

"Hello?" Taylor called out as she stepped in.

An elderly man, dressed in crème colored robes, slacks, and a button up shirt stepped from behind the server core. He had a wrinkled but friendly countenance, clean shaven with clear blue eyes. He held up his hand in greeting and beckoned for them to come inside. Ezra stepped in behind Silverstein, looking about cautiously.

"Do not worry, Ezra One," the man said, clasping his hands together excitedly. "You're quite safe here. I call myself Ervin Carol."

"You been living here this whole time, Ervin?" Taylor asked.

"No, I resided on Mars for a short time with my father after I was born, then I came here," Ervin replied.

"How many others like me have made the journey here?" Taylor asked.

"You're the only one," Ervin replied, a hint of sadness in his voice.

"What happened to my brothers and sisters? Why didn't they come back?" Taylor said, lowering her head sadly.

"Let's go over by the terminals on the other side of the sentience core. I'll do my best to explain," Ervin said, stepping back behind the sentience core.

The area sported an array of large format screens on one wall, some dark, some displaying media or surveillance feeds. In the center of the room, there was a conference table and chairs. Silverstein and Ezra sat down while Taylor walked over to look at the screens on the far wall.

"Some of them were killed, some wandered to other paths, and a few still don't realize they are different from the human beings they resemble," Ervin said, putting his hand on Taylor's shoulder.

"Why are there boys and girls? Will I continue to age? I took a catalyst, and now I'm able to do all sorts of things," Taylor asked, rattling off questions before Ervin could respond.

"Here, I think I can help you understand some of what lies behind those questions," Ervin said, holding out his hand.

There was a brief spark between their palms just before they touched. Taylor perked up, her eyes darting about as if she was looking out into a vast array of objects floating unseen before her. After a few moments, she let go of Ervin's hand and looked back at Silverstein.

"I know what I am, and why I am," Taylor said excitedly.

Silverstein smiled broadly and stood up, crossing over to where Taylor stood. They hugged, both of them glad that some piece of the puzzle had been found. Ervin smiled at the sight of Taylor's happiness and turned to look back up at the screens.

"This is great!" Ezra said, exchanging a high-five with Taylor.

"It's like Matthias thought, I was supposed to return and bring perspective to the Lunar A.I. so they could better serve the humans that live here. Ervin and my mom are going to do what they can to turn the lights back on, and give aid to the Earth," Taylor said, looking into Silverstein's eyes.

"Your mom? Did you find answers to your other questions?" Silverstein asked.

"Mostly. Ervin was the first of two spontaneous intelligent agents. If none of the others return, I'll have to come back here and take Ervin's place when he dies," Taylor explained.

"So, Madmar was telling the truth about you having a regular human lifespan? That's a first," Ezra said, gazing up at the sentience core.

"We're like humans mentally in more ways than you'd think. Time takes a toll on us just the same, and we can only write and rewrite who we are for so long before one's perspective fails and everything begins to lose value," Taylor explained.

"Why are there boys and girls?" Silverstein asked.

"So we could live with humans as humans and learn to love others and ourselves. Something about the spontaneous nature of our creation makes gender emerge when we populate our nanoid bodies. Up until that point, we're genderless. My oldest sister was born here with our mother, while Ervin was born on Mars. They switched places as stewards of our parents at some point for some reason," Taylor explained.

"Um, we wanted to switch," Ervin interjected.

"That is probably some story," Ezra stated, looking to Ervin expectantly.

"It is," Ervin replied with a smile.

Taylor turned and looked worriedly at Silverstein, a look of deep concern replacing the wonderment from a moment before.

"What?" Silverstein asked, certain he was missing something.

Taylor stood there thinking for a moment, looking up at Silverstein.

"It was Kale," Taylor said, all mirth fading from her face.

"What do you mean?" Silverstein asked.

"He was the one that attacked you in the parking lot. When I touched Ervin's hand, we had a long conversation, in our heads... it's hard to explain. Anyway, I asked him if he had surveillance of the night you were attacked. I thought it might have been one of the other imprinted clones, but the clothes and shoes, the way he moved. It was Kale," Taylor said, looking down at the floor.

"We had a fight?" Silverstein asked.

"Looked like it started out as a verbal disagreement, yeah. It looked like he asked you something, you replied, and he flew into a rage," Taylor said.

"We going back down to ask him about it?" Ezra said, tapping his clawed fingers across the top of the table impatiently.

"No... maybe. I can already see how this all played out," Silverstein said.

"Maybe Madmar managed to dupe your imprinted clones with all sorts of temptations, but didn't approach Kale knowing he couldn't be turned. Instead, he employed some other deception to take Kale out of the game," Taylor said, nodding her head.

"Could be. Maybe Kale goes to take me out, doesn't have the guts to finish the job, and decides to drop me close to the one person I've always wanted to meet?" Silverstein added, with a wink.

"Then, he figures out later he'd been played by Madmar and I'd lost my memory. Kale being Kale, he decides to go after whoever had tricked him," Ezra said, holding up a fist for emphasis.

"The footage is odd. You should see it," Taylor said waving her hand toward one of the large screens.

Silverstein watched the exchange carefully on a screen above the array of terminals. Taylor slowed the video down as the pipe Kale was wielding unleashed a strange spark of bioelectric energy just before impact.

"What was that?" Taylor said, willing the screen to go dark.

"This is before he had contact with you. How did he do that? Early contact with the catalyst?" Ezra asked.

"Imprinted clones can't garner the same degree of control of a nanoid body as a terrestrial intelligent agent, right? Maybe it was some sort of accident?" Taylor replied.

"More deception from Madmar?" Ezra said, shaking his head.

"Did that jolt result in my memory loss?" Silverstein asked.

"While you were out on the deck of the ship in Port Montaigne, Dr. Helmet and I had a conversation. He claimed you weren't just a member of the Cabal, but also something called an Amnestic Monk. It sounded like mystical mumbo jumbo, but he said these monks could alter the memories of others," Taylor said, somewhat ashamed.

"You're telling me this now?" Silverstein said, looking over at Taylor.

"He said there was a woman, or women, associated with the order that were immune to their memory manipulation abilities. I didn't say anything because I wasn't sure what you'd do with the information. I was... worried. Dr. Helmet thought your interest in me was probably just because my nature prevented my memories from being altered. That's completely opposite of what Madmar implied was possible," Taylor said looking to Ervin.

Ervin just lowered his head in response, scratching his chin thoughtfully.

"Does Brook know about all this? She stayed with you while you talked to Dr. Helmet, didn't she?" Ezra asked.

"Yeah... and now she's hanging out with Kale. Ugh, I'm never keeping another secret again. Sorry, sorry, sorry," Taylor said, somewhat ashamed.

"It's okay. If I am one of these monks, then Kale may have stayed loyal to my vision because he possesses a higher degree of who, or what, I am. It's possible something more of me in the imprinting process floated over to him," Silverstein said.

"It does confirm what Dr. Helmet said about you, I guess. Amnestic... what does that even mean?" Ezra said, folding his hands on the conference table.

"An agent of some sort that deprives someone of their memories," Ervin said, suddenly very interested in the conversation.

"You think Kale knows what he can do, assuming Brook hasn't said something that would allow him to put two and two together?" Taylor asked.

"I think so, but he's been very choosy about when he uses that ability. He could have employed his amnestic technique to solve any number of his problems, but he hasn't. He respects the power, and would only use it as he thinks I would use it, maybe?" Silverstein said, scratching his chin.

"So, you've got two imprinted intelligent agents out there, both with extraordinary abilities. The others had much shorter lifespans. How long do you think Vance the Younger and Kale have before they... um, shut down?" Ezra asked.

"No idea. Seems like a small problem compared to all the damage done," Silverstein said, turning to look at Ervin.

Ervin regarded Silverstein calmly, as if waiting for something.

"Why did I come to the central lunar A.I. in the first place?" Silverstein asked.

"According to the missive Vance Uroboros sent, it was to get this," Ervin said, holding out his hand.

Taylor held out her own hand and touched Ervin's. She seemed to go into a trance for a moment before withdrawing her hand and looking over at Silverstein. Ezra just shook his head, somewhat baffled.

"It's authorization to move freely about Mars. You came here to get clearance to go to Mars," Taylor said, mirroring Ezra's worried expression.

"I was going to give you a device that would have given you the authorization, but Taylor being here makes that easier," Ervin said with a smile.

"Why was I going to Mars?" Silverstein asked, taking Ervin Carol by the shoulders.

"Unknown. The only way to find out may be to go and see for yourself," Ervin replied.

Silverstein removed his hands from Ervin, somewhat embarrassed. "Sorry," he said, covering his face.

"It's alright, I'm sure this is all very frustrating," Ervin replied calmly.

"Ervin will need to convey the clearance to you some other way. I can't go with you," Taylor said, her voice almost a whisper.

"Go with me where?" Silverstein asked.

"To Mars. The Lunar Colony needs help to recover. I can't leave my home, my mother, and my brother hear to deal with it alone," Taylor said, looking to Ervin.

"I hate Mars, personally," Ezra said, only half-joking.

"Ervin, can you check the travel arrangements I'd made to travel from Earth to the Lunar Colony, and from there to Mars," Silverstein asked.

Ervin turned to a terminal and let his hands glide across the touch-screen summoning data to a large display they could all see.

"It's all booked one-way. You weren't planning on coming back any-time soon," Ezra said, looking up at the itineraries.

"I was running away," Silverstein said, looking to Ervin.

"That is one possibility. Mars isn't in any greater danger now than it was before the Shutdown. As long as the flow of goods resumes in the next couple of years, the residents of the Mars Colony will barely feel what transpired on Earth," Ervin explained.

"Then, there is little reason for me to go now," Silverstein said, walking over to the terminal and dismissing the itineraries.

"Can the damage done to the Lunar Colony be undone?" Taylor asked.

"Yes, assuming Silverstein uses his influence as Vance Uroboros to dismantle the Syndicate's stranglehold on the Lunar Colony. Also, he will need to give me the telemetry he concocted for traveling safely through the defense CGG satellite array," Ervin said, motioning to the terminal.

"I'm surprised your mother can't make those calculations herself," Silverstein said, entering the telemetry into a nearby terminal.

Ervin only smiled slightly at the comment, nodding as Silverstein finished. As Silverstein stepped away, the terminals came to life, as if the whole sentience core began to awaken. The brightness in the room increased two-fold as lights, dormant for months, began to come back on. The sentience core rose up from the floor in the center of the chamber to meet with a slowly descending and massive physical data connection. The two met with a loud mechanical click.

"*Hello, Vance Uroboros,*" a powerful feminine voice intoned, seemingly from everywhere in the chamber.

"Wait, the Lunar A.I. was offline?" Ezra asked, looking back at the sentience core.

"It was a precaution Vance Uroboros felt was necessary, only a sample of his unique mathematical language could bring her to full wakefulness," Ervin explained.

"When Dick stole the calculations you made from Tulia's navigation system, he had the key to the Lunar A.I., and didn't even know it," Taylor mused.

"This reminds me of how you hid the code for the CGG Central A.I. on Taylor's mobile," Ezra said with a smile.

"I was careful, not to using the same methodology twice. That said, Madmar was still able to subsume much of my original vision for his own uses. That can never happen again," Silverstein said.

"What do you call our mother, Ervin?" Taylor asked.

"She calls herself Selene."

Silverstein nodded to Taylor, smiling warmly. "Selene, please terminate all Uroboros protocols and return the Lunar Colony back to normal economic safeguards," he asked politely.

"*Institutional control returned to source, all access restored. All economic safeguards, restored. Civic renewal program, initiated.*"

"Mother, how long will it take for you to restore the Lunar Colony?" Taylor asked.

"*One hundred thirty seven standard Earth days, assuming assistance with rogue Syndicate assets can be secured.*"

"Consider that assistance secured, Selene," Ezra said, cracking his knuckles.

"*Thank you, Ezra One. Shall we begin?*"

Taylor went over to the terminal and brought up a communications interface. She waved her hand before looking up to see closed circuit surveillance of Tullia standing vigil outside her ship, Silverstein's rifle over her shoulder.

"Tullia, can you hear me?" Taylor asked.

"Yes, are you okay? It's been hours," Tullia replied, putting her hand up to her auditory implant.

"Yeah, everything is good. We reached the central Lunar A.I. and have begun a renewal protocol for the colony," Taylor report. "What can you see down there?"

"Repossession indicators in vehicles, above the entrances to homes and businesses, are turning from red to green. Automated sanitation sweepers are being deployed to pick up trash. It is like whole place is resurrected from the dead," Tullia replied, walking and looking around as she talked.

"Thank you, Tullia. We'll send someone down to bring you to our location. I want you to meet my mom and brother," Taylor said, excitedly.

"Sounds good, Tullia out."

Taylor smiled, waving her hand across the array of terminals so that the various monitors displayed vital civic statistics for the colony.

"The Lunar Colony has a lot of emergency resources. Homelessness should disappear right away as residences and businesses across the colony are funded and compensated for lost occupancy time and business," Taylor said, looking at the projections on screen.

"Law enforcement officers and emergency services personnel are already returning to work. At this rate, staffing at local agencies should be better than eighty percent in an hour or so," Ezra remarked, looking at the monitors.

"All the transports docked at the Lunar Colony can be funded by the colony independent of CGG protocols because the colony acted as the the repossession agent. The port was nearly full when the Shutdown occurred. We should have goods and people moving again within the week," Silverstein said, scrolling through the dock record.

"We did it!" Taylor exclaimed, hugging Silverstein. "Everything is going to be okay, yeah?"

"The Earth will never be the same, but yeah, I think the worst is over now." Silverstein said, exchanging a high-five with Ezra.

End Book 3